Pontoon

ALSO BY GARRISON KEILLOR

Homegrown Democrat
Love Me
Lake Wobegon Summer 1956
Me: The Jimmy (Big Boy) Valente Story
Wobegon Boy
The Book of Guys
WLT: A Radio Romance
We Are Still Married
Leaving Home
Lake Wobegon Days
Happy to Be Here

GARRISON KEILLOR

Pontoon

A LAKE WOBEGON NOVEL

To the Schraepfers.

Garrison Keillor

VIKING

VIKING
Published by the Penguin Group
Penguin Group (USA) Inc., 375 Hudson Street, New York, New York 10014, U.S.A. •
Penguin Group (Canada), 90 Eglinton Avenue East, Suite 700, Toronto, Ontario, Canada M4P 2Y3 (a division of Pearson Penguin Canada Inc.) • Penguin Books Ltd, 80 Strand, London WC2R 0RL, England • Penguin Ireland, 25 St. Stephen's Green, Dublin 2, Ireland (a division of Penguin Books Ltd) • Penguin Books Australia Ltd, 250 Camberwell Road, Camberwell, Victoria 3124, Australia (a division of Pearson Australia Group Pty Ltd) • Penguin Books India Pvt Ltd, 11 Community Centre, Panchsheel Park, New Delhi – 110 017, India • Penguin Group (NZ), 67 Apollo Drive, Rosedale, North Shore 0745, Auckland, New Zealand (a division of Pearson New Zealand Ltd.) • Penguin Books (South Africa) (Pty) Ltd, 24 Sturdee Avenue, Rosebank, Johannesburg 2196, South Africa

Penguin Books Ltd, Registered Offices: 80 Strand, London WC2R 0RL, England

First published in 2007 by Viking Penguin, a member of Penguin Group (USA) Inc.

1   3   5   7   9   10   8   6   4   2

Copyright © Garrison Keillor, 2007
All rights reserved

Publisher's Note
This is a work of fiction. Names, characters, places, and incidents either are the product of the author's imagination or are used fictitiously, and any resemblance to actual persons, living or dead, business establishments, events, or locales is entirely coincidental.

LIBRARY OF CONGRESS CATALOGING-IN-PUBLICATION DATA
Keillor, Garrison.
Pontoon : a Lake Wobegon novel / Garrison Keillor.
p.   cm.
ISBN 978–0–670–06356–7
1. Lake Wobegon (Minn. : Imaginary place)—Fiction.   2. Lutheran women—
Fiction.   I. Title.
PS3561.E3755P66 2007
813'.54—dc22   2007019553

Printed in the United States of America
Set in Aldus with Bailywick
Designed by Daniel Lagin

AUTHOR'S NOTE

This book is set in a town I've talked about for years to audiences in theaters here and there and now, sending this book out into the night, I remember how peaceful and pleasant it was, just before going out to the microphone in the spotlight, to stand in the dark backstage, next to the rope gallery and the flickering control board in the wings, the fire curtain, the hand-lettered signs (*NO FOOD OR BEVERAGES BACKSTAGE. THIS MEANS YOU.*), with my comrades, the backstage crew, waiting in the shadows for the show to start. This book is dedicated to those friends in the dark, the stage manager, the truck driver, the guard at the door, the old stagehands, the young women in black T-shirts and jeans, all the guys who did lights and sound and shared that companionable silence with me. A stagehand climbs up on the rail and grabs the rope that opens the curtain, I drink my coffee, we wait, nobody says a word. The audience gets quiet: the house lights have dimmed. The rope man braces himself for the big pull, everyone takes a breath. It's a Rembrandt painting, "The Stage Crew," and I am the one with the red socks, you can barely make them out in the shadows. —G.K.

Pontoon

1. GOOD NIGHT, LADIES

Evelyn was an insomniac so when they say she died in her sleep, you have to question that. Probably she was sitting propped up in bed reading and heard the brush of wings and smelled the cold clean air and the angel appeared like a deer in the bedroom and Evelyn said, "Not yet. I have to finish this book." And the angel shook his golden locks, which made a skittery sound like dry seed pods, and he laughed a long silent laugh and took her pale hand in his. He'd heard that line, "Not yet," before. He was always interrupting people who were engrossed in their work or getting ready for a night at the opera or about to set off on a trip. Evelyn's brother died after his wife sprayed the house with a rose-scented room freshener that made Frank sneeze so hard he had a coronary, but he made it to the phone and called the office and told them he'd be late, and then lay down and died. The angel took Evelyn's hand gently in his cool hand and off she went with him, leaving behind the book, her bed and the blue knit coverlet, her stucco bungalow in Lake Wobegon redolent of coffee and fresh-picked strawberries, her bedside radio, her subscription to the *New Yorker* paid through the end of the year. It had been a good wet summer, plenty of rain, and as she drifted out her back door she noted how green the grass was. A cat announced itself from the shadows. The smell of burning charcoal hung in the air. A red ball lay by the walk. She wanted to pick it up and throw it but the angel rose and she with him and, hand in hand, they flew up into the sequined sky, the little town arranged below, all shushed and dozy, the double row of streetlights on Main Street, the red light blinking on the water tower, the dark fastness of the lake, the pinpricks of lights from houses where they all slept, the cranks, the stoics, the meek, the ragtag dreamers, the drunks, the martyred wives, and she saw a woman's pale face at a window looking for evildoers and the single pair of headlights threading the serpentine county road, and after that she did not look down. She flew up through a meringue cloud into the mind of God and the embrace of her sainted ancestors all gathered at her grandfather Crandall's farmhouse on a summer morn, the patient horses standing in the shade of a red oak tree, white chickens pecking for bugs under the lilacs, Grandma whistling in the milk house, holding a pan of cream. The windbreak of pine and red oak, the weathered sheds and barn, the hayfields of heaven.

It was a green summer day like what a child would draw, a crayon day with a few white cumulus children's clouds, and the sun with yellow radiance lines sticking out. It was a day when after breakfast Dad did not go out to do chores but sat down at the upright piano and played by heart *O dusky maiden of the moors, my heart you do beguile—O do not hasten to your chores but stay with me awhile.* There was one day when he did that and this is that day again. The day after she was begotten.

Evelyn was a whistler, she learned it from him. The rest of the family was disposed to gloom, dark Lutherans who pitch down the rocky slope of melancholy and lie there for days, sighing, moaning, waiting for someone, usually Evelyn, to rope them in and haul them back up and comfort them with dessert. A people waiting for the other shoe to drop. Phlegmatists. Stoics. Good eaters who went for recipes that start out *Brown a pound of ground beef and six strips of bacon and in a separate pan melt a pound of butter.*

She was a finicky eater, a forager in the vegetable crisper. She'd whomp up a big feast and wait on table and have a smidgen of goose, a single stalk of asparagus, a crumb of cornbread, and that was enough for her. She was the only insomniac in a family of very good sleepers, folks who climbed into bed gladly and lay in their cottony caves and slept like stones unless awakened by heartburn. At night, she lay awake and listened to *The Bob Roberts Show* on WLT and when Bob's callers got cranking on the evils of taxation and the treachery of the media and the shiftlessness of the young, she drifted off to sleep, and if not, she switched on the bedside lamp and reached for a book and read about the Saracens and the Crusaders, about the tortured lives of great artists, Van Gogh and his prostitutes, Chopin coughing at the piano, Keats expiring in Rome, Shelley sailing in the storm, Melville languishing at the customs house, Twain and his bankruptcy and Dickens's unhappy marriage and his romances with actresses. She adored Dickens. Especially *Little Dorrit.* The weary worker trudging home from the blacking factory, the yellow glow of London street lamps, the night fog, the newshawk on the corner, the flower girl, the streetwalker in the doorway, the cabbie dozing on his hack parked by the curb, the horse's head drooping—she dozed off too. Or she got up and fixed herself a toddy and put on a recording of the Stuttgart Male Chorus singing romantic songs about moonlight and longing and the maiden who opened my heart to love and in the morning she was gone and now I can never love again, alas—that one was guaranteed to put her right out. And if not, she put on her robe and fixed breakfast.

"It's the radio and the dang books and the crazy CD player that are keeping you awake," said her sister Florence. "Turn off the radio and take a pill. You look like death on a biscuit."

Actually she looked great right up to the day she died, a Friday night in July. She had a long neck and a prominent nose and high cheekbones; after she kicked Uncle Jack out she looked even better, happier, looser, janglier, jaunty. She was tall and wiry and stayed limber by hiking everywhere and doing her Daily Dozen. She was the outspoken aunt in a family of murmurers. Other people said No. 1 or No. 2 and she said *pee* and *take a crap*. She also said *hell* and *damn* and *son of a bitch*. She had soft green eyes and gray hair like a winter sky in the morning. She cut it short. "You look like a man," said Florence. "What's got into you?" "Piss and vinegar," she said.

She was found dead on a Saturday morning, having gone out to supper Friday night with her buddies Gladys and Margaret at the Moonlite Bay supper club where she enjoyed the deep-fried walleye and a slab of banana cream pie, along with a mai tai and a Pinot Grigio. Three old Lutheran ladies, stalwarts of the Altar Guild and the quilting circle, who had put in their thirty years teaching Sunday school, and now in their dotage were having a little fun. Every second Wednesday they drove off to the Big Moccasin casino in Widjiwagan to play blackjack and take advantage of the $6.95 Blue Light buffet and catch the 6 p.m. show of Richie Dee and the Radiators and once, they entered the Twist contest (*wotthehell*) and won a night at the Romeo Motel (*hot damn*) and went and stayed, the three of them, turned out the lights, lay in the hot tub, looked up at the ceiling mirror, and drank champagne from their shoes.

Tonight the three chums sat at a table by the window and laughed themselves silly over Gary and LeRoy the town constables—LeRoy is Margaret's nephew—who got a federal grant to purchase a bulletproof windshield for the squad car and a dozen tear gas grenades and grenade launcher, six antiterrorist concrete barriers, and a bullhorn to be used to negotiate with terrorists holding hostages. They recalled the chicken salad LeRoy brought to the Labor Day potluck picnic, which had been sitting in the rear window of his car for a few hours, and the waves of propulsive vomiting it caused. Men, mostly. Big men so sick they couldn't go hide, they had to stand and empty their stomachs right there in plain view of their children. They chortled over that and then they took up Gladys's husband Leon who had discovered Viagra and now, after a ten-year layoff, was up for sex. Viagra gave him a hard-on like a ball-peen hammer. "Or in his case, like a Phillips screwdriver," said Gladys and they all cackled. Scheduling was an issue. He preferred mornings. Gladys wasn't interested in getting unharnessed at 10 a.m. and climbing into bed, but she tried to be a good sport. And then it took him forever. He'd go at it for a while and run out of breath and lie down and wheeze and then try again, and in broad daylight, the sight of the two of them in the dresser mirror struck her as hilarious. "Four hundred pounds of menopausal flesh bumping around and breathing hard. He told me the least I could do was pretend to be excited, and I said, 'For that, you have to pay me real money'"—Leon was not amused.

"So he can't pull the trigger then?" said Margaret.

"He gets all excited and then he has to stop and rest."

"And meanwhile you're checking the clock."

"The other day I had bread in the oven and I told him I had to go check it—I was baking for the Bible school bake sale—he said, 'Don't go! Don't go! I'm coming!' Then he kept at it for another five minutes—I said, 'Jesus, if you can't come just say so.' He got all mad then, said it was hard being married to someone who didn't care for sex and who kept poking holes in his confidence."

"Who's poking holes?" cried Margaret and they all three gasped and wheezed—*O God—O God I am going to die—don't make me laugh like that, I swear I'm going to wet my pants.* The busboy heard all this and was quite surprised. A good boy from a nice home. And then Evelyn said, "Tell him if he needs to hump something, you'll thaw out a chicken." And Margaret laughed so hard a whole noseful of something shot out. The busboy retreated to the scullery. The ladies wiped their eyes. *Oh I swear I am never having dinner with you two again, you are a bad influence. A bad influence.*

Gladys said she was thinking of replacing those little blue pills with sleeping tablets—they chortled over that and about Margaret's brother the aging sportscaster in Minneapolis with his hair transplant and jowlectomy. And they drove back to town in Margaret's car and Evelyn got out at her little stucco house on McKinley Street and leaned on the car and said, "It was great. See you Wednesday." There was a full moon and she stood and admired it and headed for the house. She stopped and pointed to her moon shadow on the walk and danced a couple steps as if to elude it and that was the last anyone saw of her. She was 82 and in good shape, wearing a denim wraparound skirt and a white blouse embroidered with roses and a silky red vest and sandals, and she danced in the moonlight and went indoors to lie down and die. She was a realist. At 82 you have to be. To the roof shingler who told her that the roof would be a big headache in a few years, she said, "Not my problem." The porch sagged—"Let it sag," she said. "That makes two of us." For two years, she'd been packing up her unnecessities and shipping them off to rummage sales.

Jack had died nineteen years before, leaving behind a basement and garage full of his accumulations, which had taken her months to disperse, and she didn't want to burden Barbara with the same grim chore. Barbara lived three blocks away, up the street from Our Lady of Perpetual Responsibility, alone since Lloyd drifted away to the Cities and Kyle went to college. "When I die," Evelyn told her, "I want you to be able to sweep out the place, take the sheets off the bed and the clothes out of the closet, clean out the medicine chest, and hang out a For Sale sign. Two hours and you'll be rid of me. I'm a pilgrim. I travel light."

Her name was all wrong. Evelyns should be plump ladies in spiffy outfits who collect salt and pepper sets and play canasta and fuss at their husbands. Evelyn was named after a battle-axe aunt, the pharmacist's wife who took too many pills and they made her think everybody in Lake Wobegon was out to get her. The little girl should have been a Therese or a Catherine but she got evelyned. She was a divestor, not a collector, and after the children flew the nest and after Jack left, she drew a sigh of relief and shook off her long habits of vigilance and moral correction, and she became *gleeful*. Even at 82 she could pick up a ping-pong paddle and drive you nuts. She had her ears pierced and wore feathery earrings like trout flies. She bought a computer and mastered the Internet and chatted with strangers under her screen name, HotShot82. In Lake Wobegon, most people felt you should grow more dignified with age, even sour, but she became lighthearted, even girlish. If she ate lunch with the seniors on Wednesdays at the Lutheran church where a retired pastor showed slides of last summer's cruise through the Norwegian fjords and everyone sang "Children of the Heavenly Father" and "Look For The Silver Lining" and "God Bless America," she was somewhat more Evelyn-like, but when she and her pals hoofed it up to the Moonlite Bay supper club or if she and Barbara dined at Fisher's in Avon, she smoked a few cigarettes and enjoyed a libation and told some off-color jokes and if you asked her how she felt, she cried "Never better!" and slapped her chest, and if you invited her to go for a walk she said "Delighted!" and reached for her old suede jacket. She could be exalted by a good ballgame, or by the dawn—a cup of fresh coffee, the open door, the pink and silver and pale blue sky, the inhalation of lake and grass—and she wept to hear the contralto sing, *For He shall feed His flock like a shepherd.* She could marvel at the ingenuity of screws or apply herself to polishing up her Spanish. She liked to get in her red Honda and drive away for a week or two—"to visit cousin Grace in St. Louis" or "to check up on Phyl and Earl in Sacramento," distant relations who nobody else was in touch with—and when she got home, she was vague about the details. "Oh, it was all very quiet and sedate. I was in bed by ten every night," she told Barbara, who could smell a lie as well as the next person.

She was a welcoming person in a family of wary observers. Let a strange car pull up in the driveway, she walked toward it smil-

ing. If someone died, she went straight to the house with a cas-
serole for the survivors. But she could speak her mind. She went
to the Town Council meeting when they took up a resolution to
ban nudity, and she stood up, the lone dissenter, and said, "Why
are you wasting time on this ridiculous law? So now Gary and
LeRoy are supposed to get out their binoculars and watch for naked people? What does it matter to you if I go over to the Hidden
Beach and go skinny-dipping? We all used to go over there—
should I name names? Well, so what? If you're offended by the
sight of bare-naked people, then don't go over there. And if you
have a nice body and you want to show it off, more power to
you." They had never heard anyone speak in defense of nudity
before.

When the school board took up a resolution that every child be
required to say the Pledge of Allegiance she stood up and cried,
"If you require me to go to church, then it's no longer faith, and
when you make somebody pledge allegiance to a flag that stands
for freedom—you are just being stupid." She sat down with a
thud. The school board was stunned. Finally Mr. Halvorson
moved that the resolution be referred to the executive committee
for further study and everyone said "Aye" and it was gone and
forgotten.

So she was memorable. And when people heard about her
death, they stopped what they were doing and stood, hands at
their sides, and felt her absence. A tall tree had crashed to the
ground.

2. BARBARA'S DISCOVERY

Barbara found Evelyn's body, lying in bed, face up, green eyes staring vacantly at the ceiling, long tan arms at her sides, red lacquered nails, blue cotton blanket up to her waist, a copy of *Tale of Two Cities* on the floor. Barbara is somewhat tightly wound, not the person you'd choose for the job of finding dead people. She shrieked, clutched at her mother's hand, shrank back from the bed, knocked a lamp off the bedside table, yelped and ran out of the room and into the kitchen where she tried to collect herself and took a deep breath and thought *homicide* and looked around for signs of violence. She stood very very still. Water dripped in the sink. She tightened the faucet. It stopped. She breathed deeply, once, twice, again, again, and told herself to be calm. Nobody had murdered Mother. Then she looked around for a drink.

In recent years Barbara had developed a crème de cacao problem. She liked to add it to her breakfast coffee; it put her in a gentler place. Took the edge off. She called it cocoa. It got her in the right frame of mind to go to work at the school cafeteria. She started to like work more. She sang a lot, songs from *Oklahoma* or *West Side Story* or *Music Man,* as she blended gallons of cheese sauce in with tubs of macaroni. At night she switched to brandy and called up friends and relatives, weeping for bygone times, grieving for Lloyd and their lost marriage, grieving for daughter Muffy, wishing people could get along, wishing she had been a better mom, hoping for world peace, more openness and honesty and a cure for cancer.

"Sometimes I get the feeling that I was an adopted child," she said. "I'm just so different from the rest of you." She would weep on the phone, fall asleep on the couch, and wake up feeling lousy. Now, a little buzzed from morning coffee, she looked down at Evelyn and she cried out. "I'm not ready to let you go, I need you, Mommy! I need you too much!" A horrible silence. She was all alone. *She had no mom. No mom.* And she ran into Mother's living room and tried to re-start the old life by contemplating the old coral sofa, the old rocker, the red oriental rug, the painting of the horses in the meadow (*A Blessing*), the gold fringe on the lampshade, and then she went to the kitchen and climbed up on the stepstool to look for liquor, and found the Kahlúa. She got out a jelly glass, filled it up to the third fish and sang a song Mother had taught her.

Oh the horses stood around with their feet upon the ground and who will wind my wristwatch when I'm gone? We feed the baby garlic so we can find him in the dark, and a girl's best friend is her mother.

Mother used to say, "A son is a son until he takes a wife but a daughter is a daughter all of her life," and Barbara sure knew what that meant. Roger and Bennett went their sweet way from the time they learned to ride bikes but she had to stick around and peel potatoes and clean the bathrooms. Those two couldn't clean a bathroom if you put a pistol to their temples. They went gallivanting off to play tennis and lie around by the lake and eventually off to the University and Mother was pleased if they dropped her a postcard now and then. They could do no wrong. But Barbara was held to a different standard: the assistant mother, the kitchen helper, the little manager, runner of errands.

Well, Mother was all hers now. It was just her and Mother in the house. Roger and Bennett knew nothing. Roger was in Santa Barbara, with his perky wife Gwen, hustling up customers for Milton & Merrill the hedge-fund giant, earning gold stars after his name, making pots of money, flying off to luxury spas and resorts, furnishing their second home in Vail. She would take her sweet time calling him. Maybe she would wait until Tuesday. Bennett was dragging his butt, broke in New York, fermenting in disappointment, a composer and for twenty-three years a security guard at a warehouse in Queens. He sat all night in a tiny office overlooking acres of appliances and wrote music at a computer. So far as she knew, he had never published anything except a few songs. He had written the first act of his opera, *Kitty Hawk*, and then rewritten it four or five or six times, and he had an unfinished symphony. He had followed his dream in life and gotten lost. A great talent gone to waste, sob sob.

She finished the glass of Kahlúa and went back in the bedroom. "Well, you wanted to die in your sleep. So now you have. You got your wish. Good for you. I hope you're happy. And I hope you're not expecting a big funeral because frankly I'm not up for it. I don't know if you ever noticed, Mother, in your active life befriending everyone and traveling hither and yon, but your daughter has got a lot of problems. A lot." She was feeling weepy. She thought of calling Oliver but he was working a double shift today. He'd just started clerking at Liberty Gas & Lube on I-94 over near Melrose, having gotten the shaft at 24-Hour Service in

St. Cloud, and she hated to interrupt him at work even though he said it was no problem. She just wanted somebody to tell: "My Mother, who I ate lunch with yesterday, is no more. My mama, she be daid." The day before, Mother had sat in Barbara's backyard eating a big half-moon of watermelon, leaning forward, spitting seeds into the grass, juice dripping off her chin, and now she was dead. They'd eaten a salad together. Barbara had said, "Do you want me to drive you out to Moonlite Bay?" and Mother said no, Gladys or Margaret would drive.

"I worry about you driving late at night."

"It's only five miles."

And then she was critical of Barbara's salad. "Those tomatoes you buy at the store aren't tomatoes at all," she said. "Ralph never seems to have good tomatoes anymore. These taste like they came from California. Why do that, when we have tomato growers around here? Why do people pay good money for bad food?" And Barbara said she thought the tomatoes were okay, so there was a little back-and-forth over that, and then Mother asked about Kyle, and they argued about whether Barbara was too hard on him, and Mother looked at her and said, "Well, what about you? Why don't you go back to school? You can't spend the rest of your life working in a school cafeteria." Barbara said she liked the people there and the job gave her plenty of time to work on her art. And Mother rolled her eyes and Barbara said, "I know you don't care for my art but you don't have to roll your eyes." Mother said, "Oh don't be so sensitive, I'm only kidding. Your life is your own. I'm happy for you. Wish you'd introduce me to your boyfriend, but that's up to you." And she said that if Barbara wasn't up for company, then maybe she'd go home and come back sometime when Barbara was in a better mood. "I was in a perfectly good mood until you criticized my salad and my son and my paintings," said Barbara. "Well, if I'm upsetting you, I'm sorry," said Mother, standing up to go. A thought balloon over her head, a trail of bubbles leading to it: *How did I get such a child?* Barbara said, "Where are you going? You come over here for half an hour and run me through the wringer and then you hop up and go? Why can't we sit and converse like normal people?" "We're not normal people," said Mother. "Nobody is. We're just us. And we are conversing, but you're in a prickly mood and also you've had too much to drink." Barbara said, "And now you're going to start in on my drinking—""No," Mother said, "I'm going to go home and come back tomorrow when you're feeling better." She took her salad plate toward the house and Barbara said, "You can't just keep walking away from me, Mother. You have to face me someday. I am who I am. I'm not Bennett and I'm not Roger. I'm me." And Mother said, over her shoulder, not stopping, "I'm glad that you're you and I wish you a good day and I'll see you tomorrow." She headed for the door, opened it, turned and smiled and said, "Pull up your socks, kiddo. And put on some lipstick." Her valedictory speech. And out the back gate she went and that was Barbara's last sight of her, those long legs and khaki shorts and white blouse disappearing into the mudroom and now here were those long legs, cold and stiff, under a blanket.

She wished Mother hadn't walked away like that. She should've turned and come back and sat down and let Barbara tell her about Oliver and what a prize he was if only he would slim down. He did guy jobs like disposing of deceased animals and removing bats from the fireplace and was much the same from day to day. You didn't go to bed with Mr. Chuckles and wake up with Lothar the Barbaric.

She opened the top drawer of the night stand and riffled through the clippings and postcards and aspirin packets and a poem on an index card—one of Mother's poems. . . .

Life is not land we own.
O no, it is only lent.
In the end we are left alone
When the last light is spent.
So live that you may say,
Lord, I have no regret.
Thank you for these sunny days
And for the last sunset.

Not a great poem, if you ask me, thought Barbara. *Sorry Mother.*

Under it was an envelope labeled *ARRANGEMENTS*. She opened it. The letter was typed on thin blue paper with *Par Avion* printed below and a French flag.

Dear Barbara,

I am writing this on a sunny afternoon on some French stationery I bought when I realized that I'm probably never going to make it to France, which is sad, but oh well. The neighborhood kids are tearing around outside, and it's hard to think about death now, but I feel I should write this. My parents never did and when my mother died, I had no idea what she would have wanted. So I let Flo make all the arrangements and it was a funeral horror show, a lot of lugubrious music and a hairy legged evangelist ranting and raving, and I thought, "Not for me." In the event of my death I want you to make arrangements as follows: I wish my body to be laid out in the green beaded rhinestone dress that was a gift from my dear friend Raoul the week we spent in Branson, Missouri.—

Barbara stared at the name. Raoul. Who he? Mother had never mentioned a Raoul. There were none in town. A boyfriend. Mother had a boyfriend. Good God.

—I would like someone to be sure to let Andy Williams know that "the lady in the green beaded dress" died and that his kiss on the cheek was one of the true high points of my life. I wish to be cremated. I do not wish to be embalmed and stuck in the ground to rot. I wish my ashes to be placed in the green bowling ball that Raoul also gave me, which somebody can hollow out (I'm told), and then seal it up and I would like the ball to be dropped into Lake Wobegon off Rocky Point where Jack and I used to fish for crappies back years ago when we were getting along. Odd, I know, but I *loved* bowling with Raoul, we always laughed a lot, so I want to wind up inside a ball. And I loved that part of the lake, where our town is obscured behind the trees and you feel that you might be up north on the Boundary Waters. I do not wish any eulogy or public prayers said for me, none at all, thank you, and the only music I want is Andy Williams singing "Moon River," which was "our song," mine and Raoul's, and I'm sorry to have kept all this a secret from you. I hated that my parents had so many secrets and now I've hidden so much from you, dear Barbara. Though it seemed to me that you had more than enough on your mind. I am so sorry that you never met him. He is an old dear friend who I reunited with about twelve years ago. We never got around to becoming a normal couple (long story) but we loved each other and we had some high old times. I realize that these are unusual wishes but you are a strong girl and I know you will respect them. I love you, dear. I always did and I do now, more than ever.

As for my will, it is at the bank in a safety-deposit box along with another letter that I wrote a long time ago and never gave you. Please forgive me.

Love,

Mother

The part about cremation and no eulogy didn't surprise her. Mother loathed funerals and that's why she always volunteered to make the lunch, to avoid the sermon and the crappy eulogy, which always went wide of the mark, usually pitched too high. She thought of Mother slipping off for a tryst in Branson with someone named Raoul. Barbara had been there once with Oliver. It was the only trip they had taken. A geezer resort where the face-lifted stars of yesteryear go on singing their hits like demented robots, eyes glazed, a sort of mortuary of pop music. And she thought Mother had gone to St. Louis to visit a cousin with a lingering illness. Mother lied. But Andy Williams? Mother loved choral music. She adored Handel's *Messiah* and Bach's *St. Matthew Passion*. She had never shown an interest in crooners before.

Barbara pulled the sheet up over Mother's face as she had seen people do in movies. And she reached for the phone to call her son Kyle and she saw the tiny red light blinking on the answering machine. "You have one unheard message," said the lady's voice. "Sent today at 1:29 a.m." Then a click and a gravelly man's voice.

"Hey, Precious. Couldn't sleep after I got your message on the machine. Sorry I wasn't here. Guess you've turned in. Gimme a call in the morning, okay? I saw a great deal on airfare to London and I thought maybe we could do that trip to Italy if you like. Fly to London in September—take a train to Rome. Let's do it."

Barbara stood by the dead woman's bed as the man talked to her.

"I don't know how we got this old, kid. But like you said, after you turn eighty, you've gotta live fast. Anyway, I'm sitting here thinking about you. How long does your answering machine let me go on? I forget. Maybe I'm just talking to the wall. Hey, it wouldn't be the first time, right? I was trying to figure out today when our anniversary is—I mean, do you date it from when we first met? Or is it when we got together again? Now there would be an anniversary. Does Hallmark put out greeting cards for that? Ha ha.—Thinking of you on our Special Day when you and I went all the way—huh? Ha. I think I saved the room key. Listen, I know I'm just nattering on here but what the hell. I'm not the sort of guy who writes things down. So the way I remember is if I tell someone, and who can I tell, right? You. So here I am, yakking into your answering machine. I remember you brought chocolate-chip cookies. And we got into bed and then you got up to use the bathroom and it was the first time I'd seen you without clothes on since the Dyckman Hotel in December of 1941—and you hadn't changed a bit. This tall slip of a girl getting up out of bed like a goddess rising from the ocean waves and all of a sudden that day in 1941 came back so clear, I could smell the floor wax. Nineteen forty-one. December. The Friday before Pearl Harbor. We went to the dance at Fort Snelling and that colonel made a pass at you and we got the hell out and walked along the river and talked, and we stopped and kissed and I told you that my brother was the night clerk at the Dyckman and you said, 'Let's go.' So we caught the Hiawatha streetcar and you were quiet all the way downtown and up to the room and we sort of groped around in the dark and you said, 'Not so fast.' I remember what you said, you said, 'I wish I could make this minute last for a whole day.' And then you rolled over on top of me and we went to town and when it was over you said, 'That was pretty good.' I'll always remember that. 'Pretty good.' Oh God, why do I keep going back to that? You never look back. I do. Because after that, everything happened so fast. You got that boil and you were so sick, I went to General Hospital to see you and the doctor said it was fifty-fifty, at best. They said only immediate family could see you. Your mother was in the hall crying and I went over and said I was a friend of yours and she looked at me and just cried harder. And then they shipped me to Chicago and the train stopped on an overpass and I could look down Portland Avenue to the hospital where you were and count up to the fourth floor and there was a light on in a room. And then it went out. I cried all the way to Chicago. God, I feel like I am going to cry now."

She pressed STOP. That was enough of him. He sounded like a lot of old men she knew. You put a nickel in them and they told their life story twice.

She dialed Kyle's number at his apartment in Minneapolis. He picked up on the third ring. He sounded distracted. Kyle was a sophomore at the University, an English major, and he studied all the time.

"It's Mother, honey. I'm awfully sorry but I have bad news. Grandma died."

"Omigod." He let out a breath. "When did she die?" And a girl's voice said, "What?"

"She died in her sleep. Last night. It must have been sudden. She was reading a book and it fell on the floor and she just died."

He was crying and the girl was comforting him, she said, "It's okay, it's okay." And she hugged him. Barbara said, "I know it's a shock. Me, too. I just walked in and there she was. She must've had a heart attack."

"When did it happen?" He was crying, he could hardly get the words out. The girl whispered, "Who died?"

"Last night. Late. She went out for dinner with her buddies and came home and went to bed and she died. In her sleep. She was very peaceful."

The girl was whispering to him. "My grandma," said Kyle. "Last night."

Barbara said that Grandma was not afraid of death, she looked it straight in the eye, and don't you think she had such a good life because she knew life was short and that pushed her to do more than most people her age would dream of—she talked, listening to him try to take a deep breath and compose himself and this girl, whoever she was, nuzzling him and then it dawned on Barbara that the two of them were naked. Something in the pitch of their voices. A mother can tell. Two naked young people, her freckle-faced boy weeping, and this other person—she imagined a bosomy girl with studs in her nipples and a butterfly tattoo on her butt.

She didn't tell him that she was, at that very moment, *sitting on the bed where the dead body lay.* She could see the shape of Mother's left hand under the sheet. She could have reached out and touched it.

"Are you okay?" he said. Yes, of course she was okay, she only wished she could tell him what it was like to walk in and to find her own *mother,* for crying out loud, lying in bed *with her eyes open.* "I suppose I'm in shock," she said. "I don't know what we're going to do without her."

She listened hard for the girl to say something.

"When's the funeral?" Kyle asked.

"Well, that's what I called you about." And she read him the letter. Word for word.

"That is so awesome," he said. He wasn't crying anymore, he was half laughing. "Wow. A bowling ball!! You mean, like a real bowling ball?"

"I found it in her closet. It's green. Like green marble. Expensive. It looks Italian."

"And no eulogy, no prayers. Boy. She had a whole other life, didn't she."

"I am just a little worried about this Raoul. What if he shows up?"

"Of course he'll show up. We'll invite him. He was her boyfriend. He loved her." Kyle sounded a little giddy. "God, Grandma! I always thought she had something else going on!"

"You think we should? Really? I don't know what to do," said Barbara.

"We're going to do it just exactly the way she wanted it," he said. "I'm going to do it myself." He was all excited now, bouncing around and yipping about his parasail—the one he had built from a kit—*what was a parasail? (parasol?)*—and now the girl's voice said, "Kyle, I can't let you do that. You *know* how I feel," and he walked away from her. He was naked in a bedroom in Minneapolis with a girl. Barbara wanted to ask, "Who's there?" On the other hand she didn't want to know. A redhead maybe, one of those freckled Irish beauties, howbeit with tiny silver hammers stuck in her nipples. A little trollop who could seduce and ensnare a bright but naïve young man, and lead him off to an itinerant life of miming for spare change on street corners, her smart little boy so good in school, so innocent in the ways of the world, and her eyes filled with tears at the thought of losing him. The boy who achieved Eagle Scout and who put on the white robe every Sunday morning and carried the cross down the church aisle—who had almost not gone to college but his mother made him go, who was on the road to becoming somebody—he was in the clutches of the trollop. Maybe she had interrupted them in the midst of hot sex. She tried to imagine his skinny body intertwined with a girl's. How weak men are! Educate them all you like, make them read philosophy and history and poetry, but when the waitress leans over the table and her shapely breasts hang like ripe fruit, men go blank, their pants enlarge, intelligence plummets, they are ready to buy whatever is offered and pay any price. Give them the check, they will sign it! Take their shoes, their watch, the loose change jingling in their pocket—they will look at you in awestruck wonder, little girl, and whisper Thank You as you wave good-bye.

"It's okay, Mom. Call up the mortuary. Not Lindberg. I don't think he does cremations. Call one in St. Cloud. Look in the Yellow Pages. I'll be there tomorrow morning. Do you need me to find Raoul?"

"No, I'll find him myself. Soon as I hang up."

"Promise? You can't leave Raoul out." Kyle laughed. *Raoul.* She had visions of a dance instructor in a storefront studio, Raoul's House of Samba, a lounge lizard in black slacks and flamenco shirt, his specialty: mature women, unattached. Twenty dollars a dance, no extra charge for the squeeze.

3. OBITUARY

Evelyn Frances Powell. Born March 14, 1923, in her grandma Crandall's bedroom in Anoka. Fourth child of Frank and Susan. Ruby, Frank Jr., Florence, Evelyn. Her dad farmed 140 acres near Holdingford. She grew up gardening and feeding chickens and then the farm went under. Her dad bought a tractor to replace his team of horses and the tractor sparked and the barn caught fire and the hay in the loft went up like a torch and the cows perished and that was the end of them. The bank took over and they moved to Lake Wobegon. Uncle Ev owned a machine shop there. Her dad felt "liberated" by the farm failure and pursued his true calling, which was invention. He invented a double-flange rotary valve trombone, a hawser spindle for a capstan whelp, and though his patents found no takers, he was a happy man, a fount of innovation. "Work," he told Evelyn. "That's the secret of happiness." He had a lathe, a drill press, a forge, all he needed. He invented a bifurcated grommet for an oarlock, and a two-way spring-forced sprocket. He invented the two-bit drill chuck, the semi-rigid rear-mounted eyelet, the twin-turret baffle effector. The sheepshank fish hook. Although nothing he made had immediate applicability, he went to his workbench every day with a song in his heart. Evelyn took after him.

In 1938, he went through a bad episode, hallucinations and rest-lessness and vocal outbursts (he shouted things like "Clear the decks!" and "Get 'em off me!") and Florence and Evelyn moved in with their maternal grandparents on Cedar Avenue in south Minneapolis.

When she got to Minneapolis, she took the name Eve for a few years and got a taste of stardom at Roosevelt High School. Eve played center on the 1937–38 Rosies basketball team who went to State, and she recited "The Raven" in speech tournaments, dressed in a long white gown, long wild brown hair, barefoot, and according to her sister, she was mesmerizing.

Eve had a future in Hollywood. Many people thought so. She was a natural. Like Garbo. She shone. You couldn't take your eyes off her. At the 1939 Minnesota State Fair, she was sculpted in butter. She recited "Invictus" on WCCO's "Stairway to Stardom" broad-cast at the Aquatennial, and Randolph Scott, who was Grand Mar-shal of the Torchlight Parade that year, told her she was the genuine article and she should come to Hollywood and he would get her a screen test at RKO, but nobody encouraged her. In any decent fairy tale, someone would have offered her a ride out west and dropped her on Sunset Boulevard with her cardboard suitcase, squinting into the setting sun, and she would've caught the eye of Jack Warner, driving by in his yellow roadster, and he'd stop and offer her a small part in *Babes Ahoy*. But instead she clerked at Dayton's and then went to nursing school. Three months later she got a boil on her butt that popped, which, in those pre-antibiotic days, almost killed her. She lay in General Hospital for two weeks with a 104 degree fever and came home to Lake Wobegon to recuperate.

The brush with death derailed her, and she sat discouraged in her mother's dim parlor, reading pious novels about goodness re-warded, and listened to the moaning that passed for conversation in that house, and that was when Jack Peterson walked into her life. He was the nephew of the next-door neighbor. Simple as that. He came over and shoveled the walk. He was a dark Norwegian in Navy whites, due to report for duty in thirty days, and in a burst of patriotism in the wake of Pearl Harbor, she married him.

She felt sorry for him, said Florence. He was all torn up inside about the futility of war and he believed he was going to die. He was sure that Hitler would be marching down State Street in Chicago by Labor Day and the Japs would invade Los Angeles. The Wehrmacht would blitzkrieg west across the Plains, just as they had rolled over the Poles and the French, the Luftwaffe leaving cities in smoking ruins. America was full of Germans—New Ulm, New Munich—look around you— and they formed a fifth column of spies and saboteurs. The end of the world was at hand, there was no God, how could there be? He was soaked in defeat, death was waiting for him in some stinking jungle. He wept on her hand. She fixed him a chocolate malted and he said it probably was his last. There was a Last Visit to the old high school, and a Last Ice Fishing Trip, and a Last Movie. They sat in the back row. He clung to her and she allowed him to slip his trembling hand up inside her shirt. She just wanted to bring some sunshine into a sailor's life. But some town girls saw what happened and they told and back in those days necking was sex and sex led to marriage—No U-turns Permitted—and the next day he threw himself at her feet and said she was the only ray of hope in his life, and she felt obliged to go ahead and do it. February 7, 1942, at 11:30 in the morning. The two of them and the wooden-faced minister and his cross-eyed wife and Mother and Florence. Jack looked whipped. Evelyn wore a lovely shimmery green dress that had been Mother's. The couple drove away in Jack's rattle-trap Model A, and Mother and Florence burst into tears the moment the car disappeared around the corner. They cried their eyes out.

27

"He's not good enough for her," said Mother. "So why did we let her go?" They were blinded by the uniform, said Flo. The starched cap and the gold braid. Evelyn was sacrificed for the war effort, as if she was scrap metal.

Mr. and Mrs. Peterson drove toward the Wisconsin Dells and he was half-asleep and ran the car off the road and onto a frozen pond in River Falls and they skidded to a halt and the right front tire sank in a hole in the ice. Jack tried to lift the right front end and couldn't and he flopped down on the ice, sobbing, "Nothing I do ever turns out right." They spent the night with an old bachelor farmer named Wilf who towed the car out with a team of horses. Evelyn lay on a filthy couch, her husband on the floor, and considered having the marriage annulled. But what if he died in the service? She'd feel horrible. He was going off to fight for his country in three days and she would make those days the best days of his young life. She imagined his ship would be torpedoed. She would stand by his bier in the cemetery as the bugler played "Taps" and the honor guard saluted and she would grieve for him. That was what Jack expected, and she did too. But he was sent to Los Angeles, taught Morse code, and assigned to a spotter's station at the end of the pier in Ventura where he watched for Japanese planes that never came, his finger on the telegraph key. Three years of staring at the horizon. She wrote to him every Sunday, though he seldom wrote back, cheerful letters about Minneapolis and Vocational High, where she trained as an auto mechanic and her friends there, Ina and Margaret and Grace and Ruby and Marian and Elsie, and the family they had bonded with on Oakland Avenue, the streetcar rides to Excelsior Amusement Park, the picnics in Annandale and Medicine Lake. The gas coupons they pooled to drive to the North Shore in Ina's car, the sing-alongs, the gaiety of it all, and then he came home. He walked in the door and said, "I made it." And he had. There he was. And she was married to him.

4. SEPARATION

They were married for forty-four years. Of course, it didn't escape notice among the vigilant ladies of the Bon Marche Beauty Salon when Jack and Evelyn went their separate ways or that after he died she planted him between his mother and his grandparents under a solo gravestone, a skinny slab of polished granite with JOHN L. PETERSON 1921–1986 carved in it. All around the Lake Wobegon cemetery, you saw double stones, the husband down below, waiting, his wife's name beside his, her death date blank, but she had no intention of landing next to him. Nor would she inscribe the stone "Beloved Husband and Father" or "Asleep in Jesus" or *"Takk for Alt"* (Thanks for Everything). She sat in church for his funeral, listening to him eulogized and hymns sung over him about eternal rest, like layers of whipped cream on a burnt sausage, and put him in the ground and went home and had a cup of coffee.

She and Jack split up in 1981 when he fell in love with a teen porn star named Candy Disch whom he saw in *Teacher's Pet* in a private booth at the adult-video shop in the Mall of Minnesota. It was his first visit there. A lifelong urge since adolescence, suddenly realized at age 60. When Candy strolled on screen in her teeny skirt and striped stockings to beg Mr. Baggins to please please give her a passing grade in algebra and he scowled over his wire-rim glasses and she unbuttoned her blouse and let her perky breasts poke free, Jack melted like butter on a hot waffle. She had a playful way about her that he was missing in his life. She was the girl he should have known when he was 17, come around forty-three years late. He wrote away to Candy c/o Violet Video on San Fernando Boulevard, Los Angeles, and Candy sent him a picture postcard of herself and a handwritten note ("Jack, I'm so glad you liked the movie, it really means a lot, please call me") and he got her on the phone and talked to her for $2.29 a minute. She thrilled him. He knew the meter was running but he had a big crush, which he felt was reciprocated, though she was vague about when they might meet, but he collected photos of the little honey bowling, shooting pool and sunbathing. Jack's brother Pete and his sister LaVonne couldn't comprehend this. How could a World War II vet, a member of the Lutheran church, the father of three, be consumed by passion for a frizzy-haired blonde in a red velvet jumpsuit unzipped to the navel who pursed her pouty lips and whispered, "Oh baby, give it to me, give it to me"? They refused to speak to him or look at him again. They forbade their families to speak to him.

Evelyn felt bad at first. She wept and took his hand and laid it on her breast—"Why would you be fascinated by pictures when you could have a real woman?" she cried. He turned away, flushed, embarrassed.

She had no wish to humiliate him. There was not much cruelty in her. As for fascination, who can explain it? Some men take up golf, some chase girls, some drink Hi-Lex. So she helped Jack ease into a new life as a bachelor.

"He's always felt hemmed in. He married too young. We all did, back then. He hated the Navy and he should've had a few years of freedom but he had to come back here and earn a living and raise kids. All he wants is to do things his own way in his own time. So why shouldn't he live as he pleases? He's sixty, for heaven's sake," said Evelyn.

She had been paying the Visa bill including large payments to Violet Adult Services for Candy's phone time and finally she told Jack that they had to settle up. She borrowed the money to buy out his share of the house and he bought a fishing shack on Lake Winnesisscbigosh, ten miles north, and installed a propane heater, stuffed the cracks with strips of pink foam covered with silver duct tape. He had a fridge full of beer and plenty of videotapes. He hauled a blue velour Barcalounger out there and a water bed. It was all friendly. She didn't call him names or yell or cry. She simply trundled him out to his fishing shack and kissed him goodbye. She told Florence about an article in *Lutheran Digest* about menopausal males having hormonal surges that cause phantom romances. A great big husky old farmer from Sioux Falls sold off his hogs and flew to Malibu and stood along the coastal highway with a sign saying, "Angel, I love you," referring to Angel Marquez, star of *Bolero*. It was a hormonal surge. They shot him up with estrogen and he quieted right down. She had mentioned this to Jack and he hit the ceiling. So he would have to go. His choice.

"I got tired of being supervised by my wife," he explained to his friends at the Sidetrack Tap. "Somebody always telling you to take your feet off the coffee table. It's a lousy way to live. Our ancestors in Norway knew they had a bad deal. The land was worthless for farming and the old man treated them like slaves and the pastor was yelling and shaking his fist every Sunday, and they put two and two together and got on the boat and came to America. And when they got to Minnesota, they saw they had exchanged one bad deal for another, and they didn't agonize over it, they headed for California to look for gold, but the gold was gone, so they sold shovels to people who were looking for gold, and I got about twenty relatives out there who are multimillionaires and if I wanted to I could call 'em up and ask 'em for money and they'd give it to me and you know something, I ain't going to do it, because that ain't my way. I don't need their help or yours or anybody's and I don't need you or anybody telling me what to do either."

So he sat in his shack, in a welter of junk and wrappers, his TV set shining on him, commercials in which powerful pickup trucks ran up steep mountain slopes and skinny models slunk through clouds of fog and golden beer foamed over life's big frosty glass. He lay like a pig in a pen, and dozed and awoke and peed in the sink and lay down and watched a little more. He drank all the whiskey he wanted whenever he wanted and didn't care who knew it. He called it his antifreeze. He snored to his heart's content, got up in the middle of the night to fry up a steak and have a slug of whiskey, slept until noon, it was all good.

Barbara told him once that a quart of whiskey a day was too much and he said, "Lot of small-minded people in this town, just envious of anyone who knows how to have a good time. Don't be one of them. And I'm beyond a quart anyway. Quart and a half." He sighed a long sigh. His skin was gray, mottled, as if he were rotting from the inside out and about to burst. His breath would've knocked a buzzard off a garbage truck. "Your mother never begrudged me a good time, I'll say that for her." And then he started to weep. "Do you think she'll ever take me back?" he said.

No, that was never an option. Mother was living her own life, traveling off to California, Florida, St. Louis. . . .

Dear Barbara,

It cost me $215 round trip to St. Louis and Mamie was happy to lay eyes on me so the week was well worth it and thanks for mowing my lawn. It looks great!!! I've been thinking about our talk. I know that things are strained between you and Daddy after the way he tore into you about Lloyd—no excuse for that at all—and believe me I am on your side, but you really must avoid acrimony as much as possible. Daddy never really grew up and we could talk about WHY NOT until the cows come home but it's simply a fact that must be lived with. He is and always will be 14 years old and it behooves the rest of us to accept that and not agitate ourselves over it.

Trust me when I say he means NO HARM to anyone. The man has no malevolence in him at all, he simply feels very urgent about his own needs and desires and doesn't stop to think about how this might affect others. His interests are few in number and rather simple and don't bear going into in great detail except that he has developed a vast fantasy life to compensate for the straitened circumstances of his own. I found this rather OVERWHELMING when I discovered it accidentally and now I have given up those feelings of hurt

33

and dismay (pointless, really) and simply accept that he is who he is. And meanwhile I choose to EMBRACE the meat and marrow of life, and open my eyes to the wonders around me. I have a certain wanderlust that must be satisfied and that is why I love going to St. Louis and Reno and Miami and other places I've been off to lately.

Life is so dear, dear heart. Live it with gallantry.

Daddy and I came to a parting of the ways. I handed down an ultimatum and he couldn't meet it and so we parted. I simply put him out to where he could be happy and I went about my business and that is that. And once I was shut of the worry and guilt and dismay I seemed to get back some of the old curiosity and verve I remembered from girlhood and I found kindred souls to have fun with and enjoy life and meet it with anticipation and wonder. That is what we cannot cannot cannot ever give up is that ESPRIT. That is what I admire in Bennett even though he is so lost in life, he keeps that venturing spirit. People are too easily squashed by their burdens and become dull and obedient and censorious of the esprit in others—O I could name names but I will not—and it behooves the spirited to keep dancing.

KEEP DANCING, dear.

Love love love from your mother

Barbara visited Daddy every month or so. He liked being denned up at the lake. He went shambling through the woods, collecting blueberries and chokecherries, wild plums, even sarsaparilla berries, dandelion greens, nuts, wild mushrooms, ransacking the nearby dump for usables. He told Barbara that he found roasted chipmunks quite delectable. He grew a beard. He became prophetic. He was libertarian by nature and he predicted the imminent crash of the government and an era of anarchy during which people would flock to the woods and have to learn to survive, as he had. He was quite proud of living alone, though Mother still did his laundry and ironed his shirts nicely and they spent Thanksgivings and Christmases together and when he landed in jail for drunk driving, she bailed him out. He was a mess but he was family nonetheless. She took hot meals out to him, tried to interest him in AA, and offered up his name in prayer on Sunday mornings. Once for her birthday he bought her a mink coat from a man named Shorty who was running a Fire Sale off a flatbed truck at an exit on the Interstate. A silver mink with scorch marks on the back and it reeked of smoke. And it was July. Mother returned the coat and said, "You're going to need this out at the cabin."

He said, "Well, if you change your mind, you know where to find me."

Of course people gossiped about their separation but Mother rose above it. She was a duchess. She was circumspect and unburdened herself to nobody but her childhood friend Gladys and sometimes her daughter and she did her weeping in private. In public she offered a resolute smile and plenty of small talk. She avoided scrutiny by attaching herself firmly to Lake Wobegon Lutheran church. She took over the Altar Guild after the sainted Mrs. Dalbo succumbed to arthritis, arranged the flowers every Sunday, arranged lunches for funerals and senior suppers, stood ready to step in and manage anything that needed managing. She was responsible for bringing in Ernie and Irma Lundeen and their Performing Gospel Birds, a troupe of parakeets and doves and canaries, a macaw, an owl, and a crow, who enacted scenes from

Scripture in their bird-sized costumes and picked out hymns on xylophones and wound up the show with the Blessing of the Birds—the congregation, heads bowed, heard the beating of wings as the Gospel Birds dropped mustard seeds on each person, seeds grown in the Holy Land. Some people thought the show was trashy and beneath them, but after the Birds left, people talked about it for weeks. A remarkable evening. She took on the wedding of a lapsed Catholic about to ship out to Vietnam and in a hurry to marry his girlfriend, an unbeliever, and Evelyn got them hitched and served champagne on the church lawn and tossed rice at them and paid for the motel. She chaperoned Luther Leaguers on convention trips, camped with her Girl Scouts, taught Sunday school, sponsored a Vietnamese family of four, baked for bake sales, edited the Ladies Circle cookbook, sewed for the Christmas pageant, and did the Reformation Sunday scholarship fundraising dinner fifteen years in a row. And then she buried Jack.

Jack died of a heart attack on a bitter January afternoon in front of the Sidetrack Tap. He was a little drunk and arguing with Mr. Hoppe about the authenticity of the Kensington Runestone. Hoppe insisted the stone was inscribed by Viking explorers in the fourteenth century and left in a meadow in western Minnesota, and Jack said the stone was a well-known fake, carved by a farmer with time on his hands. Anybody with an IQ of a potted plant would know that. They'd had this argument for thirty-seven years and the venom had not dissipated, but only distilled. The argument was the vehicle for Jack's anger about old age, bad luck, communism, marriage, Lutherans, the fluoridation of water. It put him in a fury, plus which he'd been thrown out of the bar that morning for yelling at someone he thought was Norbert and who was not. Wally gave him the heave-ho and a few minutes later Barbara saw him fumbling with his keys, trying to open the trunk of a car that wasn't his, and she offered to buy him lunch. Jack was gaunt, unshaven, his hair matted, his face loose, skin sagging, his teeth punky, his glasses missing a lens. He'd been in the leg trap a long time. They traipsed into the Chatterbox Café and sat at the counter and she ordered chicken soup and a grilled cheese sandwich for each of them. "I'll drive you home," she said.

"I got no home," he said. "Got no family. Used to but not anymore. Family is pretty overrated in my book. I am on my way to a place that I don't even know that I'll recognize it when I get there. Maybe the stars. Or the woods. Maybe just North Dakota. I am the Hard Luck Kid. Old and beat down and used up. That's me. Ever show you my scar?" He started to lift his shirt and she made him stop. "But I never held out the tin cup, kid. Say what you will, I never held out the tin cup. But hey, who cares? Nobody. Nobody gives a rip if you live or die. You die and they shove you down in the ground and go about their business and it's like you never existed. That's the long and the short of it. Between a man and a dog, there isn't a dime's worth of difference and you can quote me on that. People think they're so high and mighty. Ha. Vanity of vanities, all is vanity. That's in the Bible, you can look it up. Everybody in this town looks down on Jack Peterson, well, let 'em. My own wife looked down on me for forty years so I'm well used to it. Her and her books and her good manners and her la-di-da lady friends. I fought for this country. I wore the uniform. I was in California but I saw men go off to the Pacific and come back in bags. It could've been me. It wasn't but it could've been. So don't look down on me. Goddamn Norbert stole my auger and now he's trying to avoid me. What kind of a deal is that? Goddamn V.A. won't fix my teeth. Went to church to ask for twenty bucks to tide me over and they're like, 'Oh Jack, we'd love to but we gotta check with Pastor Ingqvist and he's out on a call, could you come back at four o'clock?' The hell. I'm not stupid. They got the money right there in an envelope in the drawer. I've seen it. They don't gotta get permission.

"I was born in this town, grew up here, all my buddies were from here. Married your mother, 1942, went off to war. Treat you like a hero and then you come back, forget it. You work hard, raise your kids, do your best, and you get old and they throw you away like they never knew you. I could write a book about this town that'd burn the eyes right out of your skull. I know these people. There's not a one of them better than me, not one. The Lutherans are the worst and the Catholics run 'em a close second. Myself, I am a card-carrying atheist. Proud of it. Could I borrow fifty bucks until next week? I get my check next week. I gotta go to the V.A. and have them look at my head."

So she forked over the money, paid for lunch, patted his shoulder, and as he headed off to his death, he stopped in the doorway and faced the diners in the booths along the wall, and yelled, "For all have sinned and come short of the glory of God, assholes!"

He walked back to the Sidetrack Tap and there was Mr. Hoppe who smelled of Lilac Vegetal cologne spritzed on liberally. "You smell like you're hoping to get lucky, Hoppe," said Jack, "but let me tell you: as long as it's light out, no woman is going to come within ten feet of you. And after dark, one of them might shoot you if she had a gun." Mr. Hoppe had had a major drinking bout the day before, which he had lost, so he was feeling unsteady, but he drew himself up to full height and said, "Jack, I wouldn't piss on you if you were on fire." When he wasn't dead drunk, Mr. Hoppe could be rather aristocratic. "You," he said, "are a piece of trash." They stood there insulting each other for a few minutes and then got onto the topic of Viking history. Hoppe said it was a crime that the Viking explorers were never given credit while that stumblebum Columbus had a holiday of his own. Jack said, "Well, America is named for Eric the Red. Isn't that enough for you?" Hoppe said it wasn't. And he brought up the runestone. They were standing at the curb in front of the bar, and Jack was hanging onto the town's lone parking meter (erected in 1956 as an experiment, soldered shut in 1972), and he yelled at Hoppe, "It's no wonder you never made anything of yourself. You got shit for brains." And he turned, clutched at his chest, and fell to the ground, dead, his old grizzled mug flat on the ice and snow. "To hell with you," said Hoppe and then thought better of it. He shook Jack's shoulders. "Get up, you old booger," he said. And then he smelled death. It was Bruno, the old mutt, making his rounds of garbage cans. The dog sniffed at Jack's feet, then his crotch, and his face, and then licked Jack's lips. That was too much for Hoppe. He fled into the bar and had Wally call the constables Gary and LeRoy. And then the sheriff came, and the coroner, and a motley crowd of townsfolk, many of whom had seen Jack only minutes before and were struck by the irony: there he had been and now he was no more. It was a wonderful commotion, one that the deceased would have enjoyed. They took photographs of him lying there, and then packed him up and took him away. Somebody went to tell Evelyn but she was in St. Louis. At last, the only mourner left was the dog who sniffed around at Jack's death site and scratched at the ice, and then lay down on it and took a nap.

A week after that, Wally put the Sidetrack up for sale. He told Evelyn, "I never planned to spend my life in a tavern putting mothballs in the urinal and pouring shots of bourbon and listening to a bunch of drunks talk about the good times. I got into this as a favor to my brother-in-law. I was going to run it for him until he got better, but he died. And here I am."

They were married all those years and all Evelyn would say about him was that he was who he was and never pretended to be anything else and in the end he lived how he wanted to live and it's pointless to try to change people. He liked being alone. He liked working on cars. He was employed by Rudeen's Chevy-Buick in Little Falls until the drinking got to him. He preferred a job in a town where he didn't live, which cut down on conversation. He'd slipped into marriage, and it didn't suit him, fell in love with an imaginary friend, took up the bachelor life, drank freely, went fishing, got to talk to his loving daughter at the end. And he died in an instant. It all worked out.

5 . THEY TAKE HER AWAY

The man from Waite Park Cremation Service arrived, shortly after noon. Barbara had finished off the Kahlúa. The phone rang and it was someone asking if she was satisfied with her current long-distance provider. "We're thrilled," she said. "Couldn't be happier." She didn't call Aunt Flo to tell her Mother was dead. In fact she locked the doors and pulled the shades for fear Flo'd barge in and take over. She was a great one for grabbing hold of something you were doing and saying, "Here, let me do that" and wresting it out of your hands—"That's not how you do that"—a rake, a screwdriver, a mixer—the woman would not let you so much as *whip cream with a Mixmaster* even though you were sixty years old and had raised a child, nonetheless *you were not to be trusted.* She pushed Uncle Al around like he was a lawn mower. Don't put that toothpaste there. It goes here in the green cup. Don't hang your shirt there, that's for towels. Why are you driving so fast? Do you want to kill us? Just because the sign says 45 miles an hour doesn't mean you *have to drive 45 miles an hour!* She kept a critical eye on his outfits, his grooming and hygiene, and knew everybody he spoke to on the phone and where he was every minute of the day and why—lucky for her he hadn't gone berserk and stabbed her, the old biddy. Barbara fell asleep on the sofa and awoke at three and in the meantime three persons had called Mother and left messages on her answering machine, which seemed unspeakably sad. Aunt Flo saying: "Just called to see how you're doing. You seemed so quiet the other day. Call me if you want a ride to quilting." And a man offering to clean the chimney and warning of the dangers of carbon monoxide. And the man who had called last night. "Hey, Precious. You sleeping in today? Give a call. I'm around. I see there's a fish fry in Avon. I could drive up in the RV and meet you there." And a chuckle. "Call me on the cell." His voice was low and seductive with a little tinge of the South. Could he be black?

She picked up the phone and called Oliver at Liberty Gas & Lube and he answered right away but he was with a customer so, okay, she said she'd call him right back. "Are you okay?" he said. Sure, she was okay. "You don't sound okay." "I'm okay," she said. She didn't mention that she had found her mother dead in bed. She didn't want to get into that and make him feel obligated when he was busy with customers. "Talk to you later," she said. The moment she hung up, she got teary-eyed again. *What in hell are you doing?* she thought. *You've lived in this town all your life. Call up somebody and tell them to come over here. You're in grief. They'll come and be with you. If you can't call your pastor, call the cops, call Father Wilmer at Our Lady of Perpetual Responsibility, call Sister Arvonne for crying out loud*—Sister Arvonne, now there was a good idea. A pistol of a woman in her black skirt and black jacket, her starched blouse, her sensible shoes. Sister Arvonne would drop everything and come in a minute, make some phone calls, draw up a list, turn this into a project. One, two, three, four— don't cry—that's for later—first things first.

She was blinded by tears and her left leg was asleep but she went careening into the kitchen to find the phone book and look up Sister's number at the Catholic school. The phone book wasn't in the junk drawer and it wasn't next to the phone. She looked in the drawer under the junk drawer and found clippings clipped together and some old color snapshots of family picnics and a letter—a copy of a letter Mother had written to her from Alaska. Except she couldn't remember getting it.

My dear Barbara,

Life is unjust. Here I am, goofing off and having a wild time, and sister Flo, hardworking, loyal, dedicated Florence, has no reward at all except more people asking her to do this and that, loading her up with obligations, and Al trailing along in her wake, helpless as ever. The world is merciless. Time marches on and it tromps over good hard workers and here I am skating along, the playgirl of the North.

But someday this foolish trip to Alaska will be a great asset. I flew up to Juneau in rain and low clouds and the plane glided in between mountains and the man sitting next to me was a bush pilot and out of the blue I asked if he would fly me north. Shameless. But he said, Sure. You shouldn't hesitate to ask for a ride: everybody likes a little company now and then. So the next morning I got in the back of his plane, surrounded by sacks of mail, piles of groceries, the seat belt a cargo strap, and we flew north, and he took a little detour and flew over Mount McKinley, so close to the mountain I could see strings of climbers struggling upward in the snow fields. We landed on a dirt strip next to a gold-mining camp and a man drove up to the strip and unloaded half the groceries and some mail, and invited us in for a beer. He and his wife were the only inhabitants, mining for gold by aiming high-powered hoses at the banks of a stream, and running the dirt through a sluice and collecting the gold dust, and they were starved for company, absolutely starved. Asked me where I came from and I told them about Lake Wobegon and the Norwegian bachelor farmers and how they burn their socks in the spring. And then we flew on to an Inuit village and a grass landing strip on the edge of a cliff. We came in heading for the cliff and landed uphill and used every inch of landing strip and all the Inuit kids were out, laughing and yelling and tearing around, and mail was unloaded and then Dan turned the plane around and gave the engine full throttle, and the plane hurtled toward the edge of the cliff bouncing like mad, and the engines screaming and off the cliff we went and dropped a little and then the wings caught hold and off we went. Dan was singing something that he told me later was an Inuit good-luck song. That takeoff I will always remember. The violence of it and then the silence of being airborne and banking to the right and down below the children waving, and then off to Kotzebue and the Bering Strait ahead, and beyond it Siberia and a whole mysterious world I don't expect I'll ever see.

When I am old and bunged up and living in the Good Shepherd Home surrounded by half-dead people watching TV and I rummage around in my memory bank to figure out who I used to be, that takeoff will be right there, I believe. Money in the bank. I can feel the plane shudder and buck and leap forward and me leaning forward, hanging onto the cargo strap, and then the sinking sensation and then the air picked us up and bore us forward.

Life is unjust and this is what makes it so beautiful. Every day is a gift. Be brave and take hold of it.

Love, your mother

The man from the crematorium arrived in a plain old black delivery van, no name on the side. He was young, but of course everybody was nowadays. His name was Walt. He held a folded plastic bag under one arm. "We've found it better not to advertise who we are," he explained. "Some folks are still sort of weirded out by the idea of cremation, so our customers prefer anonymity."

But how could you hide the fact of cremation? she thought—people come and there's a little jar on a pedestal.

She explained about the rhinestone dress and he smiled. "You don't want that," he said. "A lot of charred rocks mixed up with your mother." And then she suddenly could visualize Mother being consigned to the flames—rising up, mouth open in a silent scream, arms reaching out, in agony, a true Christian martyr in the flames.

"Where is your mother?" She pointed to the bedroom door. He went in there. Suddenly she wasn't sure if this was the right thing. O God. What to do? She picked up the phone but who to call? Aunt Flo was three blocks away but that would be a horror show. She'd get mad and tell you what a harebrained thing this is and how typical of you, Barbara. Pastor Ingqvist—you were supposed to call your pastor, weren't you? Yes, you were. But what was he going to add to the situation? Read a prayer off an index card. Talk about the corruptible becoming the incorruptible. And she didn't know his feelings about cremation. Probably negative. He'd come in and murmur his stuff and the upshot would be that Mother would lie waxen and cold in a $3000 coffin and Barbara would feel the whips of remorse for the rest of her life. And she knew what Pastor Ingqvist'd say about Andy Williams singing "Moon River." Not much doubt there.

Walt emerged from the bedroom holding up a diamond necklace. "You'll want this," he said. Barbara had never seen it before. He went to bring in the gurney and Barbara poured herself a little vodka and OJ.

She could imagine Oliver on his stool in the cashier's cage at Liberty, behind the candy bars, turning his great bulk to take the credit card from a customer, swiping it, shoving the slip under the glass to be signed, offering the ballpoint. He had been shot twice on duty. "Only flesh wounds," he said, chuckling. He weighed, she guessed, almost four hundred pounds and he was the sweetest man you ever met. When people stared at them at Perkins when they had breakfast after a night together, she wished she had a pamphlet she could hand out: "This man whom you stare at, who, to you, is a freak and an abuser of food, is also the kindest and cheeriest man in Minnesota. And, yes, a wonderful lover. Attend to your own shortcomings, and give this man the respect he deserves. Thank you." Oh, what a lovely amorous man. He loved to nuzzle and whisper and stroke her leg. He was a great fat man and in no hurry to get to the acrobatics. He could kiss and murmur and nestle for an hour or two before he got urgent and excited and started undressing her, which other men got to in forty-five seconds. No foreplay for them, just get you naked and in they go and a minute later it's over. The fat man was languid and tender. And then, bless his heart, when she was naked and the fat man looked at her, he imagined he saw a slender lovely girl before he turned the lights out and began to slip out of his clothes.

Walt came through the back door with a fold-up gurney, a skinny thing the size of an ironing board, and his helper, Cliff, who looked to be about eighteen. What must it be like to be so young and employed to carry the dead out of their bedrooms? She held out a hand to Cliff and kissed him on the cheek. "Oh, I'm sorry," she said. "I didn't mean to do that." The choir had stopped singing so she put on Robert Preston singing "Ya Got Trouble" and then noticed that her pants were unzipped. She took off that record and put on a choir singing something dark and slow. And then the phone rang. It rang just as Walt and Cliff emerged from the bedroom with Mother zipped up in a plastic bag and wheeled her out the back door. The shock of seeing this— the house suddenly empty—she picked up the phone and it was Flo saying, "What is going on? What is that truck doing in the alley? Speak up!" and Barbara sobbed, "My mommy's dead."

Flo pulled up in front two minutes later, her hair in curlers, as the truck pulled away in back. She'd been at the Bon Marche Beauty Salon, having it blued. She was hopping mad. She took one look at Barbara and said, "You're a souse, that's what you are! You need to get a grip on yourself, young lady. Where is Evelyn?" And then she grabbed onto a chair for support. "Oh dear God, she went to the doctor two weeks ago. She was fine." She choked and went in the bedroom and found Walt's business card and came charging out and glared at Barbara and shook her fist. "Sending your mother to be burned up like she was garbage. Why didn't you just chop her up with an axe and throw her in the incinerator? This is treachery. You ought to be shot." And Flo called up the crematorium and left a long message on the machine, to get the hell back with her sister Evelyn's body unless he wanted to be in court that evening. She, Flo, had a nephew in the legal profession who would, by God, make your life pretty damn miserable unless you bring that body back here this instant. Driving around preying on the grief-stricken who happen to be intoxicated too—

Barbara had never heard her swear before. Flo was a good Lutheran, but she tore into Walt like a dog on a bone. And then Barbara pulled out Mother's letter and handed it to Flo. Flo read it and sat down. Barbara took the phone. "Disregard the previous message, we're a little upset here," she said into the answering machine. "We'll work it out." Flo looked up, aghast.

"You should have burned this. If you had an ounce of common sense, you would've put a match to it and buried it in the garden. This is just outrageous. I ought to wring your neck." And then Flo put her old wrinkled face in her hands and sobbed. "What has this family come to? We'll never be able to hold our heads up in this town again. A bowling ball! People will think we are fools, no better than the Magendanzes. I wish I had dropped dead rather than know this. Why couldn't God have taken me first?"

She looked up at Barbara, her old eyes full of tears. "Who is this Raoul?"

"He is a flamenco dancer. He taught her to samba," said Barbara. "He took her to a casino where she won fifty-thousand dollars at blackjack and offered to buy him a drink and they wound up flying to Missouri. Mother had a whole secret life and I'll show you her confession if you like. She was an atheist and a Democrat and she thought you were a stuffed shirt with a cob up your butt. Those were her exact words, that you had a cob up your butt."

She wasn't sure why she said these terrible lies, but she found it satisfying. Flo shuddered as if stabbed with a fork. "That can't be true," she whispered. All the starch was out of her now. *Serves you right,* thought Barbara.

"Drive me home, please," said Aunt Flo. Her voice was faint. She held up her car keys. "I'm in no shape to drive."

Barbara drove Aunt Flo home—slowly, focusing on the street,

making sure not to drive across a lawn and into a flower bed—and led her inside and helped her into bed. She seemed very old and frail, not the mover and shaker of yore. "This would have killed my mother," she said faintly. "This would have done her in. I do believe that we are in the Last Days and that the world is coming to an end. I never thought so before but I do now. My own little sister— I tell you, Satan is at work among us. Pray for me." And then she grabbed Barbara by the arms, hard, and pulled her down close. "Quit your boozing," she said. "Stop it now. Shape up. For your mother's sake. For Kyle."

"Mother was never judgmental about other people having a good time," Barbara said, all cool and collected. "Mother liked to imbibe now and then herself And she went dancing. With Raoul. Mother adored him. He made her happy in her last years. She found a happiness that you and all the people like you will never know. You spent your whole damn life bossing other people around and barging in and taking mixing bowls out of people's hands. Mother found love. I'm proud of her. And I'm going to scatter her ashes exactly as she wished, and I don't care if you come or not."

She strode out of Aunt Flo's bedroom and closed the door with a bang and was on her way to the front door and then stopped in the living room and felt bad for having said all of that. What a terrible thing to do. So she turned and marched back to the bedroom door and opened it. Flo was sobbing, her face in the pillow, her white hair a big tangle. "I'm sorry for saying what I said," said Barbara, and closed the door. She was a bad person, very bad, but she had her reasons.

Out on the sidewalk three little girls were playing jump rope, two twirling and one in the middle jumping, and the two were chanting:

49

Little Joe ate some snow
He got a part in a movie show
Had a claw
On his paw
Ha ha ha he was Dracula.
Blood was dripping
Down his chin
How many crypts does he live in?
One, two, three, four, five . . .

And the jumper kept hopping as the two girls twirled faster and faster up to twenty-three and finally caught her. *Oh the misery that we have brought them into,* she thought. *They will lose their mothers and then what will become of them, poor lambies?* And she thought of poor Muffy and that old sadness came over her and she was momentarily drenched in thirty-one-year-old grief. *Oh dear God, I have got to join a group or something.* They had groups for everything now. Stress Management and Men Coming To Terms With Their Bodies and AA and a new group she'd read about that helps you deal with your issues with people who happen to be dead now. Mediums of Mercy. And another, MOCK, Mothers of Challenged Kids. It meets, as they all do, on a Tuesday night in a church basement—not in Lake Wobegon, God knows, but somewhere, Minneapolis, you could sit in a circle with other moms and cry for your lambie, your babykins, your pookster, your Little Miss Muffin.

6. THE SARAH PROBLEM

When Kyle hung up the phone, having just promised to drop his grandma's ashes in a bowling ball from a parasail, his friend Sarah was standing behind him, slipping her arms around Kyle's waist. "I'm so sorry, sweetie. You must have been really really close to her. I remember when my grandma died. I was sixteen and it really tore me to pieces. She died in Tampa and I rode a bus all night and all day to get down there and my parents got really mad at me but I couldn't help it, I had to be there. Her name was Hermione. She collected seashells. She played the piano."

Kyle unclasped her arms from his waist and headed for the kitchen. She followed, reminiscing about the death of her grandma. Sarah was like that. Anything that happened to you reminded her of something in her own life, however remote the connection. If he had mentioned Raoul, she would've remembered a Raoul, or maybe a Ramon, or a Newell, or maybe the Sun God Ra, and she could yak about it for as long as you'd let her. You were never at a loss for conversation with Sarah. She could talk for both of you. That was the nice part about having sex with her—she mostly shut up and you had a little peace and quiet.

He poured himself a cup of cold coffee and put it in the micro-wave and lit a cigarette. She hated cigarette smoke. It made her sick. He blew a little her way.

"That is just so incredibly sad," she was saying. "Have you ever thought about what it would be like to die? I mean, actually? I just can't even comprehend it. It must be terrible." She was try-ing to put her arms around him again and he slid between a chair and the refrigerator to block her and then crouched down and pretended to look for something in a low cupboard.

"Was she alone when she died?"

He nodded. "I think that she was ready to die," he said. "I think she was actually looking forward to it. People come to that point where they've lived long enough and everything around them starts to seem weird and they go, like, Okay, I'm done now, get me out of here."

It was bullshit, but he liked to b.s. her, it kept her off balance.

Kyle wasn't set on Sarah. Not at all. They had hooked up at a Super Bowl party, in somebody's apartment. She was cleaning up during halftime and he pitched in and washed dishes and when he said, "God, football is boring," it endeared him to her, and the dish-washing too, and the bridge to couplehood appeared. She invited him home and they snuggled together and did stuff that felt good and the bridge to couplehood was crossed. It was a convenience, it saved time looking for a date, and then they moved in together to save on rent. An economy move. He was happy trying out the idea of couplehood so long as she didn't take it as the first step to the Big M, which of course she did. Probing questions: "How do you feel about me?" she would murmur over the cornflakes. "Tell me the truth." Or "Where do you think we'll be two years from now?" Or "What do you think is the best age to start a family?"

"Well," he said, "unless you adopt, you have to start them at zero and let them grow up from there."

Big looping hypotheticals to which he could only shrug and make up an answer.

Still, it was better than the panicky groping in high school, in some parents' basement, the girl scared and yet egging you on, saying no no and yes yes at the same time and wanting to be violated and also to keep her innocence, pulling, pushing, pleading, protesting. Sarah was all for it. She said, "I want you." She still did. Pulled him into bed and got the show on the road.

"When is the funeral?" said Sarah. "Not a funeral. A memorial service. And it's on Saturday." He had to test his parasail. The shroud lines needed refitting. Last time he flew, it tended to drift sideways. And he wanted to paint eyes on it. He built it from a kit with money Grandma gave him a year ago to go to Europe. "Go see the world while you're young," she said. "I always kicked myself that I didn't. Got married at nineteen and had a baby at twenty and that was it, the doors closed. No reason for you to make the same mistake. I didn't even see New York City until I was seventy-two years old. What a comment!" They were driving back to Lake Wobegon from Fisher's Supper Club in Avon where she'd taken him for the deep-fried walleye. She'd had a whiskey sour and a glass of champagne. She was feeling gay. She handed him the check. "Do what you want but don't use it to pay your bills, for heaven's sake. Have some fun."

Sarah was opposed to the parasail, afraid he'd crash to his death. So many stories about homemade aircraft crashing. Famous people, rich, accomplished, going up in the air in some flimsy contraption and a gust of wind comes up and they spiral down and splatter on the rocks. "Think about me," she said. "Think how I'd feel." He'd taken it up on a test flight over Lake Minnetonka in June and it was glorious, the best cheap thrill he could imagine, better than a roller coaster.

His friend Duane Dober had an 18-foot speedboat with a 75-horsepower outboard. Duane wore pop-bottle glasses and lived in dread that a ray of sun might catch a lens and burn a hole into his brain and leave him a helpless cripple who makes ashtrays from beer cans so he wore long-billed caps and stayed out of the sun as much as possible but he loved to race around in his boat with the prow up in the air and smoke dope and listen to the Steel Heads. When Kyle called and said, "I need you to tow my parasail so I can deposit my grandma's ashes in the lake," Duane saw it as a chance to thumb his nose at the fishing community. They gave him a hard time about his wake. Well, he'd show them. He imagined he might race around at top speed towing Kyle and rock the fishing boats in his wake and they'd yell and shake their fists and then a cloud of ashes would descend on them. "I'll be there," he said.

Kyle remembered what convinced him to buy the parasail—it was a letter from Grandma, along with a check for $500—her beautiful handwriting on little sheets of pale blue paper—

Dear Kyle

I'm in Columbus GA, attracted here by the name "Chattahoochie" on my road map, which is the river between GA and AL, but you probably knew that. Anyway, it is spring and so delicious I'm stopping here and not going on to FL after all. The town is just a riot of flowers and sweetness, magnolias and the like. The B&B was full up but they gave me a little shotgun cottage across the street, tucked into a bower of jasmine and honeysuckle and I don't know what all, the air is like spun sugar. I have a little porch, a sitting room, bedroom and bath, and a tiny kitchen, plus a clock radio, a few books, soap and towels, a box of cheese straws and am happy as can be. Also a kerosene lamp in the bedroom, a real one, and last night I woke up and got a whiff of kerosene and it made me teary-eyed thinking about Aunt Josephine and her kitchen at night, her washing dishes in hot soapy water, me drying, and the lamp lit. I will tell you about her some-day. She was a saint.

This is a street of old frame cottages with lawns of silvery grass, where I know nobody and nobody knows me, which suits me just fine, kiddo. I am a pilgrim and it's good to be on the move so we don't get attached to possessions and place. I am also a romantic and we need to travel so we don't get too disillusioned by people. I am thinking of the school board's move to require the pledge of allegiance, but don't get me started.

I am also trying to escape from your mother's birthday, darling. Nothing makes you feel old like when your kids get old. That's the killer.

Deprivation is exciting, don't you think. It's one reason to travel, to strip down to essentials. I always pitied poor Flo her vast salt-and-pepper shaker collection which began when she inherited a couple hundred of the damn things from Aunt Ruth who simply adored figurines that dispensed seasoning. So Flo became a prisoner of the collection, expanded it, tended it, bought glass display cases for it, gave an interview to the paper about it, and now she is worried about vandals so she hardly dares leave the house for a day to go to Minneapolis. There is nothing in my house that I would grieve over if someone smashed it.

(Flo has never been able to throw away keys. Did you know that? She has hundreds of them, some rusted and going back fifty years. The houses they would have unlocked were never locked in the first place and the cars they started are in junkyards but she keeps them all. If you ask her, she'll deny it, but I've seen the box in her basement.

I am going to sit out on the porch and inhale flowers for a while. So little time, dear, but what there is is sweet. I hope you are getting some sweetness in your busy life and that you feel at home in this world. Lonely men tend to sink— into liquor, or homicide, religion—you name it. Don't sink, boy. Fly. That's an old lady's advice. Fly.

Love to you, dear,

Yr Grandma

P.S. Here's some money I saved by not going to Florida. Spend it on something you always wanted.

7. FINDING RAOUL

Barbara found a poem Mother wrote on the back of a recipe for ginger cake—

Go away and leave me now.
Leave me to my tears,
The long thoughts and the furrowed brow
The griefs of my long years,
And I will paint my face and blush
And turn down the light
And wait here in a holy hush—
He's coming—here—tonight.

And that reminded her to call Raoul in Minneapolis. She found his return address on letters stashed in a Scotch shortbread tin in Mother's closet. Raoul Olson, Aldrich Avenue, Minneapolis. There was a snapshot of him on a beach, grinning, flexing his biceps, an old man in crimson swim trunks, old flesh on his bones, a big head of hair dyed black black black. Mother's boyfriend. She had suspected his existence. Oh yes, many times.

There was the poem Mother wrote and recited for the Sweethearts' Dinner at church one Valentine's Day, and got choked up on the lines—

Long ago and faraway,
You and me, a sunny day—
Long ago, another time,
When I loved you and you were mine.

Well, you knew darned well it wasn't a poem about Jack Peterson.

And then there was the call from Mr. Becker at the bank. "I shouldn't say this but I'm worried about your mother," he said. "She's been spending a lot of money lately in Las Vegas and Reno and San Francisco and hither and yon, and it's her money, and I'm not saying she's overdrawn, she's not, not even close, but I just wonder what is going on here."

And then there was the urgency with which Mother packed up and left the house for a few days—"Who are you going to see?" Barbara'd ask. "You meeting a boyfriend?" Mother snorted. Well, here was her snort: an old sporting gentleman named Raoul Olson. A postcard with the Foshay Tower on it and tiny handwriting: "Dear Rosebud"—that's what he called her, Rosebud— "Youre a peach and thats for sure, kid, you deserve nothing but the best. Speaking of which didnt we have some laughs in Reno. Id say so. The motel was deluxe and so was the company in my opinion. We need not mention the clams. Never again. Those folks by the pool will not be the same since they got to see us two cavorting on the slide like a couple of kids, you could hear them thinking were do those two get off having all the fun and us sitting here like two prunes. And I sure do agree with you about the importance of 'Naps.' Two great minds are one on that particular subject. Nuff said."

She googled him and he popped right up.

RAOUL OLSON (June 24, 1923–) was the beloved weatherman and star of the children's show *Yonny Yonson Of The Yungle* on WCCO. Olson was born in Chaffee, North Dakota, and served in the Marines in World War II after which he worked for stations in California and Nevada before joining WCCO in 1958. He did the weather on radio and TV and also a 6 p.m. newscast for many years while getting into his trademark leopardskin long underwear to play Yonny, the "Scandihoovian Tarzan." The show was extremely popular and a generation of Minnesota children grew up listening to Yonny sing Happy Birthday in fractured Swedish and tell jokes to his cow Helga and his dog Rasmus. For several years, Olson also appeared as the Duke of Podunk on *Dance Party* which was carried briefly on the ABC network. He retired as Yonny in 1994. He married June Davidson in 1948 (divorced, 1964) and they had two children, John and Carmen. His son died of leukemia in 1961, which inspired Raoul to create a show for kids and to name his character Yonny, which is Johnny in Scandinavian dialect.

Yonny Yonson. She and her brothers watched him daily for years. The man who told jokes to his dog and honked a horn and showed Little Rascals cartoons and danced with a floor mop to "On The Trail of the Lonesome Pine" and at the end of every show took two steps toward the camera and said, "You kids are driving me to drink!" and grabbed a bottle of Coco-Pop soda, his sponsor, and poured it over his head. And sometimes he did it upside down, while performing a handstand, one-handed.

And now she could remember Mother watching him from the ktchen door and smiling.

And she never said a word. "I used to know him." Nothing like that.

Raoul Olson. Aldrich Avenue, Minneapolis. Barbara didn't think anybody who meant that much to Mother should get the news by phone, so she got in the car and drove to Minneapolis to tell him. She needed a drive anyway. She took the back way, down through Holdingford and Avon to the Interstate and then instead of taking it she stayed on the back roads. Cold Spring, Watkins ("Birthplace of Eugene J. McCarthy"), Kimball, Dassel. She once dated a basketball player from Dassel who took her out to an abandoned farmplace and she sat on the front step of the house, which had collapsed into the cellar, and he sat on the front bumper of his old black Ford ragtop, guitar in hand, and sang her all the blues songs he knew, which were quite a few. Pankake was his name. He was a forward with a deadly jump shot from deep in the corner and scored twenty-six points for Dassel against Lake Wobegon and she, a cheerleader, had talked to him in the parking lot after the game and given him her phone number. She had gone over to the opposition. He told her he had lost interest in basketball after reading *Moby-Dick*. He had a nice voice. He packed up his guitar and drove her home. It was 1:30 a.m.

Dassel was due west of the city on Highway 12, which suddenly became a big vacuum of a freeway sucking her in toward the towers of downtown and everybody driving as if they were on their way to shoot someone, enormous SUVs looming up in her rearview mirror, hanging on her bumper, then swerving around her though she was driving the speed limit—*what're you doing on my highway, lady? Move over!*—and she got off on Lyndale and drove north and found his address, a little blue rambler, the front door open, music emanating from within. One of the big bands playing a ballad and a girl singer spooling out the words, about a lover gone, perhaps for good—she peered in through the screen. Dark inside and a big round mirror facing the door and there she was in the mirror, hand shading her eyes. The girl singer sang, "We'll meet again, don't know where, don't know when—" She rang the bell. And a sleepy voice said, "Yeah?"

"It's Evelyn Peterson's daughter. Barbara."

He rose from the sofa where he'd been sleeping and opened the door. He was a husky old coot in a ribbed undershirt, tufts of gray hair sprouting under it, black stubble on his face, black silk shorts, flip-flops, a dead cigar in his paw. "What's going on?" he said. He looked alarmed. "Is she okay?"

"Sorry to burst in like this. Didn't mean to wake you up."

"What's wrong?" He opened the door. She wanted to tell him that Mother was okay. Waiting in the car in her beach dress, ready to fly off to Cancun and go snorkeling.

"Mother died last night."

All the air just went out of him whoosh and his face went blank like he'd been shot in the back or hit with a telephone pole.

"She died in her sleep reading a book. I found her this morning. She didn't suffer or anything. She must've just slipped away in the night."

"I tried calling her just last night—"

"I know. I listened to it on the answering machine."

He stepped out and shut the door. An elderly tabby cat looked out through the screen and made a faint scratchy meow.

"Do you think she listened to it?"

"You mean, before she died?" *Well that's a pretty stupid question,* Barbara thought. He nodded. "Did she get my message?"

"Yes, she did. It had been saved. She listened to it and then she saved it." *Lie, lie, lie.*

Big tears in his eyes. She put her arms around him and he clung to her and they sort of waltzed backward into the living room. The place was soaked in cigar smoke. Mother was death on secondary smoke. Couldn't bear it. Had she ever set foot in this house? She must have. He turned off the record player. She noticed a recent photo of the two of them in a black frame, his arm around her. She was half a head taller and grinning as if she'd just won first prize in a three-legged race. He sat down on a hassock. The cat brushed against his bare leg and made a faint scratchy meow.

"She went out for dinner last night with Margaret and Gladys and she was fine when they dropped her off and this morning I found her. She must've listened to your message and went to sleep and didn't' wake up."

He started to say something about Mother and then excused himself and slipped around the corner and blew his nose. A long-time bachelor from the looks of things. Boxes of stuff on the sofa, the glass-top coffee table, the carpet, open boxes of old clothes, magazines, gewgaws, rummage, as if he'd started to straighten up the joint and gotten disoriented. A hubcap for an ashtray and a *Mona Lisa* picture puzzle, half assembled. A picture of a wolf on a snowbank on a moonlit night hung on one wall and a wrestling poster on another—the Ayatollah Khomeanie vs. Jesse (The Body) Ventura, two gargantuans, one in a turban, one in a boa and pink glasses. And in small type: "refereed by Raoul Olson of Channel Four." The TV was on, the sound off: a newscaster in a blue suit, the state capitol behind him . . .

Raoul came back, two glasses in one hand, a bottle of Jim Beam in the other.

"We found a letter with her last wishes and everything, and I guess she opted for cremation and a memorial service, not a church funeral, so we're going to do that on Saturday. Down by the lake. I hope you will come."

"Yeah, she didn't have much use for the church. She told me that. They were too narrow-minded for her. Oh God. What are we going to do?" He choked up for a moment. "I sure was in love with her—" He dug in his pocket for a hanky and blew his nose again. He looked like he might've lifted weights at one time. A big chest and a headful of hair, newly dyed blue-black. A red splotch of broken veins on each cheek, a big nose with cavernous nostrils. He gestured with the whiskey bottle and Barbara shook her head and he poured some in a glass for himself and tossed it back and closed his eyes and shook his head hard and a long sound came out like quacking.

"Sorry," he said. He gave Barbara a long look and thanked her for driving down to tell him in person. He looked shaken. Queasy.

"Your mother and I met in 1941. I came down from North Dakota and went into nurse's training. I'd enlisted in the Marines and it turned out I had flat feet so they made me a medic and they sent six of us to Swedish Hospital and she was in my class. I was sitting on the front steps and she came walking up the walk and I went for her right away. She was tall and rangy and swung her arms and laughed and she had a way of looking you over so if she liked you, it really meant something. Oh God, she was the love of my life and I knew it. Wham. Just like that. This was back when there was a lot of dancing. Dances almost every night, and we went to every one. We were good enough that we entered contests. We jitterbugged like crazy and when we were out of breath, we sat in the corner and necked. I asked her to marry me and she wanted to but then she got sick and almost died. Infected boil. It was on her butt, she couldn't sit down. I said, Let me have a look at it, but she went and squeezed it and got a terrible infection. I took care of her for the first three days. I gave her sponge baths. I held her in my arms when she was having hallucinations, out of her head jabbering about her dad and crying and yelling at somebody to rescue the horses. I was with her around the clock. And then I took her to the hospital and I went home and slept a few hours and when I woke up her parents were there and I had orders to ship out to Chicago and then to Guadalcanal. I tried to write to her but I couldn't remember the name of her home town, Lake Wobegon. The letters kept coming back. I was in the Dutch East Indies when I heard she married somebody from home. God, I cried for three days. I met Bing Crosby when he did a USO tour in the Pacific and he got a touch of malaria. He introduced me to people and I got into radio in San Francisco. Actually, Oakland. I did a show called *Bay Town Ballroom* and played records and on weekends I emceed dances at the Alhambra and Aragon ballrooms and the Club Seville, and I married a lady bass player named June and I was doing well except I had a problem with the happy powder so June thought maybe I'd do better in Minneapolis, get me away from temptation, and we came out, and I got the TV job doing the weather and was earning good dough and we moved to Golden Valley and right then, when everything was good, my little boy got sick and died of leukemia. It happened so fast. It was like a load of rocks got dumped on me. I had a pity party for a few years. I got deep into the sauce and felt hopeless and nasty and June left and took our little girl, and that's when I became Yonny Yonson on TV. It was a heartbreaker, seeing those kids, let me tell you. All the smiling kids and I thought, 'Why couldn't mine be here? Why did this happen to me?' and one day I walked out on the bridge thinking I'd jump off it and end this nonsense, and I climbed over the rail and there was a string of barges going under that were full of wheat and soybeans and I thought how ridiculous to jump and break my neck on a pile of wheat and my body goes down to New Orleans and meanwhile I've ruined a whole load of wheat. So I crawled back over the rail and I went back to the TV studio and the secretary said, 'There's a lady in Lake Wobegon named Evelyn Peterson trying to track you down.' We talked on the phone and then we met for drinks and it was like 1941 all over again. We were like two kids. Suddenly I had something to live for. I cleaned up my act and we started dating and every day was sunshine. We were talking about going to Europe. She'd never been there." His voice broke. "I told her everything about what'd happened to me and how low I had fallen and she said she loved me."

8. QUILTERS

Evelyn made annual trips to Las Vegas with Raoul with a couple years off on account of his 1996 heart bypass and subsequent argument over his cigar-smoking. He said he knew she hated cigars and she said no, she only hated cheap ones. He said, "Don't baby me, I know you hate the smoke." She said, "Some smoke I like." He vowed he was going to give up smoking for her sake. She said, "Please don't. Do it for yourself." "There you go," he said, "you want me to quit, you just don't want to say so." He said he would quit cigars before the next trip to Vegas, a month away, and when he couldn't, he was so ashamed of himself—a guy with heart problems and he could not put nicotine aside even for the love of a good woman!—he headed out west to pull himself together and stopped in Bismarck to visit an old girlfriend but she wouldn't see him, she had gained weight and was embarrassed, so he proceeded westward to Billings where his brother Marvin lived but he was gone, his wife said, hinting that she didn't much care if he returned. "Where did he go?" asked Raoul. "You'd have to ask him," she said. He went on to Bozeman to visit his buddy George Moses who had gotten him the job on TV,

and George was up north fishing, said Lucile. So he drove off in
search of George, chain-smoking stogies, and stopped in Butte
late that night for a piece of banana cream pie, and had eaten half
of it when two idiots came bursting in with guns drawn and
cleaned out the till and then, even though it made no sense, took
Raoul hostage. "Why?" he cried. "For insurance," they said. "Insurance against what?" But they grabbed him and stuck a pistol
barrel in his ribs and shoved him out the door—"Cut it out!
There's no need to get rough! I'm seventy years old!"—but that
didn't matter to them. And then they saw a cop car parked in
front of the bank and they decided to swipe it. "Are you nuts?"
he yelled. They shoved him in the backseat behind the steel grate
and sped north on gravel roads, both of them snorting white powder and passing a bottle back and forth. In no time, there were
flashing blue lights on their tail and a chopper overhead. "I told
you this made no sense," said Raoul. They blew past a roadblock
at the Canadian border, and raced over a plowed field at 100 m.
p.h., Raoul bouncing off the ceiling, and through a farmyard,
sideswiped a chicken coop, bounced off a propane tank, and struck
a half-empty granary and were thrown from the car into a pool of
winter wheat. Like so many desperadoes, they were not wearing
seat belts. All three were badly banged up, and Raoul suffered
broken ribs and a cracked vertebra. He lay in the V.A. hospital in
Seattle for almost a month and came back to Minneapolis in a
back brace and feeling deflated, and sent her a Thank You card.
"I've learned my lesson," he said. "I am a cigar smoker, and you
are the love of my life." And she brought him a box of Muriel
Slims, and stood at his door smoking one herself, and said, "These
are good! Mild and tasty and long-lasting, just like me!"

Astonishing, Barbara thought. To look at Evelyn, most people'd never guess she had a Raoul in her life. She was a quilter. Summer, fall, winter, and spring, she and the six others in the Ladies Circle gathered in the Fellowship Room, cranking out quilts until she finally turned in her needles: she was 78 and her fingers hurt and besides, there was a quilt glut in town. "How can you?" said Florence. The Circle had been cutting and stitching since Jesus was in the third grade. The idle brain is the devil's playground, said Flo. "Remember Mildred Anderson the cashier at the First State Bank who absconded to Buenos Aires with a pillowcase full of loot and is still there today for all we know? A perfectly nice woman, or so it appeared, but she never married and so she had time on her hands that she didn't fill with hobbies (such as quilting), she just sat in her little bungalow and read books like you do, and that's undoubtedly where she picked up the idea of improving her life at public expense. Quilting might have saved Mildred from plunging into a life of crime the way she did and the cloud of shame she brought on her family." Mildred's sister Myrtle was in the Circle, along with Helen, Lois, Arlene, Florence, Evelyn, and sometimes Muriel, and they had a merry old time, chortling about this and that and ragging on each other and savoring old gossip, chewing it over, ruminating, tearing it apart like scholars. That perfectly nice girl with the bouncy blond hair who went away to college to study elementary ed and fell in with a crowd of poets and came home blanched and harrowed. So then she married a fellow she had known for all of thirty-six hours, a forest ranger, Doug, who turned out to be married already—and then, in smoking ruins, she moved to Texas and at last word was selling costume jewelry at carnivals and living in the backseat of a Honda Civic. She had aged thirty years in just seven. All from keeping bad company. The story of her fall was a favorite topic, along with the tippling of Clint Bunsen and his volatile marriage to Ilene, and the California success story of that tramp Debbie Detmer.

Debbie had broken her mother's heart and driven her father into the stony depths of depression. It was as simple as that. Her poor dad was a broken vessel, sitting glued to the Golf Channel, his wife obsessively vacuuming, vacuuming, fixing daily lunches of lima bean soup and baloney sandwiches and grieving for the beautiful only child who had turned into something else, a were-wolf perhaps. She had been Luther League state treasurer, Girls' Nation vice president, winner of numerous music trophies (she played clarinet), Homecoming attendant, the list goes on and on, and one cold January day she walked away from her sophomore year at Concordia to head for San Francisco with her boyfriend Craig "trying to figure out where I'm going." Nonsense. She was cold, that's all; Fargo-Moorhead can be brutal in January. The wind sweeps down from Canada and the sky lowers and you get depressed and gain a hundred pounds and want to kill yourself. She had read Kierkegaard in philosophy class and it went to her head. Out in California she spent fifteen years bouncing from one man to another and writing jagged letters home saying that "I now realize that my entire life was a lie"—how can a girl say such a thing to her own parents? An only child? It's not as if they had replacements.

The ladies clucked and bent to their work, turning scraps of cast-off clothing into warm quilts. (Which were bundled off to Lutheran World Services in Chicago. Where, after prayerful deliberation, they were sold for good money to a wholesale bedding house in Baltimore. The money went to buy vaccines for African children. The quilts were sold in gift shops on the East Coast as authentic handmade Amish for hundreds of dollars.)

And all the while, Evelyn was stealing away now and then to visit her cousin in St. Paul who was *non compos mentis* in a nursing home, carrying on long conversations with dead relatives, a perfect cover for Evelyn to go two-stepping with Raoul at the Medina Ballroom to the strains of Vic D'Amore and His Chancellors of Dance. Who knew? Nobody. After Evelyn's death and the whole story came out—the plane tickets, the souvenirs of the Ozarks and Branson and Reno and Daytona Beach, the matchbooks from resorts, the menus of Antoine's and Bob's Ribs and Le Coq—the ladies of the Circle wept for Evelyn and sorely missed her but they never discussed the secret life she led. That simply vanished into the Unspoken file. The subject was too painful. And that was the end of the Age of Interpretation. From then on, they discussed their grandchildren and their vacation plans. No more stories.

9. DEBBIE COMES TO TOWN

Two hours after Barbara found Evelyn dead in bed, Debbie Detmer drove into town in a blue Ford van and pulled into her parents' driveway and started unloading her bags, expensive ones, blue leather, and noticed that Mother had not planted petunias in the big white-painted truck tire in the front yard. And the tire was gone and so were the plywood cutouts of fat people bending over. Instead, there stood a sign, with reflective letters on plywood: JESUS CHRIST: THE SAME YESTERDAY, TODAY AND FOREVER. She'd never seen it before. Wrong house? No. There was Daddy's Ford Fairlane with the Bush-Cheney bumper sticker. She had come to town to get married on Saturday to Mr. Brent Greenwood, 39, of Sea Crest, California. The Detmers lived three blocks from Evelyn's little bungalow but they hadn't heard about her death yet. They had been out of the social whirl ever since January when Mr. Detmer slipped and banged his head. He was toweling off after his shower while watching the *Today* show on the tiny TV Betty gave him for Christmas, an interview with the oldest active pro ballplayer in America, a 62-year-old pitcher for the Salem Sailors named Bryce Brickel, who attributed his long career to God's Will and good nutrition. Mr. Detmer was 72, an age when a man is proud of being able to still put his clothes on standing up, and he was stepping into his underpants and caught his big toe on the elastic band. He hopped a few times, reluctant to give up on it, and fell and concussed himself against the side of the tub, and it had made him forgetful and also intensely devout and a daily reader of God's Word. He started calling his wife "Mother" instead of Betty. He might walk up to you in Ralph's Pretty Good Grocery and say "I think we are in the last days," or "I don't think women in men's clothing is right, do you?" and there is Mrs. Detmer in her jeans, and she smiles and nods as if nothing is wrong.

Debbie was lithe and lean, her hair red and spiky, she didn't look like the old Debbie at all. That Debbie was a brunette and a little chunky. And also angry and impulsive. Fifteen years in Northern California had smoothed her out considerably. She had flown from San Francisco to Minneapolis, writing the vows for her wedding while listening to a semi-famous author next to her as he consumed four double Scotches and complained bitterly about the publishing business and how it chewed you up and spat you out. "There is no place for guys like me anymore," he said. "All they want are novels by twenty-year-old girls with foreign names like Bhuktal Mukerji or something. About growing up alienated in L.A. and torn between cultures and anguishing about it and also there's a lot of shopping and long lunches." On his fourth drink, he asked for her cell phone number and she told him to get over himself, check into rehab, get cleaned up, join the real world, and find out where he fit in. She said it nicely. "You don't have any time to waste," she said. He broke down and said she was the first person in years who had dared to be honest with him, he needed a truth teller in his life. His breath was pungent, weaselish. "Have lunch with me," he said.

"We just did. I had salad and you had Scotch."

He was flying to Minneapolis to give a reading at the U. He hated making public appearances, but with a kid in college, he had to take work where he could find it. His last successful book was twenty years ago. His collection of stories got savaged in *The Times* by a guy he had voted against on a Guggenheim panel. He had a novel in the works but it was pretty rough. Notes, really. Sort of an idea of a novel. His editor kept telling him to take his time. But he was 58, for God's sake. His wife was pushing him to take a teaching job, for the health insurance. A Lutheran college in South Dakota wanted him. *South Dakota.* He shuddered. He'd lived in Berkeley for twenty-six years. South Dakota. Why not the moon? Why not a nice case of prostate cancer? His wife wanted him to take the job. She kept telling him, "You're not getting any younger."

Debbie gave him a pep talk about living one day at a time, maintaining a positive outlook, and doing what you can to improve yourself, and as she talked, it dawned on her that this was what her mother had told her years ago, after her freshman year at college.

The paint was peeling on the side of the house. She'd have to call a painter. A roofer too. Some shingles had blown off. She lugged the bags onto the porch and walked into the living room. Silent, shades pulled, musty, the temperature around eighty.

"Mom? Dad?"

The ancient oatmeal-colored couch sat under the picture of a man driving oxen across a field of brown stubble. In the bookshelf, there were rows of Reader's Digest Condensed Books and stacks of Electric Co-op magazines. On the coffee table, a bowl of plastic fruit. The TV was on with the sound off, a perky woman in a white apron frying up chicken in a pan and a smiley man with a headful of hair watching her. They seemed to be having the time of their lives. The strong smell of Lysol, and something else, urine perhaps. *Do they need live-in help? Do I need to step in and take charge here?* she thought. And then she wondered, *Should I take Brent to a hotel?* He could go nuts in this house. He was a little highstrung anyway. And without high-speed Internet access, he'd be lost. He'd have to use dial-up but maybe that wouldn't work here. Could you get Google here? Cell phone coverage? If not, there was trouble. Then she thought: *Hey. Look at it as a camping trip. Brent is a big boy. Let him figure it out.*

Brent was arriving on Thursday. She'd hoped he could come earlier and get to know people but he had meetings in Chicago. The wedding was set for Saturday at 1 p.m. although strictly speaking it wasn't a wedding, it was a "Celebration of Commitment" and the time was approximate since aviation was involved, namely a hot-air balloon and a Flying Elvis.

"Hello? Hello!" She started up the stairs, slowly, heavily, trying to make noise lest she surprise somebody coming naked out of the bathroom. "It's just me," she cried. "It's Debbie, home from the sea!"

Her father appeared at the top of the stairs, pants hitched up high, his hair wild, in stocking feet. He'd just arisen from a nap, apparently. "Hi, darling," he said. "We've been praying for you."

"I just walked in the door this minute, Daddy." She reached the top of the stairs and put out her arms to hug him and he stepped back.

"I want you to be right with God," he said. "God is moving the waters. He is bringing this dispensation to a close. We may not be here tomorrow. We're waiting on Him."

He retreated into the bedroom and closed the door. She could hear him talking in there. She crossed the hall to the other upstairs bedroom, her old bedroom, and there sat her mother, her back to the door, sorting through old photographs in shoe boxes. She had a pair of headphones on and was singing along softly to something that sounded like "Blue Moon." Debbie's old four-poster bed sat under the eaves and her white dresser and her desk. Stacks of papers and pictures covered everything, old books, catalogues, clothes piled up. "Mother?" She put her hands on her mother's shoulders and the old lady let out a squeak and jumped up, as if attacked, and fell out of her chair.

"Oh my goodness—" Mother moaned. She shut her eyes and tried to draw a breath.

Debbie knelt and took her hand. "I'm so sorry—"

"You surprised me," said Mrs. Detmer. She was dazed. She dabbed at her nose.

"I thought you were expecting me."

"Not until tomorrow."

"I told you Saturday."

"Is today Saturday?"

"Oh my God." She helped her mother onto a chair and went for a wet washcloth and there was Daddy in the hall with a pool of fresh urine at his feet and spreading.

"The Lord has given us peace of mind," he said. "I wish you could have it too."

She pushed him into the bathroom and turned on the shower. She got him a change of clean clothes. Mother mopped the floor. "He's fine," she said. "He listens to evangelists all day on the radio and he has little accidents when he gets excited."

"Where did all that junk come from? In the bedroom?"

"That's Janet's. And some of Kathy's. I'm putting them in order."

"Mother—"

As if she didn't have enough junk of her own, she had acquired sister Janet's (gone to the Good Shepherd Nursing Home) and sister Kathy's (gone to the cemetery) and was "organizing" all of it, in the sense of looking at it, sorting it, moving the stacks around, and then re-sorting.

Mother went to supervise the shower and Debbie came down to the kitchen. The old silver-sparkle countertops and avocado appliances, the glass-fronted cabinets and everything in them just so, a big bouquet of silk flowers she had sent them several years ago, and a diamond-shaped clock on the wall, the hands stuck at five o'clock.

In the refrigerator she found some brown lettuce, a carton of wrinkled baby tomatoes, yogurt way past its expiration date, a tube of expired sausage, and miscellaneous chunks of cheese. The freezer section was packed with frozen dinners. She thought of calling Brent, canceling the ceremony, and booking herself on a return flight Monday morning. So much stuff to do this week!— arrange for the pontoon boat, find a place to store the food, talk to Craig about the hot-air balloon (Where should he park? Who would help him launch?), call up Randall and confirm the Flying Elvis, meet her minister Misty Naylor who was flying in on Friday, book the honeymoon suite at the Chateau Melis on the South Shore—and now she should take Daddy to a doctor and decide whether either parent had enough marbles to run a household. Too much! Way too much!!

She said it out loud: "It would be so easy to give up right now and turn around and go back home." And then the thought, *You are home. Be strong. Make it work.*

Her new mantra: *Make it work.* Forget about world peace and saving the polar bears. Just make it work.

She closed her eyes and hummed, a low hum from her solar plexus, feeling the warm vibrations in her pelvic enclosure. The centering harmonic, a healing force using the body's own meridian powers to drive invasive toxins from the lymph system which collects every negative force around us, which can be a pool of poison, teeming with danger. The centering harmonic purifies and makes the system work. Daddy would be okay. Mother, too. The ceremony would be a beautiful gift to her hometown. People would see it and take the courage and strength to change their own lives. She sang to herself:

One love, one soul.
Here in the circle we are each made whole.
One life, one chance.
We come together in the circle dance.
Turn, turn, turn to the right.
Turn from the darkness toward our own true light.

Growing up in Lake Wobegon Lutheran church, what she felt was dread of God's judgment. God, all-righteous, his great hairy eyeball glaring down from the sky, reading your every thought and making black marks after your name. There is one way and you are not on it. Not even close. You might find it but don't count on it, not the way you're going. They said that God is love but nobody believed it for a minute. It was a culture of fussy women and silent angry men and horrified children. Now, having escaped all that, she felt happy, upheld by love, even though she was alone in her mother's kitchen. The Sisterhood of the Sacred Spirit was with her.

On the plane, trying to ignore the drunk author, she had written in her journal: *Life is partly what we choose to do and partly who we choose to do it with. Time goes on and we must live in it and on the other hand we must dwell in the realm of the timeless. We are constantly growing and changing. Yesterday's answers don't always work for today. But let us always contribute positive energy to others. Put negativity aside and put forward our most positive expectations.*

Lake Wobegon was a pool of negativity. People who believed in disappointment. Especially in marriage. You look forward to it and get all excited and then it turns into a long sad story. So, don't get your hopes up. Wanting something causes frustration, desire drives the object away. The trick is to not want it that much. Want it less. When you get to where you don't want it all, then you may get it. And if you don't get it, you won't care so much. The Lake Wobegon Credo. She was there to prove that something else is possible.

10. THE SALON WEIGHS IN

"I hear Debbie Detmer is finally getting married to somebody."

"I heard that."

"Well, she tried out enough men, let's hope she found a good one."

"I suppose it'll be quite the deal."

"Wouldn't surprise me at all. She'll probably put on a parade with a marching band and guess who gets to ride on the float and wave?"

"Think she'll invite us?"

"Don't hold your breath."

"I'm busy Saturday anyway. Got to take Lily to volleyball."

The ladies of the Bon Marche Beauty Salon could've written the book on Debbie Detmer. You can run away from home, but don't assume that your secrets are safe out there, honey. We know people in California and they know other people. Word gets around. People talk. The walls have ears. You were named in a divorce suit brought by that landscape architect's wife in Berkeley who alleged that he did your yard and garden and did you too. You were seen drunk at an Indian café, yelling at the waiter that

there was cardamom in your *jhimmi-jhammi* though you had specifically said you didn't want any and you stood up and lunged at
the manager when he tried to calm you down and in the end your
gentleman friend had to shovel you into a cab. He took a different
cab. Your cleaning lady, whom you fired, told people that you
talked to your stuffed animals and you binged on TV soap operas
all day. Also, that you hired female masseuses with crew cuts. You
were once seen sitting at a stoplight in your BMW, with your
right index finger two inches up your left nostril. Not pretty.

Myrlette and Luanne and her sister Lois felt terrible about Evelyn on Saturday. She was dead. Sonya had seen her body being
hauled away. Luanne called Florence. Florence was crying so hard
she couldn't talk. Myrlette and Luanne and Lois went in the toilet
and cried on each other and then went back to work. What else
could you do?

Six ladies sat under the beehive dryers dozing or reading *Show
& Tell* ("Angelina: Brad Won't Do It Anymore"), the smell of
permanent and bad coffee in the air. ("Have a cup of Luanne's
coffee, you won't *need* a permanent," said Myrlette.) Luanne
snipping and razoring, Lois washing, Myrlette blueing and high-
lighting, but Evelyn was on everyone's mind. They had taped to
the mirror—next to a snapshot of Lois's daughter Mary who
married the periodontist and son Todd whose greenhouse in Tul-
sa sold 60,000 poinsettias last Christmas—a big photograph of
smiling Evelyn, a rose taped below it and over it, in crimson lipstick, "Our Angel"—a terrible shock, a tragic loss, and yet—"It
was how she wanted to go, in her sleep," said Myrlette, and they
all knew that was true. No sickness, no decline, no hobbling
around the Good Shepherd Home looking cadaverous and drib-
bling coffee down yourself, peeing your pants, rocking back and

forth, a caged animal in the zoo, your mind turned to sawdust and your hip shooting with pain at every step—not for our Evelyn! A rousing good time at Moonlite Bay, a couple of drinks, some laughs, come home, wave good-bye, go to bed and don't wake up.

At Moonlite Bay, they served slabs of pie the size of trowels and the drinks are all doubles and triples. Some people finish dinner and drive off in the wrong direction. Like Evelyn. Instead of south, she went Up.

"It's what she wanted!" cried Luanne. "Bless her heart, she didn't suffer one bit. She got out of this world the easy way." Luanne's parents wound up in wheelchairs, looking like two mummies, no idea who they were or why. Every hour somebody would haul them off to pee, what was called "timed voiding," so life was just waiting for lunch and waiting to tinkle. Her mother didn't speak to her for months and then she said, "Tell Papa when he's done putting up the horses, we kept supper for him." Golden years. *Ha.*

"And she didn't have to be here for Debbie Detmer's triumphant homecoming," said Lois. "There's a bonus."

Evelyn was not fond of Debbie Detmer, especially after she wrote to Debbie and asked her to contribute to the Lutheran church, whose education wing needed major repairs after a tree fell on it, and Debbie sent a check for $100. The woman could afford a Frank Gehry beach house on stilts with a curving glass front and a fifty-foot redwood deck (featured in the January 2001 issue of *Luxury Home*) but she couldn't pony up serious money for the church that taught her about the Good Samaritan, Daniel in the lions' den, the prodigal son, etcetera. One hundred dollars! She paid more than that for her toilet seat cover! Myrlette was Mrs. Detmer's cousin and she knew the inside story of how Debbie had broken her parents' hearts. An only child who was given everything. Her father worshipped the ground she walked on, her mother waited on her hand and foot. And then somewhere around age fifteen, the princess had turned cold and cunning and spiteful and foulmouthed. A demon entered her body, and she told her mother she hated her. She went to parties and stayed out until 2 a.m. and came home drunk. She totaled the car, twice. She actually joined the Communist Party USA. She proudly announced the loss of her virginity (to the football co-captain Kirk) in his parents' laundry room on a pile of old drapes. She openly campaigned for Homecoming Queen and was elected senior-class attendant and was so miffed at Mary Ellen acing her out for Queen that when Kirk (who was Mary Ellen's steady boyfriend; Debbie was only an adventure) presented the bouquet of carnations to Debbie at the ceremony, she stuck her hand down the front of his pants.

In his pants. In the gymnasium in front of the entire student body. A wave of shock swept the crowd, amid some tittering and whistling from the boys. Kirk dropped the flowers, mortified. Mrs. Hoglund sent Debbie to Mr. Halvorson's office. Mary Ellen burst into tears, her big moment destroyed. Mr. Johnson the band director struck up the band and they played "I'll See You In My Dreams" and the ceremony was all over. Mr. H. told Debbie that he didn't know what to do with her and suspended her from school for a week. She didn't care. *She didn't care!*

At the prom, she wore her bra outside her dress and carried a pint of vodka in her little silver lamé purse and she was sent home, but she caroused in the parking lot with some boys who nobody had seen before and danced around singing "Roll me over in the clover, roll me over, lay me down and do it again." Her father had to come get her and she said something to him that made him put his head in his hands and weep. Typical.

At graduation (people said) she was buck naked under her blue gown, and when she left for Concordia College in August, people thought that now maybe she'd settle down. She got into choir, which was bound to be a good influence, and her roommate was a nice Christian girl from Bemidji, so Mr. and Mrs. Detmer were hoping for a turnaround. Mrs. Detmer was a saint. She was ready to forgive. She felt that Debbie was only immature and needed to impress other girls with her wild ways but now she would realize her innate gifts and become a teacher. Mrs. Detmer asked the Ladies Prayer Circle to uphold Debbie in prayer, and they did, and her second semester Debbie took a philosophy course and read Kierkegaard who fired up her jets and convinced her that she was not the person other people thought she was, she was a pilgrim and an artist and a free spirit and she headed for California. Mr. Detmer braced himself for a call from the Coast saying she'd been found dead in an alley.

She drove west with Craig who thought she loved him but he was only her ride. She dumped him three days after arriving in San Francisco. She took a room at the Sam Wong Hotel off Broadway and hung out at City Lights bookstore and worked in a topless bar. A good Lutheran girl and now she served drinks to old men who ogled her tits. But she loved the city. Men could wear cheery pastels there and people seemed not to brood over things that happened in the past and the climate was gentle and misty. And a pretty girl can make friends easily. A month later, tired of old men and their needs, she hitchhiked north to Bolinas, a last outpost of hippiedom, home of a Lutheran ashram run by a guru from Fargo, the Rama Lama Rasmussen, which met in a large yurt, and the Sunday sermon was about mercy, and the service was celebratory, with dancing—also it was clothing optional— Scripture said, "Think not what ye shall wear" and the Bolinas Lutherans didn't think about it at all—some dressed in shorts and T-shirts, some simply wore palm fronds loosely around the waist, some were buck naked. It was fun for a while and then she got herpes and that took some of the shine off it. She joined an alter- native dance collective called the Day Star Tribe and she became Solar Lily Daystar in a self-affirmation ritual at dawn on the beach, members of the tribe running and leaping lightly and rolling and whanging on little drums and playing their rain sticks. She lived with a man who believed in multi-headed deities, and also that dyslexic children could be helped by having them read aloud to cats. Then she got into meridians. She studied with a medium named Hadley and was in love with her for six months and then the meridians changed and she went up the coast to Eureka Col- lege to be a dorm mother, though the dorms were wide open, no restrictions, and some students kept snakes for pets, and cooked in their rooms, and held witchcraft ceremonies; filled their rooms with bizarre artifacts, boulders, neon signs, stuffed raccoons, and it was all good. Eureka banned the study of colonialist literature— all fiction and poetry by authors living in countries that exploited other peoples—and every May Day they all ran nude through the campus, and that was where Debbie met Dawn. They were naked and running and stopped to chat about yoga and it turned out that Dawn was a veterinary aromatherapist—she owned All Creatures Wellness Center in a strip mall in Petaluma—and Debbie, who was tired of listening to rich kids pour out their troubles, asked

Dawn to teach her the business of treating puppydogs and kitty-cats with eucalyptus and peppermint and chamomile.

"Smell is a primary sense for animals. Pets are forced to live in an alien olfactory environment of powerful chemical odors and the result is illness and suffering. Eighty-five percent of dogs suffer from depression caused by the psychological stress of alien odors triggering the flight reflex in animals imprisoned indoors, and what we've developed is a whole schematic of cleansing natural aromas put into a mister and the animal lies on a bed or on our lap and inhales the aroma and we cure animal depression. You can see the difference. It's the most fulfilling thing I've ever done. Making happy animals is good karma. Tail wagging doesn't mean happiness, just neediness. A dog who sleeps all day is depressed—cats overeat because of depression. We make a difference."

Dawn was the daughter of an Army colonel. She became a cat wrangler for movies, training professional cats, keeping them calm, which was how she discovered the power of aroma. Vicks VapoRub spread on the inside of the elbow: it was magic. So Debbie moved in with her in Petaluma. Got a job at Spice 'N Everything Nice. A fabulous shop where there wasn't just one of everything like back home but twenty different kinds of oregano, Mexican, Turkish, Egyptian, Moroccan—for cinnamon, there was Samoan, Sri Lankan, Slovenian. Tired of boneless breast of chicken? Put some Mexican oregano on it, some Slovenian cinnamon, why not?

She cooked for Dawn and boned up on chemistry and animal psychology. Dawn was a true idealist, but she also experienced big mood swings. Lavender made her moody. Mimosa made her lose all sense of personal boundaries. Too much of it and she'd sit on the laps of strangers on buses or in cafés. She'd go to the library and snuggle up next to men she'd never met. She was a compulsive hugger. And a strong one. She'd walk down the street and grab hold of strangers and squeeze them so tight they panicked and started flailing at her and then she hugged harder. She hugged milkmen, clerks in stores, panhandlers. She always had a bad cold. She always was late to things. People avoided her when possible. And her arms ached. Once she drove through a grove of eucalyptus and into the ditch, got out, took her clothes off, and when the highway patrol found her, she could not tell them the day of the week or the name of the President. She was ticketed for Driving While Dazed.

Eucalyptus also affected her depth perception. Six months after Debbie joined All Creatures as a therapist, Dawn swerved to avoid hitting a deer and her car plunged off Highway 1 and over the cliff into the Pacific two hundred feet below and she was killed instantly. Debbie took over All Creatures in Dawn's memory and grew the practice, as people who'd been put off by the hugging returned. She was a professional in white smock and pale green slacks, no longer the anguished pilgrim. She was earning money and enjoying it. She loved her Wednesday massage with Lala and she loved shopping for Julianne O'Connell clothes and Lauren Thavis shoes. She loved her Lexus with the three-thousand-dollar sound system. Business boomed. And then one day Tom Cruise dropped in with a big fat furball of a cat in his hands—Tom was on the verge of panic, weeping, panting—he confessed he had sat on the cat during a very intense phone conversation—and Debbie took Mumbles into the back room and gave her a dish of water and blew in her ear and the cat was fine. She sent Tom home with a chamomile-scented chew toy. But after the story appeared in *People* with a picture of Debbie in her white outfit and a grinning Tom Cruise ("There are little miracles in life that validate and center us, when suddenly we see over the edge and into the heart of things"), business boomed; she opened a branch in Westwood and another in Mountain View. She was besieged with clients. Bentleys and BMWs double-parked out front and the personal assistants of VIPs sat in the waiting room, with dogs and cats huddled in luxurious carrying cases, and others flying in from Dallas, Palm Beach and the Berkshires. In certain circles, if you were not aromatizing your dog or cat, your friends would give you a pamphlet, "Pet Stewards, Not Owners," and expect you to do the right thing.

And Debbie learned something you can't learn in Lake Wobegon. Some people have much too much money and if you charge them an outrageous amount for something, say two hundred dollars for a whiff of persimmon for Pookie—heck, three-hundred bucks—this confirms their wealth and makes them extremely happy! *Yes! Thank you for challenging my generosity*, they think as they thrust the Visa card at you. *I am a person who is not concerned about money! Not at all! I pay ten dollars for a bran muffin made from hand-rolled bran and premium raisins and baked by a French woman with a doctorate from the Sorbonne! So I am delighted to pay $2,362.50 for the well being of Meow Tse-Tung and F. Cat Fitzgerald. Other people would have conniptions at the thought, but I am beyond petty materialistic concerns! Here is your money and let me add on 25% for a tip!* She had no training, was inventing the science of aromatherapy as she went along, used inexpensive materials, and yet the animals seemed to thrive on the attention. The owners thought so. And *the higher the price, the greater the benefit.*

Growing up among nickel-pinchers, she had a hard time accepting this. She felt apologetic about taking money for what was after all her sacred duty to care for life. But Dawn had drilled into her that *Our fee is a way for our clients to know how much they love their animals.* And All Creatures grew and opened new branches and Debbie trained new therapists and took on partners and finally sold the business for ten point two million dollars and took a year off to regroup and to enjoy her home in Santa Cruz and that's where she met Brent. He was the only heterosexual male in her yoga group, and he offered to teach her to surf. He sold shared-time on executive jets. He had been a grad student in philosophy at Berkeley, working on a paper deconstructing the work of Sartre, whose subtext, he discovered, was all about a fear of dogs, and then his father, an exec at Hewlett-Packard, took him on a business trip to Morocco, the two of them aboard a 12-passenger Gulfstream, eating prime rib and knocking back some smoky thirty-year-old Scotch, served by a uniformed steward who then made up the chairs into beds with fine cotton sheets and they slept their way over the Atlantic—he thought, *I have spent enough time in libraries. Jean-Paul Sartre is meaningless. So a big dog jumped on him when he was small—so what? Who cares?* He was made Hewlett-Packard's coordinator of executive air service. And a year later, he started up a company, Shoo Fly, helping business leaders recognize the cost-effectiveness of luxury travel in private jets.

Debbie was happy at last. She was rich and in love. She made peace with her parents. She flew them to Santa Cruz, though they were terrified of flying and she took them to the Café de Mare and waved to Harrison Ford whose cat she had treated and hugged him and introduced him to her parents. Mrs. D. ate linguini with clams and got ferocious diarrhea, so they spent that whole week at Debbie's house, close to a flush toilet. Mr. D. looked at her new kitchen and asked how much the Mexican ceramic tile cost and when she told him, he was staggered and never recovered from the shock. Everything he looked at, he priced by multiplying its worth times thirty. It wore him out. She was a different Debbie, nicer in a way and they liked her red hair. She didn't yell at them about their politics—both Detmers thought the sun rose and set on Ronald Reagan—and she told them she loved them. Over and over. She hugged them numerous times. She held hands with them and invited them to meditate with her. It was odd. *How did she earn all that money?* But certainly it was better than her dying in the alley from a heroin overdose.

They hoped to meet Brent but he was away on business. She showed them his picture. He looked nice enough, but why didn't he take off the sunglasses. "Bright light is bad for him," she said, "it can trigger a manic episode. Once he got very manic and tried to tell the crew of a United flight to Chicago that he absolutely had to fly to Costa Rica and *right now*, and the way he stood with one hand in his pocket, it was a problem. A big problem. He was put on a No Fly list. Thank goodness he had Shoo Fly."

11. THE DECLINE OF
MR. DETMER

Before the naked Mr. Detmer lifted his right foot to put it into the legholo of his briefs and his big toe caught in the elastic band and he lost his balance and toppled over and whacked his shiny head on the bathtub and entered a period of religious apotheosis, he had been an amiable pillar of the community, a friendly eminence at civic occasions, a booster, a Rotarian, but now that he was convinced that the Last Judgment was at hand, nobody invited him to lunch anymore. He was the president emeritus of Mist County Co-op Power & Light, and still occupied the big sunny office on the top floor of the Central Building with a commanding view of the lake. He could look out and see men in boats angling for the wily sunfish, except now he listened to radio evangelists wail about liberals and avoiding the unclean thing. He used to be a benevolent man, handing out gifts. Everybody from the Girl Scouts to the Good Shepherd Home came pussyfooting into Mr. Detmer's office and made their pitch and he smiled and wrote out a check. No more. One sharp blow to the head ended that.

For years on the Fourth of July, on the steps of the Central

Building, it was he who declaimed the Declaration of Independence at high noon, immediately preceding the Living Flag, and every year he got a lot of compliments on it, and then the July Fourth committee asked him to edit it and he said no. If you're going to read the Declaration of Independence, you have to read the Declaration of Independence. So they shit-canned it. It was death by memo. "To: Mr. Detmer—The arrangements committee has instructed me to inquire as to the possibility of shortening your 4th of July presentation in the interest of economizing on time and making the occasion more fun for everyone, particularly families with small children." *Your presentation!* This was a sacred document of our nation!! *Presentation?* A presentation is a home economist talking about table setting! This is the manifesto that declared us a nation!

He'd been rooked. Royally screwed. "Daddy, just do the short version," said Mrs. D. No, it was the principle of the thing.

Small children, he felt, could profit from being made to sit quietly and listen to a man read the paper that made America America, but what offended him was getting a memo—not a phone call or a visit—but a *memo.* So he whipped one back. "To: Committee—I couldn't agree more. To hell with the Declaration. It happened a long time ago and who cares? Let's not force people to suffer through it, let's have a pie-eating contest instead." And so that's what they did. A pie-eating contest, an egg toss, and a three-legged race. Unbelievable.

And then the worst blow of all: nobody told him how much they missed hearing him read. Nobody. He waited for complaints to surface and none did. He thought of writing an anonymous letter to the *Herald Star* ("I was disappointed to hear that our community has turned its back on the Fourth of July, the birth-day of freedom in our country," etc. etc.) and sign it *Disgusted*, but he was not the devious type. Instead, he quietly disappeared from the Chamber of Commerce, the Boosters Club, Rotary, the church board, the Boy Scouts, and faded into the woodwork, thinking that surely someone would say, "Wally, what's hap-pened to you? Where'd you go?" And a couple of guys did, but without much real remorse.

Unbeknownst to most, MCCPL had been absorbed in 1998 by the NorCom network and Mr. Detmer's job had become ceremo-nial, which suited him fine. Minneapolis was running the show now and he was happy to step aside and let the big boys have the headaches. He sat in his swivel chair at the big oak desk and worked on an epic poem: *Sunshine in the Night: A History of the Electrification of Lake Wobegon and Environs*.

> *The glimmering lights of the little town*
> *Shone like a beacon for miles around*
> *To many a farmhouse in the gloom*
> *And folks who sat in shadowy room*
> *And tried to read by kerosene lamp*
> *Like soldiers in some foreign camp*
> *Cast their eyes to Lake Wobegon*
> *And dreamed that the swift advancing dawn*
> *Of modern times would reach them soon*
> *And turn their midnight into noon.*

A history of electrification in rhymed verse—men and women enjoying recreation and refreshment as efficient electric-powered machines performed the tasks that so burdened their ancestors—and he was halfway through it, on line 852—"The glory that was radio/Bringing opera and quiz show/With the turn of a dial/And comedians to make you smile"—and that was when he cracked his skull and suddenly electrification seemed insignificant. Man was in ever greater darkness than before. Immorality ran rampant.

LOCAL MAN SUFFERS CONCUSSION

The rescue squad was called to the home of Mr. and Mrs. Walter Detmer on Saturday morning to investigate a fall. Someone in the home had slipped and struck his head on a bathroom appliance. It was determined that he had suffered a mild concussion and he is now resting comfortably at home and is expected to recover fully.

But he didn't. He wrote the lines: "Dark shadows hover near, unseen. Men cannot fathom what they mean. They are the shadows of the wings of that dark visitor who brings Death to you and also me, despite all electricity. No device, however grand, can halt his step or stay his hand—Not light nor warmth nor radio wave can slow our progress to the grave." There his epic ended.

The next morning he tuned in *Waiting for the Call* on which Pastor Lyman found warnings in Jeremiah against the Internet and Mr. Detmer, having worked all his life to bring cheap electricity to Lake Wobegon, felt he had done the devil's work.

"You did good for us all," said Mrs. Detmer, ever the optimist, but six months later he was still feeling the imminence of the End. People who said hello to him in the Chatterbox and asked him how he was were given a gospel tract "THIS DAY MAY BE YOUR LAST," which discouraged friendly conversation. "Hey, good to see you again," they said as they walked away.

Mr. Detmer knew he had lost traction upstairs. The Lord had shown him the Truth, but the Lord had also taken away some marbles. Crossword puzzles were beyond him. He talked to Debbie on the phone and stared at the 3x5 index card on which Mrs. Detmer had carefully printed:

DEBBIE. YOUR DAUGHTER. IN CALIFORNIA.
SHE LOVES YOU, WALTER.

Walter was 72, Lutheran, Lake Wobegon-born and bred, a graduate of Concordia College in Moorhead. He had never experienced mystical visions in his life and now he was seeing one a minute. Men in black whispering, "Don't believe them. Don't you see how it all hangs together?" He didn't like this. After thinking it through, which took several hours, he decided to remove himself from the picture by taking pills. He had forty of them he had pilfered from Mrs. Detmer's prescription and they were stashed in a manila envelope on which he wrote "Declaration of Independence." It was in his desk at the office. He would do it, he thought, on a Monday, when his secretary Phyllis came in at noon. That would give him three hours to get the job done.

He was ready to go but first he needed to write a letter to his family and, in his present condition, that was hard. *Dear Wife*, he wrote. *I am gone. It was time to go so I took the quickest route. These are the Last Days and I had to get out. We had a good life with no more troubles than most people and I am glad for all our good years together. I have left you enough money to get along on and I hope you have a very nice life. But it won't last long because God is moving on the waters. I will see you very soon. Your loving husband.*

Mrs. Detmer told Debbie she doubted very much that he would ever be himself again. "This is as much of him as we are ever going to get," she said. "Aside from his references to the end of the world and the seven-headed angel and the blood covering the moon, he is pleasant and not much trouble, really. I just hope I can keep him at home for another year or two. Then we'll move into assisted living, which I dread but what can you do?"

12. ATHEISM DISCOVERED

The news spread quickly on Saturday evening, and yet on Sunday morning, during the 10 a.m. service, when Pastor Ingqvist announced Evelyn's death there were gasps and tears. Only thirty-four people in the pews and they had been pummeled hard by the substitute organist, Tibby Marklund having gone to Vermont for three weeks. Her sub was a pale thin man with colorless hair who liked to put the pedal to the metal so the prelude was like an artillery barrage before the invasion, and the opening hymn was one nobody had ever sung before in their lives, a 15th Century English plainsong, a hairshirt of a hymn, and it sounded like a fishing village keening for its dead.

The pastor came down into the congregation for the announcements, pale and blue-eyed in his big white tablecloth vestments. "We've had bad news. Our sister Evelyn Peterson passed away late Friday at home and I know this comes as a shock to many of you," he said, hearing the communal intake of breath, seeing heads turn toward Barbara's empty seat in the fourth row from the back. Mute shock. Their expressions said: *why didn't Barbara call and tell me? I was one of Evelyn's best friends, doggone it.* Evelyn gone. One more tall tree, fallen. The world we knew, turned side-ways again. *What happened? Was she sick? She sure didn't look sick a couple of days ago.* Judy Ingqvist put her head in her hands and cried, though she'd known since Saturday afternoon. Evelyn shouldn't die. She was healthy. A brisk walker. Every day. From her house down to Main Street in her trademark tomboy stride and then south past the Knutes temple and the Statue of the Un-known Norwegian and out of town past the Farmers Co-op grain elevator and the slough and over the hill beyond the town dump and then east along the lake shore and over Trott Brook and past the Magendanz place to the Indian mound where she would stand facing the water and look for the loon couple who dwelt there. The amorous cries of this faithful pair were thrilling to her. There she did her stretches, knee bends, jumping jacks, sit-ups, the whole routine, and then hiked back. Sometimes Judy joined her. They talked about everything under the sun. Evelyn was om-nivorous. And now that quick mind, that long stride, that live wire—is dead? What a dismal thought. "All of us extend our love and support and prayers to the Peterson family and to all of Evelyn's friends, which I guess includes everyone here"—he chuckled—"so what I'm saying is that we extend our love to ourselves, which I'm sure Evelyn would approve of. And of course we'll announce the funeral arrangements as those are decided."

Actually Barbara had told him on Saturday night: the arrange-ments had been decided. They would cremate her and put her ashes into the bowling ball and plop her into the lake. No eulogy. No hymns.

Florence and Al were not in church that morning. She had con-sulted with Al's nephew, a lawyer, about challenging Evelyn's let-ter (unsigned, unwitnessed) in court but as he described the procedures, the petition, the hearing, the affidavits, Florence waved her hand and said, "We'll think about it" and that was that. "I don't care anymore," she said to Al. "What will be will be."

"We could go to Chicago next weekend and visit Tom and Sue," said Al.

"I am not going to be run out of town just because they want to put my sister into a bowling ball and drop her from a kite," said Florence. "I will attend her service and I will hold my head high. I just wish she could see what she's done to me."

After church, Pastor Ingqvist called Barbara and said, "I just want you to know that we're all in shock and thinking about you and sometimes it's hard to reach out when we need help, but whatever you need, I want you to call me, okay? And I'm here if you want to talk." It sounded to her like pastor mode. Unctuous. A script from the handbook on bereavement. And she said, "It's all set. Mother made her wishes clear so there's really nothing to talk about."

"As I say, I'm here if you need me," he said.

"And vice versa," she said. Mother was clear: no eulogy, no public prayers and "Moon River" the only music. Period. Over and out.

She didn't go to church because it was a nice day and also she didn't need all those clammy hands patting her on the back. All the weepy condolences. She had no desire to get splattered with sympathy. People trying to be comforting can be weird. After church her phone rang and rang and she didn't pick up the receiver. She could hear their voices: *So sorry. Such a shock. She was such a trouper. I know how you must feel ...* " She put on a big straw hat and dark glasses and headed out for a hike along Mother's route around the lake. Dogs lay in the shade and watched her. A dog lay at the end of his chain, his chin on the ground, pawing at the grass in front of a bathub half-buried vertically in the ground, the half above ground forming a little grotto for a statue of the Blessed Virgin, arms outstretched, pity in her blank eyes. He had pawed a bare spot at her feet. A dog's homage. A car went by with two teenage boys slumped down in the front seat. Summer insects chittering and a lawn mower started up and then coughed and died and a model airplane whined, circling high in the sky. A child cried "Boogers on you" and ran behind a house with a mosaic of petunias in front. A sign was pounded into the lawn, "Garage Sale," and there in the driveway on card tables were stacks of books and encyclopedias, deer antlers, a mandolin, some golf clubs, boxes of sheet music, squirrel traps and a box of shoe trees, a chafing dish, a jigsaw puzzle of the 1965 Minnesota Twins, a Hamm's beer serving tray, a set of six maroon goblets with painted flowers ugly as sin, a framed poster of the Northern Pacific Vista Dome crossing the Rockies.

She thought she might like to buy that. Put something new on the wall. She'd dreamed of riding the Vista Dome when she was a kid, watching the mountains slide by, enjoying a nice lunch in the dining car served by old black men who call you *Darling*, your daddy sitting across from you in his nice wool suit and tie, except she didn't have that kind of daddy. She could hear the jump-rope girls out in the alley behind the garage and it sounded like—

Betty, Betty
Are you ready?
Spill your guts like hot spaghetti.
Who'd you kiss?

Was he sweet?
Make your heart skip a beat?
You're so cool
Got your groove
How much clothing did he remove?
One, two, three, four, five . . .

A heavy air of Sunday boredom. Benign, indifferent, dozy. Main Street was deserted except for five cars angled in at the Chatterbox Café. In Skoglund's Five&Dime, a window display of party decorations, crepe paper, favors, balloons, festive placemats with faces of clowns. A sign in the door of Jim's Barbershop, CLOSED UNTIL FURTHER NOTICE. He'd had a stroke, poor man. The King of the Crewcut, fading. A ballgame was on the radio, heard from an open window above the Mercantile: the crowd quiet, the southern drawl of the announcer, Herb Carneal, sounded like a string of taffy, stretching. Ralph's Pretty Good Grocery, the door propped open. A stack of Sunday papers in the rack, the top one fluttering in the breeze, restless. A woman gazing out the front window, over the TOILET PAPER 2 FOR $1 sign. Her old classmate, Marcy. She'd had some sort of operation. Maybe a hysterectomy. She waved and Barbara waved back. They hadn't been friends for years, since Barbara overheard her using the words "weird" and "schizo" and realized that she, Barbara, was the subject. Now, after Mother's death, maybe she wanted to make up and be friends. She was one of those mean women who develop hugging tendencies late in life as if that made up for everything. Well, nuts to her. Some insults aren't forgiven. Go suck your tongue, Marcy.

Barbara walked down the street past the Mercantile, the elderly manikins in their green playsuits gazing down at her, historic costumes from an old beach movie, and the hardware store where Old Man Ziegler used to stand, glowering, at the counter—all the stock was in the back room—and you had to tell him what you wanted, and if you didn't know the name of it, a chamfer or a gimlet or a reamer, with a quarter-inch burr or the ⅜ or the ¾, he rolled his eyes and groaned. An autocrat of hardware and then he died of pneumonia and his son Johnny made the store self-service. A mercy to everyone. The monument to the Unknown Norwegian. The great stone figure pointed toward the west, though all that lay west was the flat prairie, where Norwegians tended to turn mean or else go berserk, and sometimes both. There was Lundberg's Drugs that once boasted a soda fountain, where boys in starched shirts built sundaes and banana splits, but no more. One more sweet detail gone forever. And Krebsbach Chev where the old clickety-clack gas pumps were replaced and the new ones beep and are self-service so there is one less person to ask you "How are you today?" and "What do you think about this weather?" On the sidewalk the words *EAT SHIT* that somebody had tried to smudge out. She stopped and scraped it with her shoe, hard, with little effect. On the light pole was taped a poster for the Gornick & Berg carnival coming Labor Day, Ferris wheel and Kiddie Tilt-a-Whirl and games of chance. A poster for the FOURTH OF JULY DOUBLEHEADER, Whippets vs. Avon Bards—4 p.m. Wally (Old Hard Hands) Bunsen Memorial Park—which the Whippets had already lost. Skunked, twice. Barbara had dated Ronnie the centerfielder after Lloyd left. He told her a story about how he caught a 16-lb. walleye in Lake Wobegon and let him go free. "Just like I wish I were free," Ronnie said. They made love that night. She slept with him a few times, a real case of impaired judgment, then he tried to avoid her, not easy in a town this size. He'd found a new girlfriend, Janine, a perkier one, and he quit going to the Sidetrack Tap after games and switched to the Sidewinder outside of Millet, a rock'n'roll bar where the music is loud enough to keep the drunks upright, and Barbara cornered him there and he tried to hide in the men's room and she opened the door and called him names and the bartender escorted her out and then asked her for a date. She said, "No thanks." He had tattoos on his neck, not a good sign.

She'd attended that doubleheader with Mother. She ate two bratwursts and a fudge bar, downed a cold beer and talked about going to Italy in the fall. Ronnie made two errors in the first game, let a single scoot through his legs for a double and then overthrew third base by twenty feet, allowing the runner to score. And in the second game, when he chased a deep fly ball and ran into the fence and the ball hit him in the back, Barbara felt gloriously vindicated. The little bastard lay sprawled in the grass and when eventually he managed to totter to his feet, the crowd cheered, and Barbara thought, *Hope that clears up your premature ejaculation problem.*

The glimmer of sun on the water through the trees. An outboard motor in the distance.

A few pale blobs lay on the beach, nobody venturing in the water due to rumors of swimmer's itch: a parasite in bird droppings causes an itchy rash like chicken pox. So they lay in the sun getting redder and redder. She and Lloyd once went skinny-dipping there and afterward lay on the cool sand and he put his hand between her legs and she said, "Don't." But he still did. Back in the days when he couldn't keep his hands off her.

In the winter, she and Lloyd used to skate here side by side, hands crossed, and he'd swing out in front and turn and they'd skate backward holding hands and she'd lift her back leg and strike a pose and he'd turn her and they'd both skate backward in a figure 8, gliding around and around. Such a lovely feeling. People watching said, "You should enter a contest," but what's the point of that? You work your tail off and then you feel bad when you don't win.

They got married in 1976. He seemed quite plausible—who could gauge the loser in him though the slope shoulders maybe were a clue—he was a good workmanlike lover who got to the point and stuck with the job until it was done. They were in a big rush and they dashed out of the church and had sex four times a day for about three weeks and then lo and behold a baby came along and by the time they woke up and realized what they'd done, their lovely romance was over. Fatherhood hit Lloyd like a two-by-four. He never got over it. He was born to be sorry and when Muffy was born brain-damaged, half-strangled on the cord, it knocked the wind right out of him. He took it as a judgment on him for not being a good person. He sank into depression and ate nothing but cornflakes for weeks. Cornflakes and anchovies and brown beans. The little girl didn't walk until she was almost two or talk until she was three. She liked school okay until third grade, then hit a wall—Oh God, what a time. The crème de cacao set in. And Lloyd couldn't bear to look at Muffy without weeping. They never made love after that. She tried to get him to go to Antigua to relight the romance. "Why Antigua? Florida's cheaper." But he didn't want Florida either. No fare was cheap enough. Who would shovel their driveway if they weren't there? "Why shovel it if we aren't here?" she said. "I just want to go where it's warm." "So put on a sweater," he said.

Barbara got to know a lovely man, a priest. Kyle came along

afterward and Lloyd accepted him, asked no questions. *Oh God, she thought, I am just about to start bawling. Why go over the past? Much too painful. Think about the future.*

Now she had Oliver whose passion was slow to mount but once lit he got more and more excited, his great bulk trembling, and he held her close and moaned and whispered, and finally rose to engage, a great bull walrus in heat crouching behind her in the dark, his shirttails on her buns, exerting heroically, thrusting with unabashed vigor, delirious, almost out of his mind until in full passion he removed his shirt and his great belly slapped her butt *whap whap whap whap* he got panting and wheezing so she was afraid his heart would burst and he would topple onto her dead or dying, but no, he only rolled over exhausted and let her climb up and ride him while he rested, and then he was ready to go again. And when he spent, it was with a long low cry out of an ancient warrior throat, a primeval cry that made her almost weep that she could give so much pleasure to another. And then suddenly he was shy again, covering himself, slipping into the big shirt, the elephantine pants, the placid moon face. He was Lutheran, like her, brought up modest. Nowadays young girls acted as lewd as possible. Tiny tank tops, short shorts, their pretty little boobs pushed up, their cracks on display for boys to ponder. Wenching around in swimsuits made of three tiny triangles and a few feet of fishing line. A wonder they aren't all pregnant by the age of fifteen. *Don't go for the charmers, girls. Pick the smart oddball, the shy but steady one grateful for your attention. Go for loyalty.*

A boat buzzed past on the lake, towing a tall blond girl on water skis, followed by a pontoon boat with a big family standing as if riding a float in a parade and they were the winning team. She counted six fishing boats anchored at this end of the lake, each with two men, bow man and stern man, poles in hand. Catholics, probably. They got church out of the way on Saturday. In and out. Up, down, say you're sorry, pay your fine, out in time. Lloyd was Catholic. Her dad was far from devout but he got upset when she brought Lloyd home, and angry when she married him, but Lloyd switched right over to Lutheran and trotted along, it made no never mind to him. He was a churchgoer, period. Because if you weren't, it raised questions and made problems, so he went along. Clip clop, clip clop. Blessed are the meek for they shall stay out of trouble.

Fatherhood was what capsized him all right. He took Muffy in his arms like you'd hold an explosive device. He cried. She was a happy little girl, the sweetest little thing, and everytime he looked at her, he got pensive and forlorn. And then she turned fifteen and they got her in the Poor Clares Group Home, in Sauk Rapids. The Poor Clares accepted Muffy, though Lloyd and Barbara were Lutheran, because they fell in love with her. She was a beautiful loving happy person. So she never would write a scholarly book about Roman architecture, and so what? She was a peach. The Clares came for her and Barbara smiled and waved. "Bye-bye, baby," she crooned, and when the black car pulled away, she went to the basement and bawled and bawled, but Lloyd couldn't say good-bye, couldn't speak, just went upstairs and closed the door. He took it hard. The week after she left, he set out to retile the upstairs bathroom. He'd never done one before but he thought, *How hard could it be if my brother Lowell can do it?* Lowell was thick as a brick. So Lloyd got busy and started putting in ceramic tile freehand and soon the horizontal tiles started to get diagonal.

There was tile creep. Lowell had to be brought in to tear it apart and redo it. Lloyd cried over that. Had a brain-damaged daughter and he couldn't set tile straight. It was too much for him.

A stray dog came to their door one day and he took her in and named her Louise. A collie mutt, taffy-colored. She soon established dominance and trained him to get up out of a chair and bring her things and play ball with her when she brought him a ball. She put her old head in his lap and he stroked her for hours. He'd sit on the steps and say, "Life is good, isn't it? Three squares a day, good bed, birds to watch, and squirrels. Got it made, buddy." She was his intermediary. He'd say to her, with Barbara nearby, "Ask Mommy if she's going to fry up those fish for supper, willya." When the dog disappeared, Lloyd drove all over town looking for her. One more blow.

Lloyd's religion was meekness. He could outmeek anyone. He was never a problem to anybody, and that was the problem. He wore old clothes from Goodwill. He cut his own hair and cut it short, for humility. He was a meek scoutmaster. Boys made fun of his musty odor, his yellow teeth. He soaked up all the punishment he could get and asked for more. He took the boys winter camping, taught them to make birdhouses and tie square knots and sheepshanks and they tied his shoelaces together. The warehouse cut his pay, and that was fine by him. A ladder collapsed and Lloyd fell fifteen feet to the concrete floor, injured his right hip, and got right up and walked. Signed a waiver. Kept working. It broke her heart to see the man shame himself. He was in such pain. Walked the cartilage off the hip socket, kept going, bone on bone. Then they fired him, without a word of thanks for twenty-seven years of service, and hired cheap replacements for him and the other warehouse guys, and Lloyd, who'd always been dead set against unions, begged the company to hire him back for half his former pay. And was hurt when they wouldn't. He was pleasant, uncomplaining, a perfectly wonderful Christian gentleman, except that there was no Lloyd there anymore. There was no sex, no conversation, no guff, no juice, no nothing, just meals and work and sleep and his chuckling. She put up a sign in the kitchen, "Thanks for not chuckling." He didn't get it. Lloyd took his troop camping up north. A boy lied and said Lloyd kissed him and Lloyd was drummed out of Scouts. Lloyd said, "Let it go." He declined to fight the thing. She nagged him about it, not to let them get away with it. No reaction, nothing. She dropped a can of yellow paint out the bedroom window on him then, just to get a rise out of him, and he cleaned himself up without comment, and he went to stay at his sister's. She told him not to come back. "Okay," he said. "I'm sorry I made you angry. I don't know why." That was true, he didn't. He moved to Minneapolis and got a job at the ammo factory. He just sort of got smaller and smaller and then she divorced him. And then she read an article about wood ticks and the anti-libido toxin they release into your body. She read the article and wept. A good man and his life is blighted because his dad is a bully and he camps in the woods. Science! It tells you stuff too late.

She looked down. Her shoes and socks were wet. She was standing in the lake. She had walked into the water up to her ankles and the wake of the water skis washed up and she yelled, "Go away, God! I don't believe in you *anymore,* so get off my back."

The men in the boats didn't move, the pontoon boat glided away, the water-ski boat came around again.

"I never really believed in you but I tried to and that's what *screwed up my life but good*! And Lloyd! Look what you did to him! You made him a sheep! And now I'm done with it!!! It's over! I have talked to you for the *last time*! I am never going in that damn pasture again! Leave me alone and I'll leave you alone!"

Her fists clenched and she leaned into the breeze. "My mother didn't believe in you, *not one bit* and we're going to drop her in this lake and no prayers. Hear me? *No prayers, no hymns!!!*"

A man in a silver fishing boat turned and looked her way.

"One life and that's it! When you're dead, you're dead. Burn her up, put the ashes in the water! *That's what Mother wants and that's what we're going to do!*

"I wasted half my life feeling bad about you and I'm not going to waste any more!"

The man in the boat waved to her. She gave him the finger. "That's it for me! I'm done with it!" And she picked up a rock and flung it hard and it skipped on the water—two, four, five, six, eight skips. The man in the boat shouted something.

"Fish all you like! Waste your life! I'm not wasting mine!" And she turned and walked up the beach onto the grass and took off her sopping shoes and socks and walked home barefoot. She was prepared to repeat her blasphemy to anyone she met but she met nobody. As if the word had gone out, "The atheist is coming!"

Her home had not been struck by lightning. The kitchen was not infested with frogs or drenched in blood. There was not a message on the answering machine saying that Kyle had been struck down dead. She poured herself a glass of vodka on ice and stood in her little screened porch and took a few deep breaths. Bees buzzed in the asters and marigolds and a toad squatted on the walk. A snake's skin lay in the grass where a dog had chewed on it. The neighbor's cat lapped water from a dish next door. The little percussive beats of its thirst. The swish of tires on the pavement and the *whap* of a screen door and the humming of the world, machinery and wind and lake and voices, a cloud of sound. *Settle down,* she thought. *Don't bust up your best china just because you're an orphan. Listen and learn.* Mother went to church the way some ladies go to basketball games, to be sociable, not because they care who wins, and that's how Mother felt about the gospel of the Lord—it was for other people to agonize over. What she cared about was being with Gladys and Margaret and Florence and feeding the hungry and covering the chilly with warm quilts.

So she stood and listened. She felt tiny beads of perspiration on her forehead, the thump of her pulse, the grains of sand under her bare soles. And then she opened the door and swung the glass and the vodka hung in the air in a lovely long liquid arc studded with ice cubes and fell and made a long dark line along the walk and over the toad. He was soaked in vodka. He stayed squatted, thinking the situation over.

She turned and went back in the kitchen and poured the bottle of vodka out in the sink. Drunken excess wasn't her line of work anymore. She was done with it. She'd been a damn drunk because she had God problems: you live a lie, you pay a price. Maybe you shoot somebody, or shoot yourself. Or maybe you take the long way and just get good and drunk, but no more, so she poured the stuff down the drain. Every bottle she could find, in a pure righteous heat. You don't need God to get on the right road, you can do this yourself. A little wisdom now and then is enough for anybody, if your timing is right. *Ninety-nine bottles of booze on the wall, ninety-nine bottles of booze, now it is plain they must go down the drain, ninety-eight bottles of booze.* Jim Beam and Gilbey's gin and Amaretto. It was off her now, she had done her share for Seagram's, let others take up the slack. Like Dr. Dave says on his radio show, "The same energy you put into making a bad habit, you can put into breaking it and making a good one. It takes determination to be a drunk, and it takes the same determination to be sober. One or the other. You choose. You have the strength to do it." He's on at noon, taking calls from people all over Minnesota. He has a PhD in psychology and he's smart about all sorts of things. She wished she had called him when she found Mother's body. *Dr. Dave, I'm here with my mother who I just discovered dead in her bed and a note in the drawer that says "Cremation and put the ashes in a bowling ball"—what should I do?* What should she do? She kept pouring. She had bought a case of liquor after she won the Sons of Knute Guess The Ice Melt contest. First prize, $150, for coming closest to guessing when the 1949 Pontiac junker would go through the spring ice. She had an expensive bottle of Armagnac and vintage port, plus the crème de cacao and Baileys Irish Cream and Kahlúa and Amaretto and the Powers Irish whiskey that Oliver liked, the Chardonnay in the fridge, the whole shitload went gurgling down the drain and the bottles clanked into two big shopping bags and she took them out to the garbage can by the garage and plopped them in. The Andersons across the alley were setting out picnic things in the backyard. Mr. Anderson was at the grill, putting slices of cheese on hamburgers. Sonya called over, "Come and join us."

"Thanks, but I can't. Too much to do!" Sonya took a few steps toward her back fence and Barbara could feel condolences about to flutter her way, so she waved and wheeled back to the house.

She shut the door and drew the curtain. Sonya's older brother was one of the four graduating seniors who died on the Northern Pacific crossing fifteen miles south of town on graduation night, 1974. They'd gone swimming at a granite quarry, two boys and two girls, and then saw how late it was, and they raced for home to get ready for graduation, and were hit by the westbound train. Stewart and Karen and Kenny and Marianne. Two couples going steady. A week of wild grief in town, the Class of 1974 sent off numb with horror, the family of Karen consulted a lawyer about suing the family of Kenny the driver but nothing happened. The unspoken question was, "Well, were they *doing* it?" And you hoped they were, but Stewart was a devout kid and maybe there had been a rush to concupiscence—naked swimmers kissing and touching and maybe Stewart had cried out that he didn't think it was right, and maybe it was the moral struggle with temptation that took up the time and made them late. And then Kenny drove them to their rendezvous with death. Pastor Tommerdahl suggested strongly that it had been God's Will for the four that they join Him Upstairs and Mother was furious. She didn't go to church for a year after that.

Barbara stripped off her clothes and tossed them into the washer and was padding down the hall to the shower when the phone rang. She let it ring. Then she thought maybe it was the crematorium so she picked it up on the fourth ring. It was Bennett in New York. *Shit.*

"Barbara, I've got a problem," he said. "Can you wire me money to get out there? I don't have it. I've got all these bills trying to get my music copied. I hate to ask but I really need you to help me out here. It's going to cost me a thousand bucks to get on a plane tomorrow."

"Call Roger. Ask him. I don't have it."

He sighed. "Barbara, you can get it from Mother's account. Mother set up an automatic deposit for me. She sent me three hundred a month. You could get the bank to advance me four months. Please."

She stood naked in the middle of the kitchen, looking at the Andersons, heads bowed at their picnic table, thanking God for their cheeseburgers. She had just thrown a couple hundred bucks worth of booze down the drain and she wanted to stand in a hot shower and wash away her sins. "Bennett, I don't know what day it is in New York, but here it's Sunday. The bank is closed. Number two, Mother's money is all locked up in her estate right now. I have to sell her house, her assets, pay her bills, total everything up, and divvy it according to the will, which I don't even have. It takes months."

"Barbara, I wouldn't ask if I didn't need your help right now. Believe me."

"Bennett, you're an adult. You've got a job. Go borrow the money yourself. Don't ask me for it. I don't have it."

He drew a long breath and told her he had been laid off from his job. Four months ago. He was subletting his apartment to a young couple and he was living with an old trombonist friend in East Orange, New Jersey. He was living on Ramen noodles and cheese from a Food Shelf. He was finally finishing up his opera, remember the opera? The Wright Brothers opera.

"I thought you finished that ten years ago."

"It needed more work. I really think it's ready now. Soon as I can, I'm going to get some friends in a studio and make a demo and send it around. These things take time." He made it sound so perfectly reasonable. You doink around for twenty years in your sandbox, wetting the sand, making little castles with crenellated towers, laying out roads, and then people pay you for it.

"Bennett, there is only so much time and that's all the time there is. I can't make more for you. You're fifty-two years old and you're calling up your sister and borrowing money because you have to write an opera?? Get over it!"

"Don't turn on me, Barbara. Mother was extremely support-ive, you know—." He was about to whine about his hard life and she whacked the receiver on the table three times and yelled, "There is no God, Bennett. So don't expect one to bail you out. It isn't happening!" And she hung up. She felt awful, thinking of him, poor bewildered man in the kitchen of a friend who probably was even sicker of him than she was, and maybe he was down to a pocketful of small bills, maybe a Happy Meal and a large va-nilla shake, and then he'd have to take himself and his opera down to the Salvation Army and see what they could do for him.

Well, let him do it then.

Or maybe he'd walk out into East Orange and take a bus into Manhattan and walk around for a while looking at the Chrysler Building and Central Park and the Met and then screw up his courage and go into the subway and hang around until the exact right train came along and throw himself in front of it.

It's up to him, she thought. I can't be his caretaker.

She had exactly $87,450 to her name, plus her old car and the house, which she got in the divorce from Lloyd. She was 57 years old, eight years from retirement. She was bumping along on 25 hours a week during the school year, cooking in the cafeteria, delivering the Minneapolis paper three days a week, some baby-sitting for summer people, and she'd started painting plates again and was selling some of those to the This 'N' That shop in St. Cloud. It wasn't an opera, just plates with sunrises on them and the motto "Live What You Love," but people paid $21 apiece for them, which was more than Bennett could say.

The phone rang again. Let it ring. No need for sympathy, thank you very much. She got in the shower and soaped herself up and stood under the hot spray and inhaled the steam. She would kick alcohol as a sign to Ronnie and Lloyd and Bennett and all the other losers that she was one of them no longer. And then it appeared, illuminated, in a little balloon over her head. A mantra. *Love What You Live.* Magic. It was like honey on the tongue. Love your life. Love yourself. Have some r-e-s-p-e-c-t.

The phone was ringing. It rang and stopped and then started ringing again. She picked it up. "Barbara—" the voice of Mr. Smooth on his patio in Santa Barbara. "I just got your message." A fountain burbled in the background, music played, a string section.

She told him the story of Mother's Death. It was a well-polished tale by now, *Old Lady In Excellent Health Croaks.* She gave him the complete version, including the letter.

"I don't know what to say. I'm astonished." He didn't sound astonished. He sounded like Mr. Smooth.

"So we're going to do things exactly as she wished. It's Saturday afternoon."

"Saturday? I can't get there Saturday, I'm sorry."

"Roger, this is your mother we're talking about. It's not Zsa Zsa Gabor."

"I'm supposed to go in for hernia repair on Friday."

"Get yourself a jockstrap and come out."

He had an umbilical hernia. His belly button was the size of a golfball. It popped out when he and Gwen were— "Well, never mind," he said. "We were jumping around a little." They had been to Paris, at the George Sank hotel. He won the trip for breaking all previous sales records. They had such a fabulous time in Paris, he said, maybe someday they would sell their Santa Barbara house and move into an apartment so they could travel more now that the kids were grown up, they wanted to go to Costa Rica, Brazil, Vietnam, India—Barbara held the phone away from her ear, his voice sounded like a marble rolling over a linoleum floor. It sounded like someone stirring a pot of overcooked parsnips.

When he stopped, she put the phone back to her ear and told him to call Bennett. "He hates me. I've offered to help. He keeps turning me down."

"Try again. He's your brother. He's in desperate need."

She said to him, "What if the Metropolitan Opera should decide to stage your brother's opera next year, with Placido Domingo as Orville and Bryn Terfel as Wilbur and Renée Fleming as Lola the girl from Dayton, Ohio, who can't choose between them—and what if it's a huge success and *Sixty Minutes* does a long piece about the neglected genius who labored twenty years in obscurity to bring forth his masterpiece and lived on noodles and Velveeta and did his wealthy brother in California, the one with the big fake Spanish house and the Olympic swimming pool, lift a finger to help him? No, he did not. And then they cut to a shot of Roger, hands over his face, ducking and running crouched behind cars in the company parking lot, chased by the cameraman."

"It's not a fake house, it's our house," he said. "And it's half the size of an Olympic pool."

But he got the picture. She could tell. Probably he'd have Gwen call Bennett and take care of the plane ticket.

She put a Stan Getz record on and that made her think about gin so she put on the Concordia College Choir singing Christmas favorites, and "Away in a Manger" made her think of an Old Fashioned. The phone rang and she grabbed for it. It was Raoul. He sounded like he'd had a rough day. "What would it hurt if I called up Andy Williams? Worst case, he says no, but maybe he'd say yes. He could fly up Saturday morning and sing at the memorial and be home that night. Be good publicity for him." She told him she didn't want to turn Mother's farewell into a media event. If Minneapolis TV stations heard that Andy Williams was flying in to Lake Wobegon to sing for an old lady who wanted to be buried in a bowling ball, they'd be sending crews up by helicopter. They'd come by the busload. He agreed. Dumb idea. He just wanted to do something for Evelyn so the world would know how special she was. She was a peach. People their age did nothing but bitch about cell phones and computers and how terrible music is now and Evelyn was glad for everything that came her way. She mastered e-mail and text messaging and had burned him a CD in her computer. *Songs of 1941.* She was his soul mate and there would never be another for him. You go on for years thinking life will always be good like this, and then suddenly it's all over. She was gone. You thought you had an endless supply of her and you only had a few years. Barbara listened to his old husky voice and couldn't quite imagine it coming from a pillow next to Mother's head. He was a little rough for Mother, she thought. She guessed he was no reader of Dickens. She talked a little about Lloyd and what a wrong turn Christianity had been for him and his spiraling down into hopeless passivity until now he was little more than a mollusk, a scallop clinging to the rock of salvation. "Evelyn and I never had a bad day," said Raoul. "Every day was golden." And then he got choked up and said good-bye.

It was four o'clock. Barbara put on jeans and a shirt and squared her shoulders and marched over to Mother's house. She stripped the sheets and the thin cotton blanket from the deathbed and put them in a green garbage bag and tossed in Mother's undies and nylons and nighties. She worked fast. It felt good. She stripped the clothes drawers and the closet in about three minutes flat and dumped some stuff in the garbage bag and the rest she folded neatly into a cardboard carton for the church rummage sale. Old pals of Mother's would browse through the ladies' wear and find this denim skirt and this fancy embroidered blouse and think of Evelyn and mist up and blow their noses and put the items aside. They'd never buy a dead woman's clothes. Bad luck.

Hey. We've all got that bad luck, so get over it, girls. But maybe one of them would purchase this green beaded dress, never having seen Evelyn wear it. A nice dress for your silver wedding-anniversary dinner, your old hubby standing next to you, still grumpy about something, and your children, grown old and slow and careful themselves, lined up behind you, and you in the green beaded dress. The dress that says, *"Go ahead, ask me to dance, I might say yes."* *"Where'd you get that?"* You'd give them a Mona Lisa smile and say, *"That's for me to know and you to find out."*

Barbara went home, loaded the dishwasher, and poured herself a glass of tea from a pitcher in the fridge. She had no desire for alcohol, not at that moment, and she crawled into bed and said a prayer to the sky for Mother's safe arrival and repose and then reposed herself.

13. GIANT DUCKS

It was diabetes. The specialist at the hospital had suspected diabetes and given Daddy insulin and he was doing better now. He had suffered a brain concussion and there seemed to be some memory-loss issues there but he was responding well and he had told the doctor a joke so he was just fine. So Debbie drove into St. Cloud and brought him home.

He was nattily dressed in pressed khaki pants and blue shirt and blazer and she signed a receipt for him and on the way to the car he stopped and hugged her. "You mean so much to me, Pookie," he said. "I missed you." He thought for a moment. "How's your mother?" Fine, said Debbie. "I don't mean to worry you, but she strikes me as a little unsteady"—he tapped his forehead—"up here, I mean."

On the way home, just north of Holdingford, he started to snuffle. He pulled out a hanky and blew. "I'm just so happy you're here," he said, through his tears. He'd always been a sentimental guy, even before he got brained by the bathtub. He'd dissolve in a puddle of tears at a Chopin étude at a piano recital or the Mills Brothers singing "We'll Meet Again" and Christmas Eve was devastating, the first verse of "Silent Night" tore him to pieces. And now he reached over and touched her hand on the steering wheel and sang, "The wheels on the bus go round and round, round and round, round and round. The wheels on the bus go round and round, all through the town."

"Remember that one?" he said. She did. "I sang that to you when you were itty-bitty. And now you're getting married." He sat silent, tears welling up in his old brown eyes. "I would like to say a few words at your wedding," he said.

"A few words about what?"

"About you and about when you were a little girl. And about the future too. Maybe a little about Scripture."

"About the Rapture?"

"Maybe," he said.

"Daddy, do you remember those enormous ducks that they used to have on the lake? You took me to see them once. They were as big as boats. Maybe they were boats."

He remembered boats, of course. Ducks? Did she mean docks? He used to have a dock and he tied his boat to it. Remember that boat? Or did she mean dogs? They had a dog named Bailey. A black cocker spaniel. He died in the kitchen while eating his dog nuggets, had a stroke and lay down and was gone. Mr. Detmer teared up to think of it. But when they reached home, Mrs. Detmer remembered the ducks right away. The Sons of Knute had them. Ages ago. Big Boy giant fiberglass duck decoys eighteen feet long. The hunter lay on his back inside the duck and pedaled the drive shaft that turned the propeller as he looked out through a periscope in the duck's neck, scanning the skies for incoming ducks and when they came in for a landing, the hunter sprang up and threw open a trapdoor in the tail of the duck and blasted away from there. No need for duck blinds. Just climb into a decoy and go to wherever the ducks are.

The Knutes purchased four of the things and they were a big disappointment. A crowd turned out for their debut and a Knute climbed into one and it flipped belly up. So they put concrete blocks in for ballast and that helped but not much. They still were tippy. Even in a light swell they rocked back and forth to beat the band. You lay inside and it was hot and stuffy and you had to pedal and it was hard to steer and then the dang things rocked and rocked and rocked. Even on a calm day. A Knute went out in one and got claustrophobic and started yelling and he fired his gun, both barrels, and blew a hole in the side and the thing sank and he would've drowned except he was in shallow water. So they hauled all of the Big Boy decoys off to storage and nothing more was said about them. There was no recrimination, no kidding. It was too painful. The giant ducks no longer existed. They were non-ducks.

"I want one for my wedding," she said. "Or two. Two would be perfect."

"You are so creative!" Mother cried. "Where do you come up with these ideas?" She was settled in on the porch, sipping a cool drink Debbie had made with mysterious tasty ingredients that put her in a lively mood. She was feeling very vivacious and girl-ish. "Remember when we got married, Daddy?" He did not, or he preferred not to. "We were married in a hailstorm," she said. "Hailstones the size of Ping-Pong balls. It hit just as we were standing at the altar. It was in August. The minister had given a very nice talk on the parable of the vineyard and we were about to say our vows and there was a racket up on the roof and men jumped up and went to look and we just plowed right ahead and said our I Do's, right, Daddy?" Daddy looked as if he couldn't remember if he were married to this old lady or not. "They played the wedding march and we went up the aisle and out the door and it was all ice out there. August and there was ice on the ground and our car was all beat up and so were the others. And my dad jumped in his car and drove home and his corn was all pounded into the ground. Only good for silage. He had paid for my fancy wedding and now he didn't have money for gas or feed. He came back and ate the wedding cake he'd paid for and he danced one dance with me and he said to me—I'll never forget this—he said, Betty, this is the worst day of my life. If it weren't that the bank would get everything, I'd go out to the woods and shoot myself right now. He said that to me as we were dancing and then your father and I got in our car and drove to the Curtis Hotel in Minneapolis. Remember that, Daddy?" Daddy shook his head sadly. His mind had drifted off elsewhere.

"Let me tell you about *my* wedding," said Debbie. She had a notebook on her lap, everything written out. It would be called a Celebration of Commitment. Not a wedding, as such. Same thing but different. She had ordered a sign for the pontoon boat, "Celebration of Commitment."

"Boat?" said Mother.

Her minister, Misty Naylor, would conduct the service aboard the pontoon boat, *The Agnes D.* Wally's pontoon boat. She had rented it for the weekend. "What church is she from?" asked Mother. "Misty is a seeker," said Debbie. She used to be Presbyterian but she had a near-death experience during breast enhancement surgery and a door opened onto a garden full of golden light and beautiful plants and every different sort of person, Muslim and Hindu and Buddhist and Jew, all rejoicing and living in harmony, and when Misty returned to life, she dedicated herself to world peace and to Momentism—you know, the idea that all of time takes place in one moment, there is no eternity. "Very interesting," said Daddy. "I hope I get a chance to talk to her and clear up some things." He was also hoping there would be supper served soon, something meaty and substantial.

Misty Naylor was the founding sister of the Sisterhood of the Sacred Spirit in California, a church with no building, only a website. Every few weeks Misty announced a Confluence and a few hundred of the Sisterhood gathered in a park or plaza and they milled for half an hour, shuffling slowly in a circle, lost fragments of the universal divine. Openness without self-limiting expectations, no touching, no talking, just spirit essence, and as they milled, they listened for the tone as Misty blew it on a ceramic pitchpipe and they resonated with it to make the Sacred Chord, and when the entire Confluence had landed on the Sacred Chord, they held it and hummed powerfully together until they felt the Spirit from their toenails to the roots of their hair, and then they bowed, backed away, and dispersed. SOSS was Debbie's spiritual family and Misty was flying out as a very very special favor. Debbie needed to clear out the upstairs bedroom for Misty to sleep in.

"And where will Brent sleep?"

"He'll be fine on the porch."

Water and fire are holy elements to the Sacred Spirit people, she explained, and so she (and Brent) wanted to say their vows on the water. She had rented the *Agnes D* for that purpose. The two of them would sail, with Misty, and carry a barbecue grill, the coals lit—water and fire—and say their vows while cruising across the water, observed by family and guests assembled under an awning where lunch would be served.

"Lunch?" said Mother, starting to rise from her chair. "I should call up Evelyn." Visions of kitchen work, making ham salad, cutting crusts off sandwiches, frying Swedish meatballs and sticking toothpicks in them. Then she remembered that Evelyn didn't do lunches anymore. Also, that she was dead.

"Don't worry, I've got it covered," said Debbie. She had ordered ten cases of Moët champagne and four wheels of cheese, Camembert, Roquefort, white cheddar, Caerphilly, fifty pounds of French pâté with peppercorn crust, sixteen dozen giant shrimp shish kebab fresh frozen and flown in from California, and French vanilla ice cream with fresh peaches. God is within us and so when we are good to ourselves, we do a sacred act, said Misty. So there would be a wedding feast. "You can sit and put your feet up and enjoy it," she said to Mother.

"Who is going to prepare all of that? It isn't going to magically appear."

Her good buddies Georges and Patrice from the world-famous Restaurant Nantes would do everything.

"But why on a boat? Why not in a church? What if it rains?"

Because the Sisterhood believes that life is a voyage, she and Brent would vow to cherish and to support each other in their life voyages; the two giant fiberglass ducks, powered by the pedaling Swanson boys would cross their path, strewing flower petals, and then Craig would descend in his hot-air balloon and pick up Brent and Debbie and take them away—free! Drifting with the wind! And if it rains, all the better!

"Craig?"

"You remember Craig. He and I went to Concordia together. He drove out to San Francisco in 1981. He lives in St. Paul now. He teaches geometry and he flies hot-air balloons."

"Is that safe?" asked Mother. Daddy grimaced. He thought of power lines and a balloon striking one and the occupants, including his daughter, bursting into a shower of sparks.

POWER COMPANY HEAD'S DAUGHTER
ELECTROCUTED ON WEDDING DAY.

Debbie decided not to mention Craig's friend Larry who goes around the Midwest dressed up like Elvis and jumps from a plane with a loudspeaker in his pants and sings "Love Me" and "One Night With You"—Craig said they often work as a team and Debbie said okay, though she wasn't an Elvis fan. (Why didn't anybody impersonate Jerry Garcia and sing "Truckin'"?)

Mother asked about the wedding dress and Debbie got up to make more tea. She was planning to wear wedding jeans and a wedding T-shirt ("Love, Honor, and What?") but they would talk about that later.

"I'm concerned about this young man and his spiritual situation," said Daddy. "We are living in the Last Days, you know...." His voice trailed off. "But nobody asked for my advice in the matter, so I suppose I should shut up."

"Do you remember Evelyn Peterson?" said Mother. Debbie did not.

"The old lady down by the Lutheran church. The one who traveled all over and let her lawn go to rack and ruin. She died Friday night."

"Okay."

"Used to see her sitting on her porch with her nose in a book. In the morning. Let the laundry go, never mind cleaning. She sure had a vivid imagination, I'll say that. She told me once she thought she could be happy, living in Minneapolis. Minneapolis, I said. Who needs it? It's a lot of noise, if you ask me. Charge you an arm and a leg for a cup of coffee and think nothing of it. Evelyn always had expensive tastes though. Poor Jack found that out. He was my cousin, you know. All Jack wanted to do was fish and all she wanted to do was go somewhere else. So she divorced him and made him go live in that shack at the lake, poor man. He sat over there and drank himself to death. Oh, she was quite the mover and shaker. Had her hand in everything. Bossy, some people would say. I don't know. I never cared to get mixed up in all of that, the Thanatopsis Club and the Women's Circle and all. My No. 1 job was taking care of your father and keeping him happy. Just the homebody type. Evelyn told me once she wished she could just go around and live in hotels for the rest of her life. I said to her, Jeeze, Evelyn, how do ya think of those things? Oh, she was motoring in the fast lane all right. She's out in the cemetery now. Goes to show: you never know."

"She was cremated, they say," said Daddy. "If you can imagine that."

Debbie refilled their glasses with iced tea. It was seventy-eight degrees on the kitchen thermometer. Brent would arrive on Wednesday from Chicago. She hadn't spoken to him in a week. He didn't like to get phone calls on the road. She hoped he was looking forward to Saturday.

14. KYLE SURVIVES A CRASH

Kyle moved out of the apartment on Monday right after Sarah left for work. He stuffed all of his things into a suitcase and three big boxes and put them in the van he borrowed and drove away, leaving a note for Sarah on the kitchen counter.

Sarah—

I left. Sorry. It was a sudden decision and it is the right thing for now. I've been trying way too hard to make you happy and read your mood and be who you want me to be and now I have to be honest no matter how painful it is. I don't want to learn how to live a lie. I've been spending hours and hours in chat rooms, which is a pretty pitiful thing if you ask me, but I met some people there who asked me tough questions, e.g. am I happy? And the asnwer is No and what that says is that you and I don't belong together. I am extremely sorry. I am also sorry that I can't tell you these things face-to-face but any time I try to talk to you, you interrupt and finish my sentences for me and it drives me berserk. You must think I am a moron. Well, maybe so but even a moron has to live his own life. Good luck.

    Kyle

He would call up Burger King later and tell them he had quit. A bad thing to do, but he had to do it. And he would have to cancel his registration for fall semester at the U. It had all come crashing down on him Sunday, in the wake of Grandma's death. She was trapped in a life she didn't believe in and he was not going to go down that path. Live with a woman under false pretenses, work at a crummy job frying up animal parts, take courses he didn't give a rat's ass about. "Don't wait. Liberate," as Richie D. sang in *Liberty 4 U 2*, "You get on that track, don't be surprised if you never come back."

He had awoken at 2 a.m., Sarah sleeping by his side, with a great idea for a new line of work.

KYLE'S FLYING FAREWELL. Your body is yours to do with as you see fit, in this life and afterward. Millions choose cremation as a civilized alternative to mummification and entombment. Make your last rites festive with Kyle's Flying Farewell. The scattering of ashes from small planes is expensive, accommodates only a handful of loved ones, and often results in "blow-back" mishaps. Instead, hire Kyle and his red parasail to fly your ashes (mixed with sparkle dust) at low altitude over a gathering of friends and family and—out you go! In a bright cloud that will be remembered by all for years to come. The cost is a fraction of what you'd pay for a cemetery plot. Death is inevitable but that's no reason to make it burdensome and depressing for your survivors. Don't go underground. Lighten up! Fly away!

The parasail folded into an eight-foot case. He could travel the country, offering his services. Find a powerboat to tow him and he'd be in business. Collect the ashes, mix in the glitter, maybe hire a bagpiper to play "Amazing Grace"—and earn good money by giving people something they can't find elsewhere.

He drove north toward Lake Wobegon taking the scenic route up the river through Anoka. Just beyond Anoka, he changed his mind about the ash-scattering business. He was starting to think bookstore. Books about aviation and astronomy and also science fiction. *Cosmic Books.* He was also thinking about starting a cleaning service. Mom'd like that.

He needed to talk to Duane about Saturday. The guy was known to forget things. And he needed to take the parasail on a test run. On the radio, they said a seventy-eight-year-old Minneapolis man had withdrawn thirty-five thousand dollars from his bank to give to an FBI man who needed it to catch an embezzler. But the FBI man wasn't with the FBI. He switched over to music. It sounded like Mozart or Haydn. He liked it. Very symmetrical and one thing developed gracefully into another. No wonder they say Mozart stimulates brain development. He makes you believe in a fundamentally orderly world and isn't that the beginning of intelligence—a faith in order? There is no intelligence without order—

When he woke up, a few seconds later, he was hanging upside down by his seat belt and shoulder harness and the horn was stuck. He smelled grass and cow manure and something burning. He remembered the van turning over and rolling but not how it happened. He hung there, hands gripping the wheel. There was shouting nearby and someone kneeling in the grass and then a woman's face in the window, drawn and tense.

"Are you all right?" Her long black hair hung down. She looked so much like Becky Thorsen from high school.

"I don't know," he said.

"We better get you out," she said. "Can you move your legs?"

And then a man in blue coveralls appeared on the other side. He wrestled the door open and crawled in and took hold of Kyle and the girl snapped the seat belt open and Kyle dropped into the man's arms. They boosted him out and carried him forty or fifty feet away and lay him in tall grass as a fire truck came screaming up and two burly guys in gray T-shirts and jeans scrambled down the ditch with fire extinguishers in hand and shot the engine compartment full of foam.

He raised his head. "Don't move," the girl said. So he put it down. And then the cops got there, asked him who he was, shone a light in his eyes, checked his license. And then an ambulance.

"I'm okay. Really," he said. But they had their job to do. They slid the backboard under him and hoisted him up on the gurney and bucked it up the slope and slid him in the back door and off they went. He moved his right toe and then his left, his right hand, his left hand. He was okay. *Thank you, Jesus.* And now he had a cover for quitting school. A near-death experience. He swerved to avoid a smaller car and took the van into the ditch, narrowly missing a power pole. Had he hit it, he'd be a deadster. Two bowling balls, Grandma in one, Kyle in the other. As he lay there in the grass, waiting for help to arrive, he thought to himself, *I want to dedicate my life to serving others.* He didn't know just how yet, but it wouldn't be scattering ashes.

Mom would go for that. He couldn't wait to tell her.

He was wheeled into the ER of the St. Cloud Hospital and there was a man in a gold lamé suit and black wig and an enormous belt, throwing up into a blue plastic bag, heaving his insides out, sicker than a dog. He sat in a blue plastic chair in the hall and the ambulance crew wheeled Kyle right up next to him and went off to save somebody else. Kyle lay and listened to the man retching and then he said, "Are you almost done? If not, I'm going to move."

The man said he was done. He rinsed his mouth with 7Up and stretched and said he felt better.

He had gotten hammered last night and then this morning he had taken a motion-sickness drug, forgetting that he'd just taken an antianxiety drug and the three things didn't get along. "I was heading for Little Falls, thirty minutes late for a gig, and the Highway Patrol pulled me over for doing eighty in a fifty-five and I got out of the car and threw up and that's where we are. So I guess the Elks are not going to get Elvis today. Big Al is going to kill me. By the way, my name is Larry Levitz. I've been doing Elvis for thirty-two years. I was a parachuter in the service, then I got into this." He shrugged and closed his eyes. "And now I'm off to a wedding in Lake Wobegon."

"Lake Wobegon?" Larry told Kyle all about the Detmer event, the hot-air balloon, the pontoon boat, and Elvis descending from the sky with a torch and singing "Burning Love"—and Kyle told Larry about the scattering of Grandma's ashes. "She must've been some old lady. Mine died when I was twenty. Man, it busted me up something bad. I was real close to my grandma after I had this accident after I got out of the service. I was out hunting grouse with my best friend Patrick. About two in the afternoon we stopped to have a few beers and then went back to hunting and we were walking through the woods and I tripped on a tree and the gun went off and there he was with his head half blown off. God. I have a hard time talking about it even now. Forty years later and it's like it was yesterday. Man, that sure turns a guy's life around."

"I guess it changed Patrick's life, too," said Kyle.

"He was my best friend. Suddenly there he is in the dirt with his brains blown out. Hair and blood and I just could not handle it. I said to myself, Larry, you do not want to be here. This is not a good thing at all. I took off running like a crazy person. That was a bad move. Looking back, that's something I wish I could've changed."

Running away from an accidental homicide did seem to Kyle like a bad mistake, on top of mixing alcohol with hunting, and walking around with a loaded shotgun and the safety not on.

"I ran a couple of miles and made it to the highway and I hitch-hiked all the way to Texas. I got a couple of little rides and then a trucker took me all the way to Houston."

"Where did you shoot him?"

"Mississippi. Ten Mile, Mississippi," he said, looking at Kyle as if he should've known that. "Just up the road from Tupelo. Elvis's hometown. My dad grew up with Elvis. They were in Sunday school class together and helped each other memorize verses. I used to guide Elvis tours in Tupelo. Drove around in a big old bus and took 'em around to churches he sang at and the fairgrounds and all that. Took 'em to Elvis's hideout, this deep cave where he had his visions and the angel came with the silver shields. Man, that was the best job I ever had. Until this one."

"What happened in Texas?"

Larry thought for a moment, as if trying to get the whole thing straight in his own mind. "I had a buddy in Houston and I dialed his phone number but I got a couple of digits turned around in my mind so I was running out of quarters at the pay phone and there was a liquor store across the street and I still had the rifle and a couple of shells. And I was hopped up on pills and stuff the trucker gave me. Anyways, I headed for that liquor store to get me a roll of quarters and just as I stepped into the street, a cop car rolls up with a black car right behind it and the cop says over the loudspeaker for me to step back onto the sidewalk, which I did, and then this woman yells, 'He's got a gun,' which was true, and suddenly guys are on top of me, six beefy guys in suits, and it turns out that President Bush, the old one, is in the black car be hind the cop car, and these Secret Service guys throw me in a black SUV and off we go at high speed screeching into an underground garage and they hustle me into a padded elevator and it goes *down* like about five levels and we go down a hallway and into a room and they throw me in a chair and they are asking me a thousand questions, one after the other, and other guys come in with big manila folders of stuff about me, my high school record, my dad's Army records, a ton of stuff, book reports I gave, a letter to my grandma thanking her for the $25.00 she gave me for my birthday, and I'm thinking, *This is the end of you, Larry. You can kiss this life goodbye.*"

He stopped and looked around. "You see a Coke machine around here? I sure could use a Dr. Pepper right now. "

"How did you know it was President Bush in the car?" said Kyle. He wasn't sure how much he believed the story. He thought maybe 50 percent, maybe less. But which 50 percent?

"He was in the back seat, sitting next to an A-rab with a cloak over his head and he looked meaner than hell. He said, Shoot the sumbitch. I'll never forget that as long as I live. He was wanting to snuff me out on the backstreets of Houston. He climbs out of the car, real slow-like, and walks over to me, Old Man Bush, and he looks down at me on the sidewalk, arms pinned behind me, and he says something in a foreign language that's all crackly like he's eating dry toast. And I don't say anything. He's asking me a question in Egyptian or something, and I shake my head, and Bush says, 'Get him out of here.' And they took me away. Truth, man.—Hey, go get me a Dr. Pepper. My throat is all dry."

Kyle climbed down off the gurney. The pop machine was two floors up according to the ER receptionist. She was a pretty girl, brunette, with black horn-rims, who looked like she deserved better in life than to supervise this vale of tears.

"If it jams, you may have to hit it right below the coin return," she said. The pop machine worked fine, though, and the can of Dr. Pepper came bumbling down the chute and as it did, Kyle realized he had left his jacket in ER. He hustled down two flights of stairs and there was Larry, just where he'd left him, except he'd taken off the wig and glasses and was talking on his cell phone.

"I'm in the hospital," said Larry. "I had an attack of some kind. Got all woozy. They're saying it was not a stroke but they're still doing tests. I don't know where the hospital is. I'll find out and get back to you."

The Secret Service kept him for a week, flew him back to Mississippi, and he spent two years in prison for reckless disregard for human life and that's where Elvis came to visit him. The King had been dead for six years. He came at midnight and stood in Larry's cell, wearing pink slacks and a fancy white shirt and a black sportcoat and shades, very slim and his hair swept back. He brought Larry a sandwich in a white paper sack.

"What kind?" asked Kyle.

"Peanut butter and bananas and mayonnaise."

"You got that out of a book," said Kyle.

"You don't have to believe me," said Larry. "Most people don't. I don't care. It used to matter to me but it doesn't anymore. Elvis said people wouldn't believe me and he was absolutely right. He told me what to do with my life. He said to me, 'I want you to jump out of airplanes and sing.' He was standing as close to me as I am to you right now. He knew about Patrick and he knew it wasn't my fault. He knew the name of the trucker and he knew about George Bush and he said, 'It doesn't matter, none of it. Evil is riding high but God is moving on the waters.' He sang me a song to prove it was him and he gave me a Dr. Pepper. I've been drinking that ever since." Larry took a long swig of Dr. Pepper. "That sure restores a person. Bless your heart, I want to sing at your grandma's funeral. I'll do it for free. I can sing 'Moon River' for you."

Kyle said he didn't know if that was a good idea or not.

"Don't worry about it," said Larry. "It'll be my pleasure."

Larry sang a few lines of "Moon River" and actually he was good. He didn't make you forget Tony Bennett but he could carry a tune.

"What line of work you in?" he asked.

"I'm in school. Sophomore. Going to be a junior in the fall."

Larry said that he had always regretted his lack of education but there was not much to be done about it now. He was bringing joy to people and that was all that one man could do.

15. THE GROOM SHOWS UP

Brent flew the red-eye from L.A. to Minneapolis-St. Paul on Tuesday arriving at dawn and caught a limo service to St. Cloud where Debbie was supposed to meet him at the bus depot but she took the wrong road, and headed north instead of south and was almost an hour late. He was pacing outside in his navy blue linen suit and sandals, trying to get his cell phone to work. He had dropped it in the urinal in the bus depot and taken off his shoe to fish it out with but it was badly pee-soaked and meanwhile a V.I.P. was calling so Brent picked it up in a hanky which muffled his voice so the man couldn't understand him and hung up and in all the turmoil Brent had lost his dark glasses. He threw his suitcase into the back of the van and got in the passenger side and looked straight ahead, livid. "I am really pissed," he said, in case she didn't notice.

"In more ways than one," she said, and knew right away it was the wrong thing to say at that moment. "I am so sorry. You're angry and you have a right to be. I'm so stupid when it comes to directions."

He said he was not angry at her, he was angry at himself for being here. "I do not want to be here, believe me." They stopped to get him a bottle of gin and the liquor store didn't have his brand, Bombay. He said to skip it. In Bowlus, he changed his mind. He wanted gin. So they stopped at the liquor store there which only carried a no-frills gin called Calcutta, made in Toronto. Eight bucks a quart. "Cheaper than antifreeze," said the clerk. He bought it, and vermouth, and three bottles of Pinot Noir. Clearly he was settling in for a siege.

"My parents don't drink much," she said. He said he had assumed as much.

"My dad has diabetes. We just found out. They're as sweet as can be. I hope you like them." That last sentence buzzed in the air. A fatal wish. She knew it the moment she said it. He would loathe them and they would try so hard and be desperately polite and he would loathe them all the more for trying. Brent could be rude when he wanted. And sometimes without knowing it. He was in a cutthroat line of work, shared-time luxury jets were the new thing. Competition was ferocious. The Russians were getting into the market, MiG-15s had been converted to passenger jets, they'd fly you cross-country in seventy minutes. Brent had come a long way from Berkeley and Sartre. He was a Republican now, or as he put it, "a nihilist in golf pants." He made fun of the Sacred Spirit people mercilessly and God knows they were an easy target with their dinging and whanging and milling, their simple theology—children, trees, music, good; war, injustice, pollution, bad—but she loved them and they made her feel whole. They were nontoxic. How many people can you say that about?

He was slumped in the front seat, dozing, as the car came over the rise and there were the grain silos like an ancient temple and the lake and then the highway dipped into the town, and she slowed to twenty and he woke up.

"Where are we now?"

"We're in Lake Wobegon, Brent. This is where I'm from."

He looked and said nothing. They cruised slowly along Main Street, past the Mercantile and the Sidetrack Tap and the Chatterbox and Ralph's Pretty Good Grocery, all the highlights of her bicycle years. There on the corner was the old phone booth. She wanted to tell him about it. Some old mayor had insisted on the town buying one. (What sort of town had no phone booth?) So in it went and nobody ever used it. Why would you? Especially after drunks started using it as a toilet. But one day Clarence Bunsen was passing by and the phone rang. An odd high-pitched ring. He had never heard it ring before. He picked it up and a man asked for Maureen. "She's not here," said Clarence. "When is she expected?" He said he didn't know. "Oh," said the man and hung up, disappointed. So it became a saying. Whenever people complained, you might say, "Tell it to Maureen."

This used to strike her as funny, but now that she thought about telling it to Brent it seemed dopy. So she didn't. She drove down to the lake and parked under a red oak tree and snuggled up next to him. "We're going to be married out there," she said.

"But by your friend, right? So it's not exactly a wedding."

"To me it's like a wedding. What's the difference?"

"You and I agreed that we didn't need some big legal whoop-de-do. This is our commitment to each other, right? It's just between you and me."

So he was already planning to leave her. Oh God. How stupid she was. The man had played along with the thing, consented to be here and say his lines and act the part, and now he was making it clear that it was nonbinding. He was thinking beyond Saturday, wondering who the next babe might be.

"But you would marry me if it came down to that, wouldn't you?"

"What do you mean, 'if it came down to that'?"

"If I asked you to."

He looked out to the lake and he brushed his hair back and finally he said, "We don't have that sort of proprietary relationship."

"But we're going to be true to each other, aren't we?"

"Of course." He said this in an odd tone of voice, the clink of a counterfeit coin on the counter. "Let's head for home, okay? It's been a day to remember. We're starting a new print ad campaign." He pulled a paper from his pocket and read: "The aura of authority is an indispensible element of leadership, and nothing says *authority* like a private jet waiting for you at the airport—to go where you want to go, when you're ready." He put the paper away. "This is going to be big, I tell you. Let's go. I need a drink."

She backed the car up and drove around behind Ralph's and onto Main Street and up the hill toward her parents' house and she thought, *This is never going to work. How did you get yourself into this mess? You don't need this. Cut this bozo loose.* And then she thought, *Maybe he just needs a good night's sleep. Everybody has a bad day now and then. Give him a chance.*

16. IN RECOVERY

ednesday was Barbara's third day of recovery and it was rough. Monday and Tuesday were easy; she remembered how bad she used to feel, brain-dead, nauseated, guilt-ridden, dizzy. But Wednesday morning she woke up feeling pretty good and thinking about crème de cacao. She skipped coffee because of the liquorish associations and made green tea which is supposed to help counter alcoholic urges, according to something she read online.

It's a new life, she told herself. *You're doing great. Keep at it.*

She would be sober. She would exercise every day. She would go on a detoxifying diet she had read about that incorporated nutrients found in honey and locusts. She would sell her house and leave town and start Part Two somewhere else, maybe near an ocean, in a sun-swept town on a hillside, in a house with a walled garden covered with vines, on a red-brick patio under a banyan tree. She had it all clear in her mind. And either Oliver would get with the program and marry her or he would be history.

He had never set foot in her house. She had been in his house once and he was so embarrassed by the mess, the boxes of sugar wafers, a case of Spam, piles of soda-pop cans, twelve packs, empty burger bags, pizza boxes, chaos in the kitchen, that he turned around and drove her to the Romeo Motel and that had been their meeting place ever since. He'd call or e-mail her and say "What you up to tonight?" She'd play along. "Not much. You?" He wasn't up to much either. Just sitting and thinking. "About what?" Things. And then he'd say it. "Sure would be nice to see you." And she'd go, or she wouldn't go, and it was always the Romeo, room 135, in back. He could pull up in his old Caddy and walk ten steps to the door and be in the room. He'd pay over the phone and have the clerk leave the door unlocked. Oliver liked dim light and anonymity. He was not ready to stand beside her in the light of day and hold hands and be her boyfriend. She was but he wasn't.

"Come to my house. I want to fix you dinner," she said, and he shook his head. "I don't want you to go to the trouble." Lie, lie. He didn't want her watching him eat. Period. She had seen him once coming out of McDonald's with a box in his hands. It was big enough to hold dinners for six. One could only guess at the contents and shudder.

She needed some distraction from the urge to fix a drink. She had discovered a miniature bottle of brandy in the cupboard, left over from Christmas. It was there, next to the brown sugar and the cinnamon sticks. *Get out a glass, fill it with ice, have a drink. What's the big problem? Why make such a big deal over it?* And then a girl named Sarah called, asking for Kyle. Barbara went into her hostess mode— "I'm expecting him soon," she said. "How are you doing? He's told me so much about you." Lie, lie, lie. She said, "I'm worried about him. I think he has dropped out of school and quit his job and he left me an odd note—" Oh? "I think he's having a kickback or something." A kickback? "It's when you react to one crisis by creating another one." Oh. Interesting term. Are you in psychology? "No, but I'm in elementary ed. Special ed, actually." The girl paused for a deep soulful breath. Barbara could sense something coming, like a drop of water forms on the lip of a faucet and balloons—"I don't know if I should tell you this or not," the girl said. "I mean—" *Tell, girly girl,* Barbara thought. *Tell everything, open up the hatches, baby-cakes, and drop the whole load of beans on the pavement. We're big people here. Mother died Friday night. No time to waste. Let's hear it*—"I found a page Kyle wrote for a journal or something, I don't know—it was in the garbage, he tore it in pieces and stuck it inside a milk carton—but anyway, I read it and he is all confused. Stuff about currents and searching and a lot about journeys. A lot of journey stuff. I think he's been drinking, and I know for a fact he's been smoking dope. I just thought you should know. Also I found some e-mails he sent to a gay website about how do you know if you're gay or not? I think he's worried about that. But he's not. I mean, I know he's not." *Okay. Good to know, I guess. Say no more.*

"But he had sex with this other girl, somebody he met online." Her voice quavered. "He was trying to prove something to himself. Honestly, I never met anybody with so many problems, and of course he blames it all on me for interrupting him. Why does he hate me? I've never been treated this bad by anybody before. I love him. He's the only boy I ever loved." She started to cry and hung up.

Barbara had never spoken to Kyle about sex. There was a unit on sex education in seventh grade, and she remembered him bringing home a pamphlet with diagrams of genitalia and underneath it, it said: If there are questions about sex that trouble you, ask your parents or your minister. The idea of him asking her about sex scared her then and horrified her now. Or, worse, asking Pastor Ingqvist. Mother gave Barbara a book once, *Everything A Girl Should*

Know, that basically said, "When you bleed, stuff this in there. Don't worry about a thing. Someday you will be very very happy, and meanwhile, don't think about it." And that was it. Subject closed. Parents are beautiful ignorant people and a child is a miracle, and they have no idea where it comes from, only that it completes their life in a wonderful way. That's all parents know about sex. Lloyd was putting his hand down there and getting all breathy and urgent, and before she knew what was happening, she was holding Muffy in her arms and Mother was beaming and Daddy was happy and she felt like she'd been torn apart and stuck back together.

She worked the crossword puzzle and moved the sprinkler to water the flower beds. She put out fresh seeds for the finches and oriole and the bluebird who had taken up residence nearby. The sun was blazing and the grass hurt her bare feet and the neighbor's radio irritated her, that awful chuck-wacka music. *I have got to go on all day like this and nothing is going to get better.* She called Oliver and his cell phone was turned off. Probably a supervisor was hovering so he couldn't take nonbusiness calls.

What a prince that fat man was! Her cousin Joanne said, "Barbara, you ought to find yourself a nice guy!" And Barbara wanted to tell her, "I got one and you don't know it, so ha ha ha! Got a better one than you do, that's for sure." Joanne's husband Allen had a laugh like a dog bark. Imagine putting up with that woofer for twenty-five years. He was completely unself-conscious. You'd be talking to him and he'd reach into his mouth and pick a popcorn husk out of a back molar, or stick a finger in his ear and clean out some wax and examine it and roll it into a ball, and then reach around back and do some proctology. Allen was a college graduate. Big deal. He snored so loud he knocked the alarm clock off the bedside table so she sent him to a sleep clinic and he was sent home because he woke up other patients. Oliver was a high-school dropout and he didn't run off at the mouth like Allen did about the president and climate change and all, but he had his own wisdom. Still waters run deep. Mrs. Chatterley's lover was a gardener and he was no intellectual but he sure mowed her lawn. And Oliver made her feel glamorous which she never had been, not for a day in her life.

She called Oliver again and he picked up this time. "Just wishing you were here," she said. "Kind of a hard day. I'm okay. Just feeling sad. I miss my mom. Why don't you come over? I'll fix supper."

She could hear wheels turning in his brain. "I told a friend I'd help him move some stuff," he said. "I'm sorry about your mom."

"I think I may sell my house and move away," she said. "Start a new life. What do you say?"

There was a brief vast silence.

"Sounds like you made up your mind," he said. "Excuse me," and he put the phone down and talked to somebody about windshield washer fluid.

You'll never find a better lover than me, fat man. I can cook your chicken, baby, just how you like it. I can clean up your mess and never give you a hard time about it. And I can lay you down on that big bed—

"I gotta go sell somebody some motor oil," he said.

She didn't want to make a big announcement about not drinking. Better to wait until people start to notice. *Hey, Barbara, I notice you're off the sauce, huh? How long has that been going on?* Six months. *Really?* Really. *So how's that?* Not bad. *How come you decided not to drink?* I just decided, that's all. I drank my share. Time to stop.

Oh, my, how she wanted a drink. A glass full of ice and brandy— that's what she drank when she and Lloyd were going dancing at roadhouses and making out in the parking lots. And then she graduated to screwdrivers, an occasional Manhattan, and then, during the Ronnie period, she drank beer and boilermakers. She moved on to an affair with a Catholic priest who taught her to appreciate martinis. Met him at a peace rally in St. Cloud. She went with Arlene Bunsen. In front of the courthouse. A couple hundred people waving signs, WHY MORE $$$$? and WAR IS POISON, and this very cultivated gentleman struck up a conversation with her about Irish literature and James Joyce and what did she know about James Joyce? Nothing at all. But he was a beautiful talker and made her feel smart and when he asked her to join him for a drink, *No* did not seem an option. It was wrong, wrong, wrong, and she went and did it. Lied to Arlene. ("I met a friend and she'll give me a ride.") And went and had a martini at the St. Cloud Hotel. He said, "Life is a feast and most people are starving." He said, "James Joyce would have loved looking at you. You would've been a majestic presence to him. He would've sat over there and stared at you for hours and gone and invented a character who looked like you, and you know? You are more interesting than the one he would have invented." What a fine compliment! Nobody had ever referred to her as majestic before, or said she could make a man yearn for ruin, which Father had said to her in the elevator. What did that mean? He said she was an angel, she was wholesome and good and good people deserve to have sex too. *How did I get here?* she wondered afterward, in the shower, listening to him piss three feet away. *And what would Mother think? In bed with a Catholic priest, naked, his whiskers against her cheek, murmuring poetry in her ear.* "Since feeling is first, who pays any attention to the syntax of things will never holy kiss you," he said and he kissed her—so that was what martinis held in store. And two months later she was pregnant with Kyle. The father was Father. He was off in New York, the head of something, a monsignor, and there was no reason to bother him about this. And what a lovely gift to get from a martini.

And then there was single malt Scotch. Donnie Krebsbach. He was standing beside a lovely red hatchback the day she strolled into Krebsbach Chev. Donnie, an old basketball star gone to pot but still a charmer. She almost bought that car from him though she's Lutheran and Lutherans drive Fords because the Krebsbachs are Catholic and so the money you spend there goes in part to pay for diamonds for the Pope's shoelaces but she was tempted because the car was red and it was a Caprice. And because Donnie was selling it. She thought maybe it was time she had a Caprice. "It's a good car," he told her. "And we could come down on that price a little." He stood next to her and opened the door. She could smell the leather and also Donnie's cologne, a dark musky smell. He put his hand on her shoulder. "She's a real good handler," he said. "You want to get in?" He jingled the keys. So she did. They drove all the way to St. Cloud and parked the car outside the Best Western and went in. He was married, Catholic, and a lousy lover. No foreplay and he was inside her for sixty seconds and afterward he rolled over and turned on the TV. The Golf Channel. He was fascinated. Evidently he'd never seen golf on television before. He said, "Boy, look at those greens." The man had been intimate with her minutes before and now he was engrossed by Tiger Woods chipping out of a sand trap, sending a plume of sand in the air. "Wow," said Donnie. He bought her a single malt Scotch afterward. It tasted like paint remover. She didn't buy the Caprice.

Lots of liquors left, rum and bourbon and vodka, so who knew what mysterious gentlemen awaited her?

But not yet.

Not now, thank you, Lord.

A person cannot coast along in old destructive habits year after year and accept whatever comes along. A person must stand up on her own two legs and walk. Get off one bus and go get on another. Climb out of the ditch and cross the road. Find the road that's going where you want to go.

Damn, it was hard not to pour that brandy into a glass of ice right now.

But she owed this to her boy. The only sermon that counts is the one that is formed of our actions. She would quit drinking and thereby show Kyle: *life is what you make it.* A person can grab hold of her life and change things for the better. *This happens all the time.* We are not chips of wood drifting down the stream of time. *We have oars.*

She remembered Kyle's graduation. He was No. 3 in his class, wore a gold tassel, won the Shining Star scholarship, got a big round of applause. That was the year the seniors hooked up a tiny plastic hose to the lectern and when Mr. Halvorson stood at the podium to talk about daring to make a difference, he felt the front of his pants getting very wet. A great big dark wet spot. He had to do his Groucho walk back to his seat and sit with his legs crossed and let somebody else hand out the diplomas. So Kyle was out late that night celebrating with his coconspirators, and the next day, Sunday, she put on a big open house, 1 to 3 p.m., with a ham and turkey buffet, potato salad and fruit salad, punch and coffee, and a sheet cake with CONGRATULATIONS KYLE in green icing and a hundred people dropped by and slipped some money in envelopes in the big basket in the living room. Lloyd was there, with terrible back pains, leaning against the kitchen wall, tears in his eyes. She snuck a look at a few envelopes and ten bucks seemed to be the average. It made her furious. Everybody loading up on food she had made and sitting on lawn chairs she had scrounged up and admiring the yard, the opulence of the hydrangeas, the sidewalk washed, and they couldn't be a little bit generous? Would it kill you? Norwegians! The worst! Kyle strolled by, cutting a wide swathe, working the crowd, and Flo said, "So, what are you going to do next year?" And he said, "I'm thinking I might take a year off to sort of think about it, and I'll stay with my dad in the city and get a job and earn some money for college or whatever." *It was such a lame reply*, she wanted to throw fruit salad in his face— and then she overheard him say something similar to other relatives. A sunny June afternoon in Lake Wobegon with her cheapskate relatives and her martyred ex-husband and lackadaisical son and the whole air of *Okay Then Not So Bad Hey* and visions of that bright boy adrift and some little trollop latching onto him, a romance like a brain tumor, and in two years he's working in retail for $8.50 an hour and in debt up to his eyebrows paying for the chintzy rambler and the crummy furniture. She took Kyle aside and said, "You can tell people whatever the hell you want, but you're not living with your dad next year and you're not working. You're going to enroll at the University as you told me you would and you're going to make a 3.8 grade point average and in return I am going to pay for the whole thing. That's the plan we agreed on and that's what you're going to do. Just so you know."

He said, "It's my life, you know," which was also lame.

And she said, "It is and I won't let you piss it away. Be as angry at me as you like but I'm not going to let you piss away your chances in life and wind up wearing an apron, putting price stickers on cans of creamed corn. And that's that."

He started to say something about needing to find his own way. "Listen," she said. "The world has enough slackers, and featherbedders and thumbsuckers so don't become one of them—it's really very simple—there are the doers who go at the job and get it done and there are the folks who find a comfy spot and surf the Web and download more pictures of themselves onto their website"—this was a dig, she had seen his website. Dreadful. Stupid. Vulgar. "You give me the next four years, and you can do as you like with the rest. And you'll have more to do as you like with," she said.

And after some stomping around and slamming doors and muttering at her, he, by God, went to the University and studied and got good grades. Not a 3.8, but 3.4, sometimes 3.6, acceptable. Once he tried to pledge a fraternity and she put her foot down: he wasn't going to join a gang and live in a house smelling of beer and livestock, dirty clothing strewn, underpants with skid marks in the seat, sink full of empty beer bottles, pizza boxes stacked six feet high. She found him a studio apartment, a little cell, white walls, tile floor, a futon, a door on sawhorses for a desk, no curtains so you wake up with the sun. And she mortgaged her house and paid his way. A pretty straight deal. If necessary she would rob a bank. Why not? Find one in a shopping center and walk in with a nylon stocking over her head and a pistol in her purse and tell them to hand over the hundreds and make it snappy. Most bank robbers got away with it. They don't tell you that on television but it's true. You could pick up $50,000 in a lunchbag and walk away and that night on *Eyewitness News* they'd be talking about the Larceny Lady and here she'd sit in Lake Wobegon cool as a cucumber, the loot in a Tupperware dish tucked away in the box of Christmas decorations. The ladies at church would say, "I can't imagine who would do a thing like that."

Two o'clock. She needed a drink. Really and truly. If a girl in a frilly apron walked in right now and asked, "What'll you have?" she would order a brandy sour. Slice of lemon. So delicious on a hot day. And what harm would it do? None. We are poisoning the earth, blasting the ozone layer, the Arctic ice cap shrivels, polar bears perish, and why not have a drink, Barbara Peterson?

Three o'clock, the doorbell rang. Front door. Nobody used that door except Mormons, Jehovah's Witnesses, and the UPS man. It was the boy from the crematorium, the one she kissed. With a big heavy box that the moment she took it she knew what was inside. It was Mother. She set it on the desk in the living room and cut the box open and lifted the bowling ball out. It was wrapped in heavy clear plastic which she cut off. The ball felt light, with its core drilled out and Mother's ashes inside. The hole that held the ashes was covered with a plaster patch. She thought maybe she should have the patch waterproofed to keep it intact. But why? Why preserve the ashes? It didn't matter. Mother was extinguished, her fire was out, let the water in.

She went and fetched the blue loose-leaf binder of Mother's letters. She had rounded up a few dozen and was keeping them to give to Kyle someday. That morning she'd found one from last December.

Dec 9

Dear Barbara,

I am in Reno, beat, absolutely knackered, and am trying to make this hotel computer work. I wrote you one letter already and then hit SHIFT for a new paragraph and the screen went blank. A thousand words of deathless prose, lost in a single stroke. Ah, progress.

As I said in that letter, I left Tuesday all of a sudden when I realized that if I didn't, I was going to get roped into baking forty dozen saffron buns for St. Lucia Day. I could feel the phone trembling—Sonya getting up the nerve to call me and pour out her troubles and how hard it is to get people to bake anymore—but I have baked my last bun and am done with it, so to make that clear, I vamoosed. I tried to call and your line was busy. I cleaned out the fridge, hauled away the deer bones that somebody's dog hauled into the yard, locked the house, and put sunflower seeds in the feeder for the birds to gorge on. Did you know that chickadees eat their weight in sunflower seeds every few days—think of a truckdriver ordering the 200-pound cheeseburger,—but I don't need to eat one more saffron bun, and that's why I had to get out. Christmas depresses the daylights out of me. All that damn food. Gladys came home with a mouse tail hanging from her mouth the other day and she was moaning the next morning so on the odd chance she was poisoned, I took her to the vet in St. Cloud, the lesbian one, and there she was in her white lab coat and offering a Comprehensive Care Analysis for $150—I said, "But it's only an old cat!" She winced at that. She listened to Gladys with a stethoscope for awhile and reported that Gladys has a heart murmur. She said that surgery is an option to consider. (Did you know about Medicat? It's health insurance for cats.) I said, "Not on your life." And I paid her twenty bucks and took Gladys out to Rollie Hochstetter's who owed me one for the times I lied to his wife about his whereabouts when he was running around with the horse-faced lady. He was in the machine shed dinking around with one of his antique tractors and I set Gladys down and told him to shoot her. So he did. It took him a minute to get the gun and I patted her and told her that it was for her own good. Her hips are stiff and she whimpers when she sits and I can hear her wheezing at night and life for her just isn't the feast it should be and I am not going to pay money to have her be a biology experiment. I said, "I'll join you soon enough, but there's one more dance in the old girl yet and so I'm off to Reno. And you are off to the Great Meadow in the Sky." She didn't believe a word of it, of course. She gave me a scathing look that I'll remember to my dying day and Rollie set her up on a stump and I turned my head and he blew her little head off. And now here I am, in the Business Center of an enormous hotel, weeping for a dead cat. It's a mistake to have a pet—they're so dear and you get to know them too well and then they turn into a tragedy in which you are the betrayer. I can't forget how she looked at me, her disdainful look, and today I saw that same exact look on the face of a fat old lady on her way to the slot machines. She glared at me just like Gladys did and I thought I saw whiskers on her. She said, "Where you been? I've been looking for you." I said, "I don't think I know you." She said, "Oh, Pffffft." A cat hiss.

By the way I stopped in Sauk Rapids and saw Muffy who is very very happy and has a blessed life and you should know that. She can't read the newspaper or do math and I can't ride a bicycle on a high wire, and life goes on.

I love hotels, even ones with slot machines jangling everywhere and old fat ladies with jangly bracelets and music dripping from the ceilings and grinning Filipino bellmen who are your instant best friends. There is dancing here and men to dance with and that's exactly what I want to do instead of sit in the church kitchen baking saffron buns and listening to people lament the dead. I want a gallant man to lead me out onto a dance floor with a prom ball sparkling and the band playing a rhumba and I want to do steps and turn and be turned, over and over again. But meanwhile I am missing my old accusatory cat. Anyway, that's why I didn't bring her over to your house. She is dead. I ain't. Neither is Muffy. She saves all my postcards so I will write her another, soon as I say,

    Love, your Mother

Drinking had gotten Barbara excused from kitchen duty: people were afraid she would drop glassware. It also got her out of teaching Vacation Bible school which was good. She had hated that for years, teaching innocent little kids about Noah's Ark. The kids were doped up on chocolate, vibrating like hummingbirds, so they really didn't pay attention, and the science was transparently weak—a gene pool of one male and one female means monstrous inbreeding—and then there is the issue of genocide. Judy Ingqvist said, "Yes, it's a hard story for children. So don't dwell on it." So one year Barbara had God send snow and cold instead of rain and instead of an ark Moses built a fort and God gave him fire, which the wicked did not have and so they froze to death.

Moses in the bulrushes, okay. A child destined to lead the uprising, raised by the very family who he will overthrow. Sweet. Or David and Goliath. An all-time favorite. Abraham and Isaac, on the other hand, this was madness. She told Judy Ingqvist, "A god who tells you to kill an innocent child is not a god to be worshipped." Judy smelled liquor on her breath. She frowned and turned away and Barbara was not invited to planning meetings the next year.

The next morning, she was trimming the trumpet vines and then Kyle arrived. She wrapped him in a warm embrace that he tried to wiggle out of. "Mom, people are looking," he said. Their little joke. He said he had spent the night in Mother's house. He let himself in through her bedroom window and slept on her sofa. She had come to him in a dream and told him to live his life and go out in the world and travel and meet women.

"Horse hockey," said Barbara. He looked sleepy, unkempt, unclean, and she embraced him tighter. "People are gonna be thinking incest," he said. She told him that he was her treasure in this world and she didn't care who knew it. "You screw up though, and I'll pound the crap out of you."

Roger's boys Jon and Sammy were spoiled rotten in Santa Barbara, drifting along, writing dopy songs, working dead-end jobs, going through girlfriends like rats through crackers. They were almost thirty and they went around in those damn droopy shorts and untied shoes and backward baseball caps and wires coming out of their ears. They owned every expensive piece of junk there was and Roger kept buying them more. They had the attention span of a fruit fly. The thought of sitting down and reading a book was alien to them, like tinkering with a car or growing vegetables to eat. Why would you do that?

She sat Kyle down in the kitchen and she poured him a glass of OJ over ice, got out the butter and eggs, tossed a big chunk of frozen hash browns in one frying pan and fried two eggs sunny-side up in another along with four strips of bacon. Kyle's favorite breakfast. The kid ate like a wolverine and was slim as a snake. Go figure. He was so beautiful, the dark lashes, the curly hair, she had to make herself stop staring at him. He had Mother's cheekbones and the priest's eyes. He was movie material. She was not going to let him fall asleep and go drifting over the dam. God, it was hard being young today. Holy Mother of God—the distractions.

But it was hard for Lloyd too. Lloyd, the ball-handling guard on the Leonard's basketball team, the good boy with the big grin, the ready lover, and then after they married and he went to work for his old man in the machine shop, he got eaten up. Tried to win his daddy's love by jumping higher and higher but there was no love to win. Lloyd was blamed for every setback. He should've walked out after a week, but Lloyd just got meeker and meeker. He made himself inoffensive. Kyle had that meekness in him and she didn't want him to get eaten up like his dad. Lloyd worked nights in a factory in New Brighton where he ran a machine that dipped shell casings in an acid concoction that gave him ferocious headaches. He accepted this as his due in life. He came back to his apartment at 5 a.m. and took a fistful of Advil and a sleeping pill and slept, and then got up and watched TV and ate cold cereal. He accepted any overtime hours they threw his way. He had no life.

So when Kyle told her, mouth full of egg and bacon, that his near-death experience on the highway had shown him the preciousness of life and he was dropping out of the U and reading Thoreau and searching for something meaningful to do with his life, she felt sick to her stomach. She drank her coffee, leaning on the counter, thinking, *Don't scream. Don't yell. Don't wave your arms,* looking at Mr. Anderson mowing his lawn across the alley, back and forth, back and forth. "Get to the point," she said quietly, not yelling, her arms at rest.

He had totally abandoned the ashes-scattering idea. That just didn't seem practical. Too much overhead. He wanted to make a documentary about Larry the Flying Elvis. To just sit him down and get him to say what he'd said in the ER, especially the part about Old Man Bush. But he needed $50,000 and he thought maybe Debbie Detmer would like to invest in him.

"I always wanted to make movies," he said, "and this is the perfect time. Like Grandma said, 'if you don't live life now, when are you going to live it?' I want to get a digital camera, it's great, it looks like film but you can shoot stuff for peanuts. I can do this. I really think I can. And if it doesn't work out, fine, I'll go back to the U next spring semester. But not in English, I'm done with that. Maybe history."

"Maybe you could make a documentary about somebody doinking around and wasting his time," she said. "How about a good masturbation movie? The world could use one of those, I'm sure. A camera and a tube of Jergen's and you're in business."

"I'm serious," he said. "Larry is fantastic. He's got a story to tell. He shot his best friend. He did time in prison. He had a visit from Elvis. And that Bush family is a bunch of thugs and gangsters. I'm going to ask Debbie Detmer to be the producer."

"Oh for pity sakes—the woman puts Vap-O-Rub on cats!"

"I met her once, five years ago, when I was mowing her parents' lawn, and we talked— she knows Tom Cruise. And a lot of others. She went out to California with nothing but the clothes in her suitcase and she made a big career out there—."

"Sure. Running a scam on cat owners."

"She can open doors. That's how it's done. You can beat your head against the wall for years, or somebody opens a door and suddenly somebody wants to make a movie with me. What's wrong with that?"

About ten things, actually. Sucking up to the Detmers, for one, and going off half-cocked on a hare-brained scheme instead of buckling down and finishing college and getting a degree. Some people spend their lives chasing hare-brained schemes. Why be one of them?

"Why bolt from the barn when you are only two years away from finishing? One thing at a time. And we have a task at hand. Don't forget. We're scattering Grandma's ashes on Saturday. *You* are scattering them. We are watching *you* scatter them. We can talk about it after that."

"I'm there," he said. "I just want to go talk to Debbie Detmer about making a movie. It'd be cool." And he put his plate and silverware in the sink and went off to take a shower.

Be firm, Barbara thought. *Don't start making threats. Don't weep. Be cool and firm.* She wanted to put up a marker: DO NOT GO THIS WAY. It leads to a life of bad bounces, perpetual tardiness, invincible ignorance. She filled up a bucket with soapy water and got the sponge mop and washed the kitchen floor, just to steady herself. The kid had canceled fall registration. A done deal, so don't bother talking about that. *You can't argue with what's done.* The goal was to get him back on track. He wants to change majors, quit English, take up History? Okay. History is fine. She'd never seen him crack a book of history, but never mind. She needed him to set a goal for himself and she would offer a clear reward for completion. She would sell Mother's house and put her share of it in an account and the moment Kyle got his degree, the money would be his. Twenty or thirty thousand dollars. A young man could keep himself focused for two years, with a pot of thirty thousand dollars waiting for him. Couldn't he?

"Oh, by the way, somebody named Sarah called for you. She asked you to call her back. She said it was important." Kyle looked stricken. "Is she your girlfriend?"

"Was my girlfriend."

"Well, she was very upset. And she asked how to get up here."

Kyle shook his head. "No way," he said.

"Well, there are roads, you know. You can buy maps at gas stations. You look up Lake Wobegon under L in the list of towns and it says C-7 and there we are."

Mr. Hansen called as they were sitting down to supper. "I wanted to express my condolences," he said. *Fine,* she thought. *Good.* He said he had a quilt that Evelyn had made forty years ago and it was as good as new. *Fine,* she thought. *Thank you very much. That's what happens if you don't ever use a quilt: it stays good as new.*

And then he got around to the point. "I'm on the county board, as you're probably aware." She was, Mr. Hansen had been there forever. "And we heard tell that you were planning to bury your mother in the lake and I just wanted you to know that there are ordinances about that. So if that's your plan, you'd do well to speak to one of us. I hope you understand." She thanked him for his concern. "I don't want to tell you what you can't do, but on the other hand, we don't want to set a precedent, if you know what I mean."

He was one of the old guys who'd run the county for fifty years and whose passion was roads. They loved to drive around and inspect the roads and shoulders and ditches and bridges and then meet and discuss things and plan new projects. Roads were what government was all about in their book. They took a boyish fascination in the subject. Land use didn't interest them, except they were against zoning, it was all about roads, grading roads and paving roads and repairing them in the spring, and God forbid you should spend money on the library or a public tennis court, or turn the old firebarn, with the sandstone around the door and the inscription A.D. 1892, into a museum—no need for that. No telling how much that could cost. You want money for that sort of thing, go have a bake sale. Roads on the other hand, you could never spend too much on. You need good roads.

She called him back after supper. "The lake was actually our second choice. What Mother wanted was to be buried in a pothole in County Road F. She told me that two years ago. We were driving home from Holdingford and talking about funerals and the car hit a pothole and she said, 'Bury me there where I'd do some good.'" Mr. Hansen laughed uneasily and said he didn't think it was a good idea to dig a hole eight feet deep in a county road. "Oh no," Barbara said. "She's been cremated. She'd fit in a pothole very nicely." He still didn't think it was a good idea. "It would cause controversy," he said, "and we've got enough on our plates without people coming to complain about that."

"Then I guess we'll have to do it in the lake," she said.

"You'll need a permit first," he said. "I hope we're not talking about scattering ashes. I don't think the fishermen would go for that."

"We're going to put her inside a bowling ball," she said. "We'll drop it in and it'll go straight to the bottom and stay there. Promise."

And the next day he brought over a county waste-disposal permit, signed and sealed. Permission granted to dispose of one (1) bowling ball in Lake Wobegon, containing ashes of decedent Evelyn Peterson and properly sealed in a watertight manner. He waived the permit fee of $35—"I always liked your mother," he said. "She was an original, that's for sure." He asked if he could see the bowling ball. Barbara brought it out to him and he held it in his arms. "By God, you've got something here," he said.

17. BREAKING UP

The wedding invitations were hand-delivered by Mr. Detmer's nephew Chuck on Thursday morning. The bride had forgotten all about invitations. They had to be rushed through by Clint's Print shop in St. Cloud, no time for raised lettering or creamy paper—it was a 3x5 brown card (brown was all they had in stock) with small lettering—you had to hold it up at a certain angle to make it out:

> Deborah Detmer and Brent Greenwood will publicly de-
> clare their love in poetry and song on Saturday the 11th
> of July on the waters of Lake Wobegon with a feast to
> follow in Pioneer Park, under the striped awning. Please
> be at the park by 2 p.m. to watch as events unfold and to
> share in our great good fortune as we celebrate our com-
> mitment to each other. No gifts, please. Casual dress.

It was an odd invitation—what events? Athletic? Long speeches? The rejection of gifts—what sort of arrogant nonsense was that? And "declare their love?" Is this a wedding or some sort of performance? If you want to get married, and you don't elope,

163

you're supposed to send out nice invitations to people you expect to come and who should bring a nice gift. It isn't a cattle auction. And "great good fortune" is a phrase one should never use. It is begging for trouble.

People felt bad for Mrs. Detmer that her only daughter hadn't a clue how to put on a wedding and then word got around via the Chatterbox circuit that chefs in big white hats were flying in from San Francisco to whomp up a flaming gourmet dinner and that the *Agnes D* was involved and an Elvis impersonator and a nondenominational minister named Froggy who had played keyboard in a rock 'n' roll band. It was headline news along the lunch counter. They feasted on that all day. And reminisced about their own weddings and unreliable groomsmen who got into the schnapps and what weird pumpkin-colored dresses bridesmaids were required to wear long ago and the long-gone custom of tin cans tied to the bumper and cheese smeared on the door handles and bride-kidnapping and LeRoy the town constable suggested they kidnap Debbie and take her up north to come to her senses and Myrtle Krebsbach hollered, "And what would you do with her if the groom didn't want to come get her?" Good question. Dorothy was one of the first to lay eyes on the groom. She described him as handsome in a bedraggled sort of way, unshaven, jeans and T-shirt and sneakers, and she took him for one of the summer people from across the lake, people with expensive boats they never use except to fish once a year with night crawlers flown in from Thailand and drink $100 bottles of scotch. Anyway, he'd come in and asked for cappuccino and she made him one from hot water and a packet of Folger's powdered cappuccino and he dumped some sugar in and drank half and ate a yogurt. He smelled of cinnamon. He kept trying to dial somebody on a cell phone.

"We don't have good coverage here," she told him, "but if you go up the hill behind the school it helps."

He kept dialing as if he fully expected to get lucky. She passed him a copy of the *Star Tribune* and he glanced at the stock listings. She said, "Congratulations on your wedding" and he gave her the strangest look. Like he was embarrassed that she knew. "You got yourself a real nice girl," she said. "How did you meet?" He said they were neighbors in Santa Cruz, California. "Well, whose house are you going to live in?" she said, kidding him. But he wasn't going to be kidded.

"We're going to build a new one," he said. "I think we are. It's up to her. It's her money." He gave a wave of his hand, as if the whole business were up in the air at this point. And he plunked a ten on the counter and got up and walked away.

"You forgot your change," she said.

"That's for you," he said and out the door he went. Dorothy gave the tip to Darlene who had the day off and who could use the money. "To make up for all you cheapskates," she said.

"Pretty well stuck on himself, like so many these days" said Rollie, and heads nodded. Myrtle had spoken to Mrs. Detmer who said that Mr. Greenwood was a wonderful young man and doing very well in the aviation business.

"Well, she would have to say that at this point, wouldn't she," said LeRoy.

"I don't know about the real nice girl part though," said Gary. "You could get some argument on that."

Dorothy said she believed in letting bygones be bygones and each to his own and live and let live. "There is too much backbiting and malicious gossip in a small town and that is the truth and everybody knows it," she said. "It wouldn't hurt people to be a little more forgiving and tolerant. That was how Evelyn was. She used to say, 'There's a lot of human nature in everybody.'"

At the mention of the deceased, the patrons got quiet for a minute or two. LeRoy said that Evelyn was the salt of the earth and a good soul and she'd done a lot of little unsung favors for kids who might've been headed down the wrong path and she set them right and not by preaching at them but by offering them a kind heart and a friendly ear. "Including me," he said.

LeRoy was from Rapid City. He worked for the post office there. One day he saw a package in the mail that he thought contained money and he took it home in his lunch bucket. It wasn't money, it was a heating pad. The postal inspectors arrived five minutes later and he got three years in prison for a heating pad. People had heard this story before—LeRoy told it once in Men's Bible Study—and now he got choked up as he told it again. Evelyn heard about him and campaigned to get him out of prison and then got him to Lake Wobegon and wangled the constable job.

"She was a bulldog," he said.

"Well, that was right," said Gary. "And once she got rid of that idiot Jack she was able to live her own life and get a little happiness."

"What do you mean, happiness?" said Dorothy.

"Well, I think you know what I mean," he said.

"Raoul?" she said. He nodded.

"Who was he?" He shrugged. "Her boyfriend," he said.

"How do you know?" Dorothy said and the moment she said it, she held up the palm of her hand. "Don't tell me. I don't want to know," she said.

Thursday morning, Pastor Ingqvist called Barbara to say that some of Evelyn's friends at church wanted to hold a little service in her memory, nothing big, not a memorial service, just a few friends gathering to remember her, and of course nobody wanted to offend Barbara—it would be a small private thing, really—"It's Florence, isn't it," said Barbara. He said that a number of people had suggested it. "It's Florence. She just can't stand not to have her way. I don't care. They can do whatever they like. I just wish they'd remember her as she was, but I'm not going to be there, so I don't care."

So that afternoon, fifty members gathered in the basement around the piano and sang a few songs for their old pal—"When The Roll is Called Up Yonder" and "Let The Rest of the World Go By" and "I'll Be Seeing You"—and Pastor Ingqvist, feeling a little sheepish, gave a talk about Evelyn and what a blessing she was, his eye on the stairs, waiting for Barbara to appear and read him the riot act. He was talking about what a blithe spirit Evelyn was and what joy she carried with her every day and more and more as she got older, when LaVonne appeared at the side door and motioned to him, and then motioned again with some urgency. "God bless her memory and all she meant to this church," he said, and walked to the back of the room—"Somebody to see you," said LaVonne and rolled her eyes to indicate *Nut Case* and right behind her was a man in black leather pants and an enormous black leather jacket with a dozen zippers and a lot of silver doodads. His hair was gray and he had fashioned a ponytail out of what remained of it and it hung down on his back. His face looked like an old pumpkin after a couple of hard frosts, and he took off his dark glasses and said, "This where the wedding is taking place?" His voice sounded like rough gravel in a cement mixer. "No," said Pastor Ingqvist. "I think you want to talk to Debbie Detmer."

"That's the one. So she ain't getting married in the church?" He squinted at Pastor Ingqvist who shook his head. He explained that Debbie was making her own wedding arrangements. The man handed him a business card: AL GARBER, EXECUTIVE PRODUCER, PREMIER ENTERTAINMENT. "YOU'VE GOT A PAL WHEN YOU CALL AL." He said, "If I can ever be of use, I'm in and out of this area all the time—" And then the piano struck up "Blessed Assurance" and he perked up his ears as the friends of Evelyn raised their poor quavery voices—*Blessed assurance, Jesus is mine, O what a fore-taste of glory divine, heir of salvation, purchase of God, born of his spirit, washed in his blood*—and the man closed his eyes and rocked back and forth with the music, his ponytail swinging back and forth—and he looked at Pastor Ingqvist and said, "My mother—" and then he couldn't speak. *Perfect submission, all is at rest, I in my Savior am happy and blest. Watching and waiting, looking above. Filled with his goodness, lost in his love.* Tears rolled down his old pumpkin face and he gave Pastor Ingqvist a terrible brown grin, his teeth like a rotted log, and he exhaled a blast of beer and whiskey and cigarettes, and he said, "Is it okay if I join you?"

"Of course," said Pastor Ingqvist. Jesus didn't say to check sinners for firearms, though for a moment he did flash on the shooting in Pennsylvania at the Amish school, a troubled loner with voices in his head steps into the midst of Christians and starts shouting and suddenly you're in the news, *Six Slain In Minnesota Church*—he followed Leather Man, thinking *Hold on just a moment. Not so eager, sir*—all the ladies looking up as Leather Man walked down the aisle to the front, black leather swishing, zippers flashing, and he listened to the last chorus—*This is my story, this is my song. Praising my Savior all the day long*—and when the hymn ended, and it was all silent, he punched the air and said: *"Yeah."*

The Lutherans looked at the man in black, gave him their standard welcoming look—here, evidently, was one of Evelyn's more interesting friends, come to tell about the difference she made in his life. He walked out in front of the pews and stood and chuckled. "My heart is full," he said. "Though I sure as hell am surprised."

A few ladies laughed nervously and he bowed his head sheepishly and said he hadn't set foot in a church in forty years, and he pulled out a filthy hanky and gave his nose a liquid honk and said that his mother used to sing that hymn and it tore him up to hear it again. He had drifted far from his Christian upbringing and was in the entertainment business now and living the road life estranged from his kids ever since his wife left him—and for good reasons, too—and he didn't know if he'd ever see them again, but somehow the hymn gave him hope. Out of the blue, these old lines—*born of his Spirit, washed in his blood*—Oh yes, you wouldn't know it to look at him but once he was just like you: followed the Christian path, and then got lured into show business and suddenly he was managing Muddy Waters, and then Joan Rivers, and Dinah Shore. The Beach Boys. Cliff Richards. Wonderful people and they paid him lavishly and he snorted it all up his nose. He was moving in the big leagues, Vegas, New York, Hollywood—he had Earl (Fatha) Hines, The McGuire Sisters, Joyce Brothers, The Mothers of Invention, the Boston Pops—then Alan Alda, Bob Barker, Chevy Chase, Doris Day, Gladys Knight, Dawn Upshaw, Sonny Rollins—Pastor Ingqvist was edging forward to thank the man for coming and nudge him toward the door but he was on a roll—"I tasted of every evil drug and liquor, every pill, every hallucinogen known to *man*—you name it, I did it twice—I had girlfriends left and right and all the desires of the *flesh*—I was a slave to them. I thought I was *free!* But I was utterly *bound* by my own cravings for pleasure—I needed more and more—it wasn't *enough* to have everything I wanted—I craved more and more—and I signed up The Eagles, the Orioles, the Ravens, Flanders and Swann, Ethan Hawke, Rita Dove, Russell Crowe, Steve Martin, Jay Leno, Marty Robbins, the Byrds, Dan Quayle—"

"I think it would be best if you left now," the pastor said quietly, taking Leather Man's great jacket by the elbow. The Lutherans perked up—their pastor was bouncing somebody out of church! He was telling a sinner to get the hell out! Bravo! He should've done this years ago, with some others. They could name names.

"What's the matter? What did I say?"

"This is a memorial for somebody you didn't know," said Pastor Ingqvist. "We're not interested in your life story. Not here. Thank you." He took Leather Man's arm in both hands and tried to steer him toward the door. A couple of men stood up, Clarence and Clint and Clint's brother-in-law George, and Leather Man eyeballed them. "Where I come from, it's not considered Christian to refuse a man who's witnessing for the Lord, but maybe here it's different. Okay. But don't be surprised if Elvis pays a visit to you," he said. And Leather Man struck a karate pose. He scowled with his pumpkin face and furrowed his big eyebrows and bared his brown teeth. "You are gonna be all shook up." And he shook his cheeks *brbrbrbrbrbrbrbrbr* and let out a whoop and shook off the pastor's hands and stalked out the door. They heard the roar of a motorcycle and it revved up a few times and then it raced away. Myrtle Krebsbach jumped up and said, "Let's not get down in the dumps! Let's sing!" Old Lutheran men looked down at their shoes—they'd have preferred to bend over and spread their cheeks to singing with Myrtle—but she was already warbling "Let me call you Sweetheart." "Louder!" she cried, her old eyes glittering.

The motorcycle went blasting past the Chatterbox Café at sixty miles an hour and the windows shook and people looked over at LeRoy in his constable jacket and badge and he said, "Long as he is headed *out* of town he is okay. I am not going to chase him down and bring him back."

"Probably a friend of Debbie's going for more champagne," said Darlene.

Myrtle said she'd like to know how much that champagne cost that was sitting in the Detmer's garage. Donnie saw them unloading it. Ten cases of it. French. "Don't tell me they got that wholesale." And somebody said there was a hundred pounds of cheese, also French. "Who is going to eat all that? I wasn't invited, I know that. Are they flying people in from California or what?"

"Well, I'll bet you ten dollars they aren't going to get married at all," said Dorothy.

She had just emerged from the kitchen, wiping her hands on a dishtowel, her hair pasted to her forehead, two silver bracelets on each forearm with crystals in them which are supposed to help her lose weight.

"My sister heard them last night and they were snapping at

each other and he referred to her as a bitch and he was walking away and she was running after him and hissing at him, something about his whole attitude making her sick."

"Sounds like they already are married," said LeRoy, ever the comedian. "Maybe they are only renewing their wedding vows before they expire."

"She threw the car keys at him and hit him in the head, and it was a hard throw. She told him the whole thing was a big mistake and they might as well stop right now. He was on his cell phone. He found a place next to the Unknown Norwegian where he got a pretty good signal and he was all excited and she was telling him he was the great mistake of her life."

They all sat stunned. LeRoy said, "Sounds like she read our thoughts."

But oh boy. Those poor Detmers. Ten cases of French champagne in the garage and Mr. Detmer had gotten himself a white linen suit for the occasion and now this.

"Better to find out now that you don't like each other than figure it out over a lifetime," said Myrtle, looking at Florian who was digging into a slab of apple pie.

Barbara was out for a walk and passing the Lutheran church and saw all the cars in the parking lot and remembered the memorial service and put her head down and almost sprinted to the end of the block and around the corner. She did not want to be spotted. She thought of stopping at the Chatterbox for coffee and a cinnamon roll but what if some busybody said, "How come you're not at your mother's memorial service up to the church? Didn't you know that was today? In fact I believe it's starting right now." So she started across Main Street and a blue Ford van came straight at her—it was turning onto Main Street and it swerved toward her as if intent on killing her and she shrank back and the van slammed on the brakes and she saw the assassin—a pair of sunglasses talking on a cell phone, one hand on the wheel—a screech of rubber and the van stopped and she put out her hand and touched it and he yelled, "Okay! I didn't see her! Okay?" and then he said to the cell phone, "It's okay. Never mind." And then he looked at Barbara and said "Sorry" and backed up and drove away. He was yelling, "Oh so I suppose you never made a mistake in your life!" as he drove past. Barbara saw the license plate but didn't think to remember it. She stood, stunned, frozen. The guy never got out of the van. He came within an inch of killing her. Or maybe putting her in an electric wheelchair that she'd steer with a stick held between her teeth and people'd see her go by and think *There but for the grace of God* and the sonovabitch never turned off the engine or got out, just muttered "Sorry" and off he went. Just like a lot of people nowadays. Barbarians. Their sense of ethics depends on who they think is watching at the time.

Thank you, Jesus. Somebody said it out loud. It was her. She said it. *Thank you that I still can walk and climb the stairs and take my own self to the bathroom.*

She did not feel up to crossing the street now, so she turned around. Her legs felt like wooden posts but she swung them, left, right, left, took three steps and got up onto the sidewalk and put out her hand and braced herself against the lightpole. Her legs were shaking. She thought she might faint, so she sat down on the pedestal of the lightpole, a narrow ledge, and then she slid down onto the sidewalk, her knees up in the air, her skirt up around her thighs, her hands on the ground. "How you doin'?" It was Mr. Hoppe, sitting tranquil as a fencepost on the bench in front of Ralph's Grocery. He gave off a strong fragrance suggesting he had passed away several days ago. "It's me," he said. "I was a friend of your father's." She held up a hand: *Peace. Thank you, Jesus.* For not making me a quadraplegic. For not making Kyle have to bury me *and* Mother in the same week. For not leaving Kyle motherless and rudderless in the world. For letting me go on as before, except now with a grateful heart.

And it dawned on her that if she had been struck by the van, people would've said *Oh how horrible* but they would've thought *Well, it was Barbara and you just have to wonder if she wasn't drunk.*

And then it dawned on her who the assassin was. Debbie Detmer's fiancé from California. The bridegroom.

18. SHE SENDS HIM PACKING

Debbie Detmer was fine. She was just fine. In fact she had never felt better. She had broken up with Brent and that was that. Done. She had seen the light. It wasn't a sudden thing. It was a number of little things. Brent was simply not ready to make a life with a bowl of goldfish, let alone someone with the power of speech. Such stupidity and selfishness she had never witnessed before, it was almost incomprehensible. He told her last night: "I came here even though I didn't want to come. I want you to know that. This is your show, not mine." He accused her of being angry and controlling. This man who treated her mother and father like unwashed peasants and refused to engage them in conversation had accused *her* of anger. He said, "The whole past two weeks when I was on the road, I felt so good and then I come here and it's like the door has slammed shut on my life and suddenly I am like a character in a movie or something and it's not my movie!"

"Movie?!" she said. *"Show?! This isn't make-believe. It's marriage."*

"You keep saying that! Why don't you marry yourself?"

She thought he was just acting out but he wasn't. They got in the van to go find a bottle of red wine for dinner and he almost ran over a lady in the crosswalk. He was on the phone with his office and ratcheting at them and in his anger he cranks the wheel and comes within six inches of pasting a lady to a lamp pole and then instead of apologizing to her, he yells at Debbie for warning him that the woman was there!!!

He yelled at Debbie for yelling at him that he was about to kill somebody.

So she told him he was an asshole and to get out of town and the sooner the better.

"Whatever," he said.

She told her parents the wedding was off, as she tried to reach her travel agent and get herself on a plane back to California and call Misty and Georges and Patrick and wave them off though it was too late to cancel the giant shrimp shish kebabs, which had arrived that morning and were resting comfortably in the freezer at the high school, courtesy of Mrs. Halvorson, the superintendent's wife, a friend of Mrs. Detmer.

Mr. Detmer kept asking where Brent was. "Gone home," said the Mrs.

"Good," he said.

"Good riddance," said Debbie.

Oh, she had seen this coming for six months and she had denied it and denied it and denied it, trying to make things work out, and then today the man had left for good, having barely avoided a manslaughter charge, and she couldn't be happier. Except she wished she could call the lady they'd almost killed. A tall dark-haired lady in her fifties or early sixties, dangly earrings, maroon University of Minnesota T-shirt, shorts, sandals, knobby knees.

"No idea," said Mrs. Detmer.

Debbie fixed them a meat loaf en croûte, meat loaf encased in a light pastry crust, and sautéed green beans. She was happy. She had cut herself loose from the Misery Express and told the engineer to take a hike, which she should've told him back around Christmas. He'd been waiting for her to cut him loose and now she had. It was all clear in her mind. She had succumbed to an illusion. Craving a happy domestic life, she had invented Brent as Mr. Husband and coaxed him along and prompted him, giving him easy tests, watching him, and then came the big test—Lake Wobegon—and the boy failed miserably. Because he was a jerk.

She had an appointment to teach aromatherapy at the veterinary school in Davis as an adjunct professor—she'd sell the house in Santa Cruz and buy a little farm and raise llamas and teach. She had come to a seam in her life and once she had crossed over it, she would move forward, no regrets. She was centered, she was directed, she was intact.

"I first knew it yesterday when we were talking about what to read at the ceremony and he insisted on reading this long poem by a friend of his called 'Diptych of Desire' so I said okay, I'll read Whitman. So he says he hates Whitman. As if I am supposed to know that. 'I celebrate myself and sing myself, and what I assume you shall assume, for every atom belonging to me as good belongs to you.'—What is the problem there? It means nothing, he says. It's just a lot of gas. Okay, I said, fine, no Whitman. It'll be Whitman-free. How about the Song of Solomon? 'Come away, my love, for lo the winter is past, the rains are over and gone.' And so forth. He says, 'What about "Your neck is like a tower of David and your breasts like two small rabbits"?' I said I didn't think it was appropriate. We didn't have to get into breasts. We could do 'Comfort me with apples' or one of those. Why breasts?

He says, 'Why do you have to be in charge of everything all the time? Down to the last detail. You can't give an inch. We're always fighting over the smallest things.' 'Fine,' I said. 'You read anything you want. Go ahead. Knock yourself out.' 'Oh no,' he says. 'I've been down that old passive-aggressive road with you before. I read about breasts and you'll be very cool and distant for the next six months.' I said, 'Go ahead. Read it. It's not important to me.'

" 'No no no,' he says.

"So then we haggle about the music. More of the same. He wants this, he doesn't want that. Okay, okay. I'm trying to go along with him. And then he says, 'You're not really going to have that creep come down in the hot-air balloon, are you?' 'What creep?' I say. 'You mean my old friend Craig?' 'Yeah,' he says, 'your ex-boyfriend.' I said, 'Sure, that's the plan, you knew that.' He says, 'I never knew that.' 'Yes, you did,' I say. He says, 'Couldn't you have found *somebody* to pilot a hot-air balloon whom you have *not been intimate with*?' I said to him, 'Brent, I am not going to start a life with you in an atmosphere of jealousy and distrust.' And he says, 'Okay, then don't.' I said, 'What is that supposed to mean?' He says, 'I came here even though I didn't want to. I came here for you. It's not for me, that's for sure. I want you to know that.' And I said, 'Baby, you are out of here. Right now.' So he is out of here."

"Maybe you only need some time apart," said Mother. Hopefulness was her style.

"We need a lot of time apart. Like thirty years for starters. Maybe more." Brent was high-maintenance and she had known it, she just hadn't known the extent. He was so completely wrapped in luxury-jet time-shares. His head was full of it, the

break-even point of X number seat/hours, the turnaround sub-
lets, the overage fees, and talking to him was like interrupting a
man playing chess. Brent was business and he had no time for
life. He was fine as long as he was on the phone, moving and
shaking, but you put him in an alien environment—Lake Wobegon—where people live at a stately pace, and his sneering, bully-
ing side came out. He was in love with her only in certain loca-
tions under favorable circumstances. A temporary regional
romance.

"Well," said Mother, "whatever you want, dear, we're certainly in support of. Isn't that right, Daddy?"

Debbie didn't mention what she had said to Brent as he packed
his bag. She stood in the guest room door and said, "You are so
putrid." It was a word she liked to use in high school. It just came
winging out of the past: putrid. He turned, stunned, and said,
"What?"

"You're not a person, you're a pathology," she said. It felt
good after all of the humming and harmonic converging, to haul
off and sock the guy.

"If I'm so bad, then why did you almost marry me?" he said.

There wasn't a good answer for that so she reached for the
antique china pitcher on the bureau and as he cringed and ducked,
she flung it at him and it shattered on the side of his head. He
dropped to his knees and clapped his hand to his temple where he
was bleeding. Slightly. But he groaned and made the most of it.
She seized his bag, an expensive soft brown English leather thing,
and walked to the open window and pitched it out the window
unzipped and his shirts and underwear flew out and fluttered
down on the Larsons' yard next door. Mrs. Larson knelt at her
flower bed, as if praying for her geraniums. She jumped when the

bag hit the ground and glanced over her shoulder and then re-sumed work.

"Why did you do that?" he said. He was sitting on the floor, nursing his head.

"Just wanted to make the day a little more real for you, so you'd remember it, shithead."

"Where does all of this anger come from? Explain that to me!"

She thought about it as he trotted over next door and recov-ered his undies. Mrs. Larson did not look up from the flowers as he collected his clothes. He stuffed them in the bag and headed downtown, forgetting his cell phone on the night table. Debbie threw it in the garbage where, a few minutes later, it rang a few times, weakly.

She pondered the question further that afternoon, and then the answer came to her: he had been unkind to her mother and father, her family, her people. He had asked if her father had al-ways been "that way"—and he said, "If your mother asks me one more time if there's anything she can get me, I am going to scream." He was sneering and supercilious toward them and their home, their books, their art, the food they ate, their conversa-tion—he accepted their hospitality and he laughed at them be-hind their backs—that was the reason for all of the anger. *You don't look down on people who are good to you. Maybe you can love your enemies, maybe not, but for sure you can be decent to your hosts, you prick.*

And then she recalled her own cruelty at age 17. And also 16 and 15. And 18 through, oh, 31 or so. It was dizzying. She had to lie down on her bed. The white chenille bedspread of her youth. The yellow sheets with the flowery borders. The maple desk that

Carl Krebsbach had made for her 14th birthday. The old bureau that had been Grandma Berg's. The old photos of the Beatles and Leonard Cohen and Anne Frank and Juliet Greco and Jacques Brel.

Someday she might come back here, when she was done with California, and move into this house and live out her days. She could be an old lady here and little kids would visit and she'd give them cookies and tell them stories about when she was very bad. Once upon a time there was a young woman named Debbie and she ran away from home because she was afraid of being normal. That was the worst thing she could imagine. So she hurried out to California and lost her virginity as soon as she could, to an older man who was very sad about something, and then she learned to be a freak, making it up as she went along, and then she held cats and dogs on her lap as they breathed in healing smells. Oh, and she also used a lot of cocaine at one point, children. And she ate some mushrooms that gave her dramatic visions of ocean waves and rainbows rising from peninsulas and gargoyles falling out of trees. She was original and creative and vibrant and independent and praised by one and all and then one day she suddenly got very sick of herself and had to get away and she came back here. It's peaceful here. You don't have to be wonderful here. You can just be who you are.

19. A PASTORAL CALL

Pastor Ingqvist had talked to Barbara on the phone and left messages for her, offering help, and she had left a message for him—"We are all doing very well, thank you, so don't feel you need to be concerned." On Thursday he thought he'd better walk over and knock on her door and see how she was doing. Maybe she had heard about the fiasco at the Evelyn memorial and he should assure her: it wasn't that bad. The man was harmless and left peacefully. Mrs. Ingqvist had heard via Dorothy at the Chatterbox that Barbara was planning an outdoor memorial service on Saturday at which the ashes would be fired from a cannon, but she wasn't sure how. So that was that. Lake Wobegon Lutheran was entertaining a group of twenty-four Lutheran pastors from Denmark on Saturday and if Barbara wanted to change her mind and hold the funeral in the sanctuary, he might have to wave off the Danes. Funerals had right-of-way. If she had something else in mind, fine. He just wanted to make sure.

The little memorial service at church had raised $225 in Evelyn's memory to go to the flower fund and he should make sure that was all right. So, he walked over to see if she was at home and accepting visitors.

And he wanted to explain about the Danes, if she was curious why a busload of visitors was coming on the day of Evelyn's memorial service. The Danes were on a two-week tour of the United States. They had been sent over by the Danish Lutheran Board because they had signed a profession of doubt—there was a great stir about this in Copenhagen, big newspaper headlines (PRIESTS DENY DIVINITY OF JESUS)—and then the Hellerup 24, as they were known, took a more radical step and denied the Queen's right to be head of the Danish Church, and then all hell broke loose. Agnosticism was acceptable, but not an insult to Queen Margrethe, so the Hellerup 24 had been packed off on a junket to America for a cooling-off period. The Danish Lutheran Board thought it important that the troublemakers should visit Minnesota and Wisconsin. The twenty-four, given their druthers, would've focused on the coasts, but the Board had reminded them that the Midwest is the Lutheran homeland. It also reminded them that their pensions were at risk and they might be forced to live in rented rooms in Ahlborg, the Danish Omaha. So the twenty-four had relented. They would land in Minneapolis on Thursday night, go to Walker Art Center for the Poul Henning exhibit and attend the Minnesota Orchestra on Friday, and board a bus Saturday morning and come up to Lake Wobegon for lunch.

The guy in Bishop Ringsak's office called on Monday to suggest that the Danes might appreciate salmon and small red potatoes (boiled) and a light salad to start and perhaps homemade pie for dessert. And he suggested a California Chardonnay.

"I think we'll serve a tuna noodle hot dish," said Pastor

Ingqvist, "just as we would for anybody. I'm not going to spend church money on a California Chardonnay."

"It's only a suggestion," said the Bishop's man. "But these are Danes. Not Norwegians. And the head of the delegation called me yesterday specifically about the menu. They're in Boston now and he was a little concerned that you might be serving lutefisk."

"Lutefisk never crossed my mind until you just mentioned it."

"Well, don't, is my advice. His name is Mattias Paulsen and he's a nice guy but he said that if it was going to be lutefisk, they'd prefer peanut butter sandwiches."

"I'll take it under advisement."

Lutefisk is cod that has been dried in a lye solution. It looks like the dessicated cadavers of squirrels run over by trucks, but after it is soaked and reconstituted and the lye is washed out and it's cooked, it looks more fish-related, though with lutefisk, the window of success is small. It can be tasty but the statistics aren't on your side. It is the hereditary delicacy of Swedes and Norwegians who serve it around the holidays, in memory of the ancestors, who ate it because they were poor. Most lutefisk is not edible by normal people. It is reminiscent of the afterbirth of a dog or the world's largest chunk of phlegm. Pastor Ingqvist wrote on his calendar for Saturday: "Lutefisk?"

He then headed to Barbara's, four blocks from church, her little bungalow with dead flowers in the flower beds and the grass long, thistles and crabgrass rampant. A bad lawn: a warning sign of personal distress. She had long been a sort of recluse in the congregation. Came to church less and less often and exited out a side door to avoid shaking hands with him. Sometimes he'd glance up from a sermon and catch her scowling at him. He counselled her when she divorced Lloyd—his standard talk: marriage is a story and it gains richness with time—"Not this one," she said. A life-long Lutheran and a complete mystery, not so unusual, come to think of it. Lots of sphinxes in the ranks. According to the church secretary LaVonne, Barbara was a heavy drinker from time to time and was dating a cashier at a convenience store, an obese man named Oliver. LaVonne liked to pass these things along.

He knocked on Barbara's front door and a young man opened the door, shirtless, his hair wet, a towel around his neck. "Hi. I'm Kyle," he said, forgetting that Pastor Ingquist knew him, had baptized him, had confirmed him in the faith. "Come in. Excuse the mess. I'll get my mom." He remembered Kyle from confirmation class. Very bright, asked if God caused war and famine and if so, why, got confirmed, and never showed his face in church again.

A big painting hung over the couch, swatches of orange and purple like tropical leaves, and he could see another in the dining room, similar but brighter, almost neon. Newspapers spread on the dining room table, and a wooden tray full of little jars of paint, and a stack of white dinner plates, unglazed.

"Pastor."

He jumped. She had come up behind him. She was wearing baggy old jeans and a sweatshirt flecked with paint and she looked as if she hadn't slept in days.

"I came to see how you're doing, Barbara, and see if we can offer any assistance with your memorial service—I hear it's on Saturday—" She nodded. "I thought a lot of your mother. We all did. It's been a big shock to everyone. Evelyn was the genuine article. She had a big influence on the lives of a lot of people. We're going to miss her."

Barbara said, "Did you get my letter?"

He shook his head.

"Probably because I didn't send it. I wasn't sure if I had or not. Anyway ..." and she waved for him to sit down at the table. "Mother left me a letter that leads me to believe that none of us knew her, Pastor—"

"Call me David."

"David—my mother lived a charade, if the truth be told. She was faithful to a loveless marriage and a loveless town and she went to church every Sunday like an old firehorse but she didn't discover her true self until she was almost seventy. When Daddy keeled over who had been her ball and chain, she was able to fly, and that's the woman I want to celebrate. Not the Sunday school teacher and Girl Scout leader, but Evelyn herself. The old broad who said what the hell and took a lover who took her dancing and traveling and they went to shows and played roulette and God knows what. She had pieced together enough damn quilts and she wanted to live before she died and by george she did. That's her, by the way, over there."

A green bowling ball sat on the desk, on a folded yellow bath towel. A big plaster patch covered the top and on the patch was written "MOM."

He said that he didn't agree about the "loveless town" part but he wasn't here to argue, only to offer whatever help she needed— what about lunch? Would they like a funeral lunch? She shook her head. He was relieved—he didn't know how he'd merge the Danish pastors and the grieving Peterson family—and right away he felt bad about feeling relieved. "What about lodging for family members coming from far away?" She shook her head. "Got them all taken care of," she said, "except for Roger and he's strictly a hotel type of guy."

He wanted to say more. *Life is complicated. We're all leading double and triple lives. Everyone has secrets. We'd be happy to celebrate Evelyn's life in all its complexity.* But it seemed trite, unnecessary, so he said his good-byes and wished her well and Kyle walked him out on the porch and shook his hand again. He was turning to go when Kyle said, "I have to ask you about something—it's not about my grandma, it's about something going on with me." The boy glanced left and right in a confidential way. "It's about sexuality," he said. "I've been living with this girl for almost a year."

Pastor Ingqvist nodded.

"It wasn't anything I planned exactly—things just sort of went in that direction." Kyle was looking him straight in the forehead, as people in confession so often do. "Anyway, she's sort of thinking about marriage, and I just don't feel that excited by her—I mean, we have sex and everything, but she just really doesn't turn me on that much—I'm sorry—" He turned away. "I shouldn't even be saying this. And taking up your time ..."

"It's fine," said Pastor Ingqvist. "This is what I do. I listen to people—I do it all the time."

Kyle stuck his hands in his pockets and looked at the ground. "So I slept with this other girl who I met in a chat room. She was really hot. I met her in a coffee shop and we talked and then we went for a walk and we had sex. On a nature trail. In broad daylight. And what I wanted to ask is: when the Bible says to confess your sins, does it mean you have to do it out loud to everybody? Or can you do it privately?"

"Well—I guess it says somewhere—"

"Confess your sins, one to the other. James 5:16," said Kyle. "I read that."

"Yes, but I think the manner of confession isn't as important as having a genuine contrite heart."

"But if you can't confess out loud, doesn't that mean you're too proud to admit to it? And so you're not contrite. Right?"

"Well, what are we talking about? Having sex with that girl?"

"Unnatural sex, to be specific."

Pastor Ingqvist nodded. He had counseled erectile dysfunction and bitter anger and sheer disinterest but never unnatural sex. He imagined an orgy, naked people glistening with oil, torches stuck in the ground, dogs barking.

Kyle pulled out a pen and a slip of paper from his billfold and he wrote on it. He handed it to Pastor Ingqvist. It said, *I had oral sex with that girl. I went down on her.*

The pastor put a hand on Kyle's shoulder. "Do you know what I mean by that?" Kyle said.

"I do and it's not unnatural. A lot of people do it."

"It felt unnatural to me. And I don't do it." He looked Pastor Ingqvist in the eye. "I don't think I'm saved," he said. "If I had to say, I'd guess that I'm not. I don't think that was a Christian thing to do."

"We've all sinned," Pastor Ingqvist pointed out.

"I know but I need to figure this out, if I'm supposed to tell everybody what I did with that girl. I wrote Sarah a note."

"You wrote her a note?"

"I can't talk to her. I never could. I moved out and left her a note and now this other girl's boyfriend, actually her fiancé, who she told, is looking for me except he doesn't exactly know who I am. She says she thinks she may be pregnant."

"So you didn't use condoms?"

"She didn't have any."

"When did you have sex with her?"

"A week ago."

"I don't think she can know this soon."

"We were kissing and I didn't think we were going to do it because it was broad daylight and we were on a nature trail—"

"A nature trail."

"A nature trail in the Cities. Near the airport. Airliners flying over at low altitude. And we sat down in the grass and nobody was around and we were kissing and necking and she undid her jeans and she wanted to so I did what she wanted me to do and she was moaning and twisting around and then we heard voices and we stopped."

Pastor Ingqvist tried to look impassive, attentive, professional. "Did you ejaculate?"

"Not quite," said Kyle.

He looked up at Pastor Ingqvist. "I know this is going to sound crazy, but—I read an article that said that compulsive sex is a way for a guy to evade the fact that he is gay."

"I don't think that having sex with that girl means you're gay if that's what you're asking," said Pastor Ingqvist. He put a hand on Kyle's shoulder and then thought better of it and took it away. But not too suddenly. Eased it away.

"I don't know," said Kyle. "I'm also sort of particular about my hair and I hate football. What if I were? Everybody I know would turn against me. It just scares me."

"Don't worry about it," said Pastor Ingqvist. "These things

have a way of sorting themselves out. The girl on the nature trail isn't pregnant by you so don't get fussed up over that. What you did was perfectly normal. Did you send Sarah the note?" Kyle shook his head. "Don't. Burn it."

"You don't believe in confession of sin?"

"In principle, yes. In practice—I don't know. I don't think people need to go through each other's garbage."

"I just wish I felt like a Christian." Kyle turned to go inside. "Anyway—thanks."

"I wish I could help you," said Pastor Ingqvist, who also wished he could come up with a better line. *I wish I could help you.* Pitiful. But he did wish he could. *Come to church,* he thought. *You want to find out about sin—hey, we talk about it all the time.*

20. HOMECOMING

Roger and Bennett finally arrived on Friday afternoon, having driven up together from the airport in Minneapolis. They walked into Mother's house, where Barbara had fixed tuna salad sandwiches and cole slaw, and Roger looked as if two hours in a car with his brother had driven him beyond the edge of tolerance. Fratricide glittered in his eye. Bennett plopped down in the living room, doughier than last summer, seedier too—the black turtleneck stained, the blue blazer smelled of mothballs, the black sneakers torn. He'd lost most of his hair and shaved the rest. He still had the big black horn-rimmed glasses. She shook his hand. Roger stood by the door, restless from being cooped up, his eyes flicking, his right foot twitched. Surely you couldn't sell a gazillion dollars worth of mutual funds to people if you twitched like that. She shook his hand too. In most families you might've hugged your brothers whom you hadn't seen in more than a year. And she hadn't. And wouldn't. Couldn't, somehow. Mother was a hugger and she was not. She had been close to Bennett when they were kids, before he got tangled up with being an artist. She had never cared for Roger at all.

"Gwen was so sorry she couldn't come," said Roger. "She had plans to go to Palm Springs with some women friends, and she couldn't change it. Another time."

"Oh," said Barbara. "Well maybe we should hold on to the ashes and schedule it for a time that's more convenient for her." She wanted to take them both by the neck and boink their heads together. She remembered their roughhousing as boys, and how Roger always won with his arm-twist hold, inflicting unbearable pain, Bennett weeping and refusing to surrender, and how she would scream at Roger to let him go, and Roger, as cool then as now, would say, "Of course," and give one last twist, and Bennett would shriek and the arm fall limp at his side, and a few weeks later they'd do it again.

"I sent off a demo of my opera to ten different opera companies," he said. "Audio files. You send them by e-mail attachment. It's amazing. Sent them the Orville/Wilbur duet, 'It's All a Question of Balance.' I think you heard that—" Barbara shook her head. "Maybe you forgot. It's where they're waiting for the wind to die down and Wilbur says, 'Let's try flying into the wind.' Remember?" She didn't. She imagined operas got scads of submissions from various bald, horn-rimmed geniuses with bad breath. She couldn't imagine her own brother ever succeeding and dressing up in a tux for a premiere and taking a bow. It just wasn't going to happen.

Roger had a big head of curly hair—she didn't remember the curly part—evidently he was under a beautician's care—and looked as if he'd stepped right out of an L.L. Bean catalogue, tan chinos, loafers, pink cashmere sweater, and a shirt with little anchors on it. Mr. Casual. He had sewn his wild oats in Miami, four solid years of bad behavior, and then got lucky and found his niche in sales, where persistent denial of reality is 90 percent of the game.

"And Jon and Sammy send their love. They're in the midst of mixing a CD. They started a band together. Lemon Tree. It's good. Folk. You know. About the environment, relationships, lots of things. Good stuff. I should send you a copy."

"When did they become songwriters?"

"They've always written songs. They're very talented. Sammy is going to songwriting camp this summer in Idaho."

She set out the sandwiches on the table and opened a bottle of wine. Mother's. An Oregon red wine with a portrait of a lady on the label. She poured two glasses. "I'm not drinking anymore," she announced. "And I'm not a Lutheran anymore. Just so you know."

"Gwen read that a glass of red wine a day pays big dividends for your heart. She likes those Italian wines, the Montepulcianos, the Amarettos and Barolos."

Bennett asked her when she stopped being Lutheran. On Sunday afternoon, she said. "What happened?" She said that things suddenly became clear for her, thanks to Mother.

"Is this wine one of Mother's?" asked Roger. She nodded. "Not bad," he said. "A little oaky and the finish isn't as smooth as the Italians but it's okay. I had no idea they made decent wine in Oregon."

"Mother took up wine right after Daddy died," she said. "She took up a lot of things. Dancing. I found a blue ribbon in her dresser drawer for a tango contest at the Miranda Casablanca Hotel in Las Vegas. Bet you never knew your mother did the tango, did you?"

Roger said that dancing was an excellent exercise, one of the best. He wished that he and Gwen could get out to a ballroom more often. There was a beautiful one in Santa Barbara called the Santa Margarita with electric stars in the ceiling. Dancing, three nights a week. Unfortunately, in his line of work you often needed to work nights too.

Barbara stared at him. *Shut up, shut up, shut up. Shut your dumb mouth.* He leaned back and crossed his legs and spread his arms on the sofa back and said that he hoped to retire in another four or five years and then he and Gwen would start living the life they had always wanted. Keep their home in Santa Barbara for a base, and travel from there to all the places they'd hoped to see—Japan, Rio, Vancouver, Shanghai, Tuscany—maybe buy a country house in Tuscany, near Siena, or maybe Provence. Gwen loved country houses, terraces, gardens.

"Does anybody in town know we're here?" said Bennett. "Like regular people? I'm afraid that if I walk up Main Street, I won't remember anybody's name. Maybe we should review."

"They won't remember you either," she said. "Thirty years is a long time, sweetheart."

"Is Miss Falconer still around?"

"She's ninety-two, kid. She moved to Fergus Falls to live with her sister. There were a lot of kids in choir. Thousands. I don't think she's holding her breath waiting for you to call."

Bennett gave her a bleak look. "She and I used to sit in the choir room after school and play duets. She was the one who encouraged me to study music. The first real compositions I ever wrote, I wrote for her. I was looking at one the other day. It's not bad."

"That whole world is gone," she said. "Mother and all her friends in the Thanatopsis Club, the ladies who put on the musicales, the Community Concert series. It's all gone. Speaking of which," she heisted herself up in her chair, "I hope one of you wants to say something at the memorial, because we don't have a speaker. I don't think we should throw Mother into the waves without saying a few words."

"How about you?" said Bennett. She shook her head. She couldn't. Just plain couldn't. She was going through too much now, being in recovery and everything. And she and Mother had had a lot of issues. A lot. She couldn't honestly stand up and talk about Mother's good points without referring to the others.

"What were the others?" said Bennett.

"Essentially she lived a lie and all of us had to live it with her. And now we're all paying the price for it. Look at us." Roger and Bennett looked at her.

"Mother messed us up good, and now we just have to deal with it. That was her gift to us. She gave us problems. I'm dealing with mine, I suggest you do likewise."

"Hey," Roger said. "Remember how to play Battleship?" He got out graph paper and explained the rules and that's what they did. They shot at each other's ships and Roger won and went to the bathroom to take his Compazine. "It keeps me level," he said. He was in the bathroom a long time. She could hear him weeping. "Family reunions!" said Bennett. "Guess this is the last one, huh?" She couldn't disagree with him there.

21. MEANWHILE

In Barbara's living room, under the big leafy painting, Kyle reclined on the couch, rehearsing telling Sarah that it was all over between them. Nothing to talk about. Their living together was a big accident and didn't mean anything. She wept, clutching his hand, begging him not to destroy something so precious with these terrible words, and he went right on —he never loved her, he was only using her to try to run away from himself. His true self.

"What do you mean?" she gasped. "Oh my God." And then she understood. She stood up, pain written large in her face. "Oh my God." And she turned and bolted out the door. And a moment later came the gunshot. . . .

His mother entered, with a pitcher of iced tea. Peppermint. "I know you'd prefer beer but work with me on this, all right?"

At the Detmers' Debbie stood on the front steps, watching Donnie Krebsbach pack her blue luggage into his Chevy van. Donnie, good soul that he was, had agreed to drive her to Minneapolis and drop her at the airport out of the goodness of his heart. She had offered him money but he declined. Not necessary. His pleasure. He was Florian's son and it was his day off at Krebsbach Chev and it was his pleasure to help her out.

Mother and Daddy stood in the doorway behind her. They hoped she would come back for a good visit soon. She was always welcome, they hoped she knew that.

"I'm sorry about the wedding," she said, for the tenth time. "Not that it was cancelled, but that it was ever scheduled in the first place. Sorry for the embarrassment."

They laughed and threw up their hands. Don't give it another thought. She had given Lake Wobegon something to talk about for the next ten years, right, Donnie? Donnie nodded. He had the bags all stowed and was ready to take off.

"What about the cheese and the champagne and the pâté?" said Mother.

"Keep it. It's good. And the shrimp shish kebabs. It'll keep for a few weeks."

"We don't have room in our freezer, though."

"Give it away then."

Mother took Debbie's hand—"That's what I thought too," she said. "I thought it'd be nice if we gave it to the Lutheran church. Maybe you've got your own opinion of Lutherans, but—they do so much good, you know."

"Fine. Whatever. Not a problem." And she kissed Mother on each cheek and then Daddy and told him to take his medicine, and got in the car and off they went to Minneapolis.

Watching the Chevy van turn the corner of Elm Street and head down the hill, Daddy knew in his heart he would never see his daughter again, and he got teary-eyed. She would be killed in a freak accident, sideswiped by a semi, the van rolling and rolling, Debbie's neck broken, lying crumpled under the coroner's blanket, leaving her parents to grieve. Or she would go down with the airliner. An item on the news, "Passenger jet missing over the Sierras," and they would spend 48 hours waiting, hoping, praying, and then search parties would locate the wreckage. No survivors. A freak accident. Possibly an aileron malfunction. Investigators trying to piece the parts together. Or she would be killed by Brent late at night in her home. He would slip in through a sliding glass door and smother her in her bed and take the body out to sea and drop it in, weighted with chains, but in his haste he would not secure them tightly and the body would slip free and wash up on the coast and be found by surfers and Brent would be arrested and tried. A long trial. Only a thin web of circumstantial evidence—a vague threat overheard by a waitress, his thumbprint on the glass, seaweed in his shoes. The tabloids would play it up big and they would print a picture of Debbie's lifeless body. He wanted to marry her for her money and now, in a towering rage, he wreaked vengeance for her cutting him loose. Or she would drown herself in the ocean. She had put on a brave front for her old parents but her heart was truly broken. She flew home to Santa Cruz, wrote a three-page anguished letter to them, put on a heavy canvas jacket, fastened chains to her ankles, and rowed a kayak out to sea and rolled over. Her body would be returned to Lake Wobegon and Daddy would ask permission to make their double plot into a triple. Bury them in a stack. Debbie on the bottom, then Mother—dead of grief a year later—and finally Daddy. He wasn't sure when he would die. Maybe not for a few years. He would come and trim the grass over their grave every week with a hand clipper and brush the clippings off the stone and tend the geraniums in the pot. He would sit and talk to them and people would see him and think, *That poor old man. He lost his daughter and then his wife, all within a year. His life, gone. Everything.* And then he would die himself. He would die at home, listening to Chopin, the light fading, and then there would be Mother and Debbie, all happy and dressed in white and welcoming him to an enormous mansion full of happy people where there would never be suffering or grief ever again.

He sat on the porch, comforting himself with these bleak thoughts, as Mother called up Pastor Ingqvist and made the donation, and five minutes later, Pastor rolled up with Clint Bunsen in Clint's big blue Ford pickup, and they walked up to the house, grinning. Pastor shook his hand. "This is just one of the most generous things I ever heard of," he said, and he and Clint went back to the garage and started hauling the cases of Moët champagne to the truck. They had already loaded the cheese and would get the frozen shish kebabs from the high school.

"Don't forget we're going to need a receipt," said Daddy. "For the tax deduction, don't you know." Suddenly his mind was clear as could be.

22. SATURDAY MORNING

Barbara had got wind of the Detmer nuptial cancellation and though she was glad the homicidal groom had left town, she thought the wedding would've been a nice distraction and drawn all the gawkers and rubberneckers and humorists—plenty there for them to stare at, between the giant duck decoys and the Elvis impersonator—and let Mother's ashes quietly splash into the beyond far from the cruel gaze of town. Maybe they should postpone the memorial until after dark. "We could just row her out at midnight and drop her over the gunwales," she said to Kyle. "Why do we need to do it from a great height?"

He shook his head. He'd gone to a lot of trouble: why back out now? Grandma had a flair for drama, she went in for big Christmases, a ten-foot tree and caroling with candles, and bottle rockets at midnight on Christmas Eve. You sang "Deck the Halls" and lit the fuses and a trail of sparks whooshed into the winter sky. Birthdays were big, large packages with bows and ribbons, stripey hats, horns blatting, and "Happy Birthday" *and* "For He's A Jolly Good Fellow" *and* the Minnesota Rouser, everybody marching around the table banging on pans and then the birthday boy and

Grandma hooked little fingers and farted for good luck. For his 19th, Grandma got a belly dancer swathed in veils with a diamond in her belly button and her bosom jiggling, gold silk pantaloons riding low on her hips. Flo and Al were embarrassed but not Grandma. She told the lady to "shake, shake, shake," and then Grandma got up and danced with her. Flo had to leave the room.

"The ladies in the Bon Marche are going to feast on this," said Barbara. "They'll be cackling for a week."

"So let 'em cackle. Who cares?" he said.

Actually she didn't. She intended to put her house on the market as soon as she sold Mother's and look for a new job somewhere warm. Work up a professional resume on her computer: *Experienced Problem Solver & Life Coach. Tired of the textbook clichés of so-called "experts"? Wish you could discuss your life situation with someone who's been there and done that? Look no farther.* In Lake Wobegon people wouldn't dream of asking her advice. People in Lake Wobegon imagined that you needed to be the Virgin Mother or the goddess Athena to be worthy of consultation—well, guess again, people. *It takes a broken person to heal broken people.* These Christians cocked their snoots at anybody who'd ever embarrassed herself in public. Well, tough. She had once, in a giddy mood, got dressed up and strolled downtown twirling a parasol— okay, an umbrella—and singing "Good morning, good morning, to you" from *Singin' in the Rain* and doing some of Debbie Reynolds's steps and trying to get passersby to dance with her—and yes, she was drunk. But so what? Get over it! It happens!

Aunt Flo called to ask what time the service would begin. "It's not a service," said Barbara. "Mother didn't want one, remember? Anyway, we hope to get going around eleven." And then she said, "We'd love to see you and Al there." Poor Flo was a changed woman. Evelyn's secret romance had humbled her. The bossy quarrelsome Flo who relished a good sharp retort, the Flo who could bring you to tears—that battle-axe Flo had been replaced by a sweet Flo who dropped by the day before with a basket of peanut-butter cookies. She handed it to Barbara, who said, "Come in." "I can't," said Flo, and then she did. And once she got inside, she melted into tears. She sat on the couch and bawled and Barbara held her in her arms and after ten minutes, Flo got up and said, "Thank you," and left. She probably had cried more this week than in the previous fifty years. Ten minutes was about all she could take, bless her heart.

Barbara put on a fresh blouse to replace the one Flo had wept on and got out the car keys. "I'm going to get your sister," she told Kyle, eating his Wheaties and reading yesterday's paper. He grunted. "I'll be back in an hour. If Raoul comes, be nice. Remember he's family." She headed for Sauk Rapids and went through her Muffy checklist. Muffy liked classical music on the radio, German, Brahms or Beethoven—the nuns had influenced her big time—and she needed to sit in the backseat where she didn't get so scared and the backseat had to be neat and clean. Muffy didn't tolerate disorder very well. She could not sleep away from the Poor Clares convent either, which broke Barbara's heart: she wished that her little girl could spend a night with Mom now and then. But no, it wouldn't work. Too much stress. And Muffy was 31 years old, a big strapping lady who looked a great deal like her grandma Evelyn. Whether she remembered Grandma clearly, Barbara wasn't sure, Muffy lived in the moment, but she would attend the memorial and then Flo and Al would bring her back to Sauk Rapids.

Oliver could not come, it simply was beyond him. He sent

flowers and a note. "My thoughts are with you today." Red carnations and a sympathy card. No note. Just signed Oliver. Not even "love" or "XXOO" or even "O"—just *Oliver*. He couldn't help it. He was a man and his social skills were rudimentary. Medieval even. And he couldn't bear to be around strong feelings. Crying drove him right up the wall. Once at the motel she said she was afraid of him having a heart attack and she got weepy and out the door he went.

Raoul arrived in town around 9 a.m. Dorothy saw the maroon Pontiac pull up in front of the Chatterbox and the old man in mirror shades climb out and she checked the clock in case he were a serial killer, she could make an accurate report to the police. He wore yellow plaid pants and lizard-green shoes and a sportcoat that looked as if it had been made from the skins of a thousand rainbow trout. It had a liquid glitter to it that caught the eye. Below it was a Hawaiian shirt, tails out. Pink hibiscus. Certainly festive. He took off the mirror shades and put on blue-tinted glasses. He was smoking a small cigar and carried a boom box that was quietly playing, an opera tenor singing love songs in Italian. He extinguished the cigar as he came in the café and wrapped the stub in tinfoil and put it in his pocket for future use. He gave off a strong aroma, sweet and musky, some exotic plant not grown locally. He sat down at the counter, studied the menu, and ordered a stack of buckwheat with two eggs on the side, scrambled, and an 8-oz. sirloin, rare. Black coffee. Cranberry juice. An English muffin, with a slice of cheddar. And then he opened up the Minneapolis paper and scanned the stock listings.

He ate his breakfast, mopped up every drop of syrup, accepted two refills on the coffee.

"You're here for Evelyn's funeral, I suppose," said Dorothy, probing.

"She and I were in nurses' training together. Minneapolis. Fall of 1941."

"She was quite a lady."

"She was a fine lady."

Dorothy got a cup of coffee for herself and perched on a stool. "I don't mean to intrude on your privacy," she said, "but weren't you on TV? I think my kids watched you on Channel Four."

He smiled and nodded. "I was Yonny Yonson."

"I knew it!" She threw back her head and laughed. "*You kids are driving me to drink!* They cracked up every time I said it."

"I had a nice long run with that show," he said. He explained that that was how he and Evelyn got back together, after he divorced June and she split up with Jack.

"Well, that's nice," said Dorothy.

He said Evelyn wasn't afraid of death and she just wanted to go quickly.

"And she got her wish," said Dorothy.

He nodded. "My ex-father-in-law took about six months to die. Went to the hospice and June sat and held his hand and he started improving. She never liked him that much so holding hands was a big novelty. He was near death when he arrived and they took him off antibiotics and he bounced back, and got up and started walking around. She thought maybe he was postponing, waiting for the ground to warm up. It was February. She had this handbook on death that said you should talk to the dying person about his life but Arne wanted to talk about his car. He wanted her to go start it every morning, especially when it was colder than ten below. This was in Duluth. Death isn't easy in Duluth. People cling to life out of sheer cussedness. Arne came home from the hospice and sat around watching TV and that kept him going another six months. The irritation. He watched my show every day and sent me messages like 'Get some new jokes' and 'Your Swedish accent is lousy. What a fake' and 'Don't sing anymore unless it's with other people and they're louder.' Once I left my fly open and sure enough he called up and said, 'Your fly is open.' When he died, I felt like I'd lost my biggest fan. I pissed him off but I sure held his interest."

He got up to go and paid his check and slipped a couple ones under the coffee cup, a nice tip. "You say hi to Barbara for me," said Dorothy. He crossed the street to the Mercantile, studied the beachwear on the manikins in the front window, and strolled down to Ralph's Pretty Good Grocery, where he asked Cathy the cashier where he could find flowers.

She didn't immediately grasp the question. "We have seeds. . . ." No, he wanted flowers. "I'll call my sister," she said. "Are irises okay? Or maybe she's still got some begonias." Her sister wasn't home and then Cathy remembered she'd gone to Hibbing. So Cathy drove him over to Deanna's and picked him a bouquet of glads and he was happy with that. He tried to give her a twenty but she waved it away. "My pleasure," she said. He thrust it at her. "I couldn't take money for that. They aren't even my flowers. It'd be stealing."

So when he appeared at Barbara's door, he held a dozen gladiolas in one hand and the boom box in the other. A boy answered the door and said, "You're Raoul." "I'm Raoul," said Raoul. He fished a picture out of his pocket, of him and a radiant Evelyn in their salad days, on the steps of Swedish Hospital, Minneapolis,

June, 1941. They looked like they'd just won the bedroom set and the kitchen range. "My mom'll be home in a few minutes. Come in. You care for breakfast?" Raoul had had breakfast. He saw the bowling ball sitting on the desk and he got tears in his eyes. "I knew I was gonna cry today," he told the boy. "I knew it."

A little after 10 a.m., Barbara rolled up in her old Pinto. She pulled into the garage and Muffy whimpered in the backseat. "Sorry," said Barbara. She backed out. The garage was too threatening, dark, cluttered. She parked the car in bright sunlight and opened the back door and Muffy climbed out slowly. "Remember Mom's house?" said Barbara. "Remember all the fun we've had here?" Muffy wore a black skirt and a white blouse and a white hanky on her head; she was trying to look as nunlike as possible. She was more buxom than Barbara recalled from her last visit in April. Maybe the blouse was too tight. Her hair was pulled back severely. She wore black horn-rimmed glasses, a new thing too. "Will we have lunch?" she said quietly. "No, baby, not now. We're going to bury Grandma first." She had explained Grandma's death over and over on the way home and Muffy kept forgetting it. The Poor Clares said she had not been herself lately, more distracted, more obsessive, sometimes going off to her room to weep.

Barbara had to remind herself not to weep with Muffy around because it distressed her so deeply. You had to keep control of yourself. *So why did you bring her to the funeral, lady?* Because Mother loved Muffy dearly, and vice versa, and because it was the right thing to do. "We'll eat lunch later," she said.

Barbara gave Raoul a big hug. It was just too much. Oh it was too much. She had been dreading this day and now here he was— and she introduced him to Muffy who had taken a seat in the middle of the couch and sat, hands folded, waiting for something, lunch or something else. A breeze swept in and riffled Muffy's hair and she put her hands up as if warding off a blow so Barbara went to the window to close it and she heard the jump-rope girls out on the sidewalk.

Jenny Jenny
Found a penny
Looked for gold but there wasn't any
Just a nickel
And a dime
Not enough for a real good time
She sat in her yard
And cried so hard
Because it hurt
And teardrops ran down her shirt
And how many teardrops hit the dirt?
One, two, three, four.

"You probably want to come over to Mother's," Barbara cried, and she told Kyle, "Talk to Muffy" and she pushed Raoul out the door and took his hairy hand and headed up the street—Bennett and Roger were camped in her house and she wanted Raoul to herself. "You're too polite to ask," she said, "but yes, Muffy is retarded. She's 31. She lives with the nuns. They're saints. She loves it there. It was the best thing I could do for her." She steered him up McKinley Street and then detoured down the alley to avoid the Lutheran church. "When she was born, it absolutely broke my husband's heart. And his will. He couldn't take it. I think she's a perfectly fine person. She's just different." She walked fast and he stumbled trying to keep up. Past the old garages, the incinerators, the back fence and the little gardens. "I'm putting Mother's house on the market and as soon as I sell it, I'm going to sell my own," she said. "I'm out of this town. Lived all my life here. That's enough."

"Where you going to go?" He was wheezing slightly, making his old legs move, his plaid pants going *swish swish swish.*

"Mother went through Columbus, Georgia, a few years ago on her way to Florida and I thought I'd take a look at that," she said. "I've been in the north long enough. Time for a change." She had never said this out loud before. Had never even thought it. It felt good to say. So she said more. "I think it's much more enlightened than here. They just seem gentler people. They don't throw you away just because you aren't rich and successful. I'm more of a socialist. I'm starting to realize that.

"I am also an atheist. I think my mother was a sort of agnostic, and I've gone the rest of the way."

"I think she believed in God," he said. "She said she did. I think she just got tired of church."

They were almost to Mother's now—three houses away—and she decided she'd save her big announcement for later. She had planned it for now but she didn't feel up to it now. She hardly knew the man. Nonetheless facts are facts. Mother had told her, "You were born a little early. Not out of wedlock, just not far enough in." And Mother winked. Their old joke. But Barbara had figured it out now. They came to the back gate and she opened it and up the long walk they went past the garden, the pole beans and cucumbers all neatly weeded and hilled up, and onto the back porch. "Muffy loved this yard. I'd bring her over here to play because Lloyd got all quiet and weird around her—" Barbara felt hot tears in her eyes. "My mother was so good to her. She was so good." She was crying so she could hardly get the words out. "That's why I brought Muffy to the funeral. Or whatever it is. It was just the right thing to do." Raoul was very still. She threw open the kitchen door and he walked in, probably expecting the dead to rise and give him a big smacker, and she said, "Do you think I did the right thing?"

"I don't know," he said.

"Mother said that Muffy was our greatest trial and our greatest blessing." And they stepped into the bedroom and looked at the deathbed from which her spirit had risen to worlds unknown and Barbara thought, *Oh God I can't do this. Why am I doing this? What does it matter?* and she turned to him and said, "Maybe you already know this but I only figured it out this week." She put her hand on his shoulder where he stood studying the bed and the slight hollow made by Evelyn over the years. "You are my biological father. I read your letter. You made love to my mother in December 1941. I was born in September, 1942. Mother married Jack in February. I just want to point that out."

He stood frozen still for a long minute and there was only the low whisper of breathing, hers and his.

He looked as if a camera was about to flash and he had to compose himself and form some sort of expression. His brain was brimming over and then it overflowed and he squeezed his eyes shut and cried.

And she cried. She was already crying, so why not some more. He turned toward her and put his arms around her and they held each other for awhile. She said, "I love you, Daddy." His face went all rubbery then and he had to take his glasses off and blow his nose. "She married Jack because she was pregnant," she said.

"That's the answer to the big family mystery. Any port in a storm. Went from the frying pan into the fire. All because of a night at the Dyckman Hotel." He put his hands in the hollow of the bed and slid them down it, caressing it. He didn't hear her. He was miles away, off in the past.

The bus carrying the Danish clergy rolled up in front of the Chatterbox Café at 11 a.m. and a nervous young man named Fred Samuelson emerged, clasping a clipboard. He was fresh out of Luther Seminary, interning at the synod office in Minneapolis, wondering if he actually had a call for the ministry or if maybe he should go into creative writing instead, and his boss Bishop R. W. Ringsak had dumped these Danes on him and told him to show them rural Minnesota and not lose any in the process. Bishop Ringsak had had it with the Danes. What a bunch of princesses! Finicky about food and fussy about hotels—their head honcho Mattias asked if the hotel in Minneapolis would have organic conditioner as well as shampoo and how late would the bar in the lobby be open and where is the nearest newsstand and would they offer the London papers? As if Bishop Ringsak had *no other mission in this life* but to look after visitors from other lands. Renegade pastors whom the bishop of Copenhagen wanted out of her hair. Well, Bishop Ringsak had other fish to fry, as a matter of fact. He had a scandal brewing out in Minnesota where an interim pastor fresh out of seminary was evidently dating an elderly widow who had deeded her farm to the church via a living will and now that she had romance in her life was thinking of changing it. The pastor, to complicate things further, was a poet (good God!) and had written fairly explicit love poems to this woman that he had read at a poetry reading in Marshall, not far away. There were rumors that the two of them were shacked up together at the End of the World Motel in Canby. And this man was charged with bringing the gospel of Christ to the farmers of Lac qui Parle county!! The Lutheran church was short on pastors and instead of closing up these little country churches—consolidation, a wise business decision, no matter how you slice it—they were sending moral cripples into the field of battle.

Oh no, Bishop Ringsak had plenty on his plate without babysitting twenty-four agnostic Danes, so he handed them off to Fred and said, "Don't let them preach and keep them away from women. They can booze all they like. They will anyway. Just try to keep their names out of the paper." The Danes sat in the bus and Fred stood outside the Chatterbox and looked around for any Lutheran-appearing persons who he could ask for directions to Pastor Ingqvist's house. The bus had stopped at the church, which was locked, and he needed to know where to take the group for the lunch which, according to his itinerary was scheduled for 1 p.m.

They were two hours early because the Danes had revolted against the scheduled tour of the hog operation in Melrose. They had gone to the turkey farm in Annandale and marched through the sheds, led by a laconic young man who stared at his shoes and mumbled, and the whole thing horrified them—it was a concentration camp for birds disfigured by genetic engineering, birds with enormous breasts like Hollywood porn stars, breasts like backpacks, breasts so huge that the birds couldn't keep their balance and many fell and broke their ankles. And the invalid turkeys were not euthanized but sedated and put in hammocks and fed intravenously and brought to market weight in a comatose condition and then slaughtered and sold. The obscenity of it aroused the Danes to a high pitch and they sat on the bus ratcheting and snarkling about it in their skritchy language with the weird chuckling vowels and meanwhile Fred was urging them to please stick with the program, the hog people were expecting visitors. But no, they wouldn't. "We have seen swine farms in our own country," said Mattias. "There is no need to see more." Some of them were afraid, he explained, of inhaling airborne genetic material that would enlarge their own breasts and make them freaks. They were serious.

Fred knew they were looking forward to Los Angeles. There was a Lutheran surfer mission in Ventura, a Danish film star Virginia Madsen, who would throw a big pool party, Meryl Streep would come, Lily Tomlin, Kevin Kline, Lindsay Lohan, the Danes whispered a long list of names. Minnesota was an obligatory stop, like you might visit your grandparents' grave on your way to L.A. They were sick of Minnesota. So flat, so boring and the food—so *bleecchhh*. Fred had been with them for all of three hours and he had come to loathe them heartily. Their carefully trimmed hair and moustaches, their pastel clothing, their superciliousness, their smoking, their *unLutheranness*. He was the only one in ecclesiastical garb—the others looked like a gang of insurance men on holiday. They looked more French than Scandinavian. They had insisted on stopping for coffee in Sauk Center so the bus stopped—some kind of democracy was in force, and whatever authority Fred thought he had was gone—and they trooped into the coffee shop of the Main Street Hotel and inspected the menu and saw the word "Danish" and were amused and ordered those, which, of course, turned out to be inferior stuff, just like everything else in America. The pastries came on plates and the Danes poked at them with knives, as if conducting an autopsy, and sliced off tiny morsels and tasted them and wrinkled their noses and jabbered in a dismissive way and drank the coffee, which was inferior too. They asked about Sinclair Lewis, whose hometown it was, and asked Fred if he had read *Main Street* or *Babbitt* which, of course, he had not. They had. "It wasn't assigned to you in school?" asked Mattias. "No," said Fred. He was pissed. Where was the fellowship you expected of Lutherans? The humility? They were the Examining Committee from hell. A tall bald man with black horn-rimmed glasses asked, "How much philosophy did you read in seminary?" *Quite a bit.* "Did you read Play Dough?" "Who?" said Fred. The man peered at him over his glasses. "Greek philosophy?"

None, actually. You don't need Plato to minister to the sick and troubled. They're not asking you to discuss the nature of Beauty; they need you to hold their hand as they die. What Fred disliked about the ministry, was the suck-ups who wanted to talk theology and show off by quoting Kierkegaard.

"Is this the Danish delegation?" He turned around and there was a sandy-haired man in T-shirt and jeans. The T-shirt said "Lutherans: It could be worse." He held a Jacques seed corn cap in one hand and an ice-cream cone in the other.

"I'm David Ingqvist," he said. He climbed aboard the bus and said something to them in Danish that made them all laugh.

And then a parade of people came marching around the corner, led by a gaunt man in a Viking helmet with horns and wearing a cape and a silken sash with blue fringe, carrying a sword and a sort of torch made from a cheese grater. He marched with an airy hauteur, followed by a woman in a blue robe carrying a green bowling ball, a man in a sparkly sportcoat, a young man in red swim briefs and flip-flops carrying an enormous red parasail, a young woman playing Dvorak's "Going Home" on the trombone, and an old coot waving a couple of sparklers. And a gaggle of others, most of them elderly. And an old lady in a purple pantsuit, wearing a jet-black wig and scratching her butt. They crossed Main Street and disappeared behind a brick building with manikins in the window.

The Danes came trooping off the bus, all twenty-four, Fred counting them off, and Pastor Ingqvist led them across the street and down to the lake. "We've been looking forward to your coming," he yelled back over his shoulder, and there indeed, tied to a long dock, was a pontoon boat, the *Agnes D,* with a sign hanging from the rail, *Velkommen Danskere,* and little Danish flags and *Celebration of Commitment* painted in green leafy lettering on a white muslin sheet stretched between two steel poles in the bow, left over from Debbie's wedding. Two dozen bottles of Moet champagne sat in three big washtubs full of chipped ice and smoke rose from the barbecue in the stern where giant shrimp shish kebabs were grilling. Pastor had put them on the grill moments before, still frozen, a mistake perhaps, and so he took them off the grill, dropping a few on the deck, and had to wash them off in the lake, which had an oil slick from the motor, but he splashed them around vigorously and tossed them on the grill, leaving them in the Lord's hands, and went to meet the bus. Wheels of cheese and tubs of pâté and a basket of baguettes sat on a white cloth on a table along the port side.

"Lunch aboard ship!" he cried. *"Frokost paa skibben."* Their eyes brightened. They moved slowly down the dock toward the boat.

"I am attending a memorial service for an old parishioner at noon," he said, "so help yourselves, enjoy the champagne, take it easy, and I'll be back and we'll go for a cruise."

He peeled the foil off a bottle, popped the cork which flew into the lake, poured, peeled, popped a few more—"Any nondrinkers?" he cried—the Danes laughed.

The boat, Fred noted as the Danes trooped aboard, was riding rather low in the water. He thought he would remain on shore. They wouldn't notice his absence, now that the champagne was uncorked and they were pouring a round in little plastic cups. He thought he would repair to a shady spot on the grass under a red oak tree and observe from a distance.

23. PHYSICS

The north end of Lake Wobegon is where the town lies, the swimming beach, Al's Baits, the fancy summer people's houses. The south end is smaller, rockier, weedier, less visited, and so nobody has ever removed the skeleton of the wing from Wilbur Scott's plane, the one that he flew nonstop the length of the Mississippi River in 1952. He was a dairy farmer who was looking to do something remarkable in his life and the nonstop flight was going to be his big moment and then he crashed the plane when he fired a signal rocket over Bemidji and shot off one of his struts. They gave the wreckage to his wife and she dumped it by the lake, a violation of the dumping law, but she was a grieving widow so nobody bothered her about it. And it was the south end of the lake, after all.

The Evelyn Memorial troupe stood a little north of the abandoned wing. The bowling ball was cradled in Barbara's left arm, a chain attached to it. Muffy stood to her left, between her and Raoul, the boom box in hand, and Bennett and Roger to her right, and then Aunt Flo and Uncle Al, silent, dabbing at their eyes, trying to keep composed, Flo in dark glasses for possibly the first time in her entire life. Enormous wraparound goggles that made her look extraterrestrial. The trombonist was her daughter Karleen who had offered to play "Beyond The Sunset." They stood together in tall grass at the edge of the rocky beach and looking across Lower Lake Wobegon toward the Indian mounds and the marsh where the loon couple lived. Myrtle Krebsbach fussed about the low turnout. "I know fifty people who'd be here in a minute if they knew this was going on," she said. "Jesus, Mary and Joseph, you shoulda told me, I'd've rounded them up."

"It's perfectly okay," said Barbara. "It's not a contest."

"I would've thought the Bunsens'd be here, but some people think they're too good to breathe the same air as the rest of us."

"They're out of town, dear. They went to Houston to help out their son who broke his leg on the basement stairs."

"Well, it's always something, isn't it." Myrtle was experiencing shooting pains in her left leg. "It feels like it's on fire," she said. "I may have to call Florian to get the shotgun and put me out of my misery. And he'd do it too."

Duane sat at the wheel of his silver runabout, the motor idling, emitting blue smoke, his pop-bottle glasses shadowed by the great brim of his yachtman's cap, and Kyle adjusted the trapeze of the great parasail, which Mr. Hoppe, in his Viking outfit, and Wally of the Sidetrack were holding gingerly by the tips of the wing. Kyle had set the waterskis in the water. He wore a fluorescent green Velcro belt around which he would wind the chain that was fastened to the setscrew he had drilled into the bowling ball. He explained that he was making last-minute adjustments to guard against a sudden nosedive.

"Darling," said Barbara, "Grandma would be horrified if you hurt yourself doing this, you know that. She didn't specify that she be *flown*, honey." He looked rather fragile in his red swim-briefs, her pale slender dappled son with the light down on his arms and legs shining in the sun, sliding the aluminum trapeze assembly a few inches aft on the bracing struts. "Shouldn't you be wearing a life jacket?"

"I'll be harnessed in. Don't worry about it."

There were twenty-four of them there, including six ladies from the Ladies Circle who looked faintly horrified but had come out of true loyalty. And then Pastor Ingqvist arrived. He nodded at Barbara and she nodded back. He stood, hands clasped behind his back, as if about to launch into prayer.

"Do either of you care to say anything?" she whispered to her brothers. Roger shook his head and looked away. Bennett nodded yes. "Would it be out of place for me to say a word?" said Raoul. Muffy put an arm around Barbara and whispered, "I love Grandma so much. She takes me for ice cream and we go swimming but I don't swim because there are fish in the lake. And there are dogs. I don't like dogs. I like some dogs. I swim in a pool. Wednesday and Saturday. I do the backstroke and the butterfly."

A quarter-mile away, the Danes were on their second or third glass of champagne which they agreed was as good as any they had tasted. A little warm, perhaps, and the plastic glasses were not so charming, but it was lovely with the Camembert and the Raclette and the blue cheese and the lovely paté. Half of them stood on the *Agnes D* and the others on the dock, studying the little town spread out on the slope, the high brick bell tower of the Catholic church, the lesser wood steeple of the Lutheran, the blue and brown and green roofs of houses. "Why is there so little color in America?" cried one. "Is there a fear of color?" "A fear of art and culture, if you ask me," said another.

Fred sat under his tree, trying to shut out their jabbering and then the word *"puritanisk"* rang out, which he heard before on the bus. Several times. Puritanical. An obsession of theirs. Evidently they'd read *The Scarlet Letter* once and it summed up America for them, that and *Death of a Salesman* and "The Waste Land." They probably thought Joe McCarthy was still in the US Senate. He wished he could piss in their champagne. What jerks. He vowed never to drink Carlsberg or purchase Lego toys. On the other hand, they were drinking steadily and that meant he might be able to shovel them on the bus and get back home early. He pulled out his cell phone and dialed his girlfriend Helen in the Cities to tell her. When he was in college, he borrowed his uncle's pontoon boat on Lake Minnetonka and invited a girl he had a huge crush on to come for a sunset cruise and out on the lake he dove from the boat and surfaced with a huge erection, a ball-peen hammer between his legs, thinking, *How am I going to climb aboard?* And then he noticed oil leaking from the outboard. He unsnapped the cowling to adjust the oil flow and suddenly the engine started up with a roar and the pontoon went racing away with the steering cranked to port and it came around and charged him like a huge bull, and she was sobbing for somebody to please please stop this and he grabbed hold of the pontoon as it came by and hoisted himself aboard and got the boat straightened out and she clung to him, weeping, and there he was, naked, erect, and a grateful woman in his arms, and that was when the boat skewed into the swimming area and got tangled in the floats, and a powerful beam swung out from the beach and caught the two of them in its glare and ten minutes later the deputy had written him a ticket for public lewdness and that was when he decided to go into the ministry.

A mangy yellowish Labrador came walking past him along the

shore. The dog stank to high heaven. You could almost see stink waves rising from his scraggly burr-infested fur. He was carrying a dead fish in his mouth and it appeared to have been dead for a long time. The head hung by a thread and then fell off as the dog strolled down to the dock and headed for the Danes. *Good for you,* thought Fred. *Go get 'em.*

A man standing at the upstairs window of Ralph's Pretty Good Grocery saw the dog and whistled to him and the dog didn't notice. The dog was deaf and practically blind. He had a lot on his mind, having been to the town dump and foraged there and found nothing, an old mattress, some rope, gunnysacks of junk from the garages of dead farmers. He had picked through it all and found nothing worthwhile. He was hungry. His name was Bruno and he was eighteen years old and a legend in the town. As a pup, he had caught a two-pound walleye while wading in the shallows and he had wrestled it to shore and hauled it to Inga, his owner. He carried the fish by its tail, four blocks to Inga's front porch, set it down, and barked. She made a big fuss over him. His picture was in the paper. She cooked the fish for him and let him sleep on the couch. This imprinted him with his mission in life, to catch big fish. He had been wading in the shallows ever since and had not matched his early success. The only fish he brought home were ones who lay on the beach or floated on the water. Inga turned against him, and so did everyone else in town. "Get the hell out of here, Bruno!" people yelled whenever they saw him. He was rejected on every hand, like an old drunk, on account of his rank odor of rot and mildew and algae, but he persisted. Half his teeth were gone, his eyes were rheumy, his ears leaked pus, but the dog kept fishing, and now he made his way toward some men who smelled fresh to him, who had never rejected him, hoping to find a pat on the head, a scratch on the belly.

The Danes smelled him right away and turned and stiffened. One of them shouted at the dog in Danish which didn't impress him. One of them waved a giant shish kebab at the dog but that only piqued his interest. As he approached the boat, the Danes on the dock, cornered, decided to go aboard, all of them, in a big rush, and to cast off the lines and start up the motor.

Fred was gratified to see the boat almost sink under the weight of twenty-four Danish pastors. Water glittered on the deck and a few pastors cried out a warning and then one succeeded in starting the motor and revved it up and away went the *Agnes D*, its deck awash but making slow progress, the Danes crowding in tight in the middle, so as not to push the bow any lower or to bump into the barbecue in the stern, the red coals glowing under the giant shrimp shish kebabs. Fred thought that this might make a good story for a sermon someday. It looked like twenty-four men walking on water, carrying an awning, and towing a barbecue. The sermon would be about pride and how we cannot make ourselves more buoyant simply by wishing it so. He got up and walked along the shore so as not to miss anything.

"Who's on the boat?" yelled the man in the window.

"They know exactly what they're doing," yelled Fred. "They're Danish, after all. They're excellent sailors."

At the lower end of the lake, Pastor Ingqvist stood ready to say a prayer—either a Christian one or an all-purpose one addressed to the Spirit of Love and suitable for mixed audiences—or to bless the bowling ball or to lead them in the singing of "Kumbaya, My Lord, Kumbaya," but Barbara wasn't looking his way. She was gesturing for her brother Bennett to step forward and face the group. Kyle had attached the bowling ball to himself, wrapping the chain around the green Velcro belt, and Duane had thrown the towrope out of the stern of the runabout and the show was about to start.

"My mother was a woman of great kindness who knew how to pay attention," said Bennett, reading from an index card in his hand and stopped, trying to decipher his own handwriting. Flies buzzed in the air and the water lapped gently on the stones. The motor rumbled. "She went through life tuned in to everything around her and I feel, as perhaps you do too, that she is still tuned in to us, but from another place, and perhaps at a deeper level." (*Oh get off it*, thought Barbara.) "I'll always remember Mother taking me downtown to line up for the Living Flag on the Fourth of July. There was a man up on the roof yelling and trying to get everyone organized into red stripes and white stripes—a stripe was about a hundred feet long, three people abreast wearing red or white hats and Mother and I always wore blue hats so we could stand in the corner of the flag and hold the big sparklers that made the stars. And when the whole flag was formed and everyone was holding still for the picture, Mother said to me, 'I can hear them breathing, can you?' And I could." He stopped again, and turned the card over. The other side was blank. He said, "I meant to finish writing this, and I forgot to and now I forget what the point of it was, but anyway it's what I remember about Mother." And then he stepped back into line and Raoul stepped forward and faced them. "I was a friend of Evelyn's from our days in nurses' training," he said. "Nineteen forty-one. A big year in our country. I loved her then, and I was lucky enough to reunite with her late in our lives. So I knew her as a young woman and as a mature woman, and she was the same at 82 as she was at 21. She was the same lively and curious and fun-loving person that she always had been. Sometimes it takes an outsider to see a person clearly"—he looked around in a meaningful way—"and I found her delightful." He looked at the green ball hanging from Kyle's chest. "You were a delight, old girl," he whispered. "There will never be another like you. Not for me." He choked on these words and stepped back into line. For a second or two, Barbara considered making a speech of her own—Mother was a free-thinker, it's as simple as that. *There is no God, we are free agents, each one of us, and if you want to go around with a big knapsack of rocks on your back like a person in a cartoon, okay, but I choose to be free, just as my mother, in a lucid moment, wanted you to know that she is free.* But her left leg would not step forward. She leaned slightly but her foot wouldn't move. She turned to Muffy and put her arms around her. "If I cry, don't get scared, okay, baby?" Muffy nodded. She was looking straight ahead, standing straight as a soldier, her hands pressed together in prayer.

"Okay, Grandma," said Kyle, "let's get the show on the road."

He waded gingerly into the water, on the sharp rocks, harnessed to the trapeze, the great parasail above him, and he staggered a couple times, pushing the skis ahead of him with his feet and then his knees until he was in water up to his thighs. He sat down and slipped his feet, first the left, then the right, into the foot holsters, and Duane gunned the motor and the towrope went taut and Kyle rose up on the water and skied over the waves, his knees bent, the towbar lashed to the trapeze. The little crowd watched the slender figure in the red swim briefs go skimming across the water and Roger said, "Mother would have loved this." As the boat made its turn, Kyle appeared to adjust the trapeze, the towbar clamped to it, as the bowling ball swung between his knees, and Barbara pulled out her camera. Raoul had a videocam out. "Here he comes!" said Raoul. But something was wrong—he wasn't lifting off the water. Mr. Hoppe waved his arm in a circle to tell Duane to pick up speed. "He must've adjusted the trapeze wrong," said Roger.

And then the speedboat swerved, and they saw why—two giant fiberglass ducks were racing across the water, strewing pink flower petals from their butts—*Was the Detmer wedding now on again?* There were people inside, pedaling, propelling them, crookedly, slewing around.

The speedboat was racing due north when it swerved again. The *Agnes D* had just come into view from behind the point, its deck crowded with men in pale blue and green and violet shirts and pants, a trail of black smoke rising from the barbecue. The men on deck were singing lustily what sounded like a hymn to alcohol, their arms linked, the boat riding extremely low in the water but that troubled them not at all, they were brothers united, champagne can do that to you. Loping along the shore, plunging through bushes and tall weeds, came the young theologian Fred, followed by Bruno the fishing dog; stink waves rising, a dead fish in his mouth, he was wheezing. The *Agnes D*'s prow was a couple inches above water and the engine was almost submerged. It gave off a sucking and sobbing sound. Duane cut sharply to the left to avoid the pontoon boat and at that moment Kyle lost his balance—the bowling ball between his legs swung to the right and he fell, still harnessed to the trapeze—Barbara cried out, *"Jesus Christ"*—the skis flew off him and he disappeared under the parasail which came skimming over the waves with him in the harness, dragged at high speed underwater. They could see his pale body racing submerged through the water—"Stop! Stop!" Barbara cried, clutching Muffy—and then they saw his red swimsuit and the Velcro belt and the green bowling ball, all three, torn from his body by the sheer force of the water—and then the parasail lifted into the air, carrying Kyle aloft. *Oh God have mercy. Oh Jesus have mercy.* "Holy Mary, Mother of God," said Muffy. Kyle hung from the trapeze, entangled in the towrope, stark naked, his legs pedalling, fifty feet in the air, and that blind idiot Duane at the controls with his eyes on the pontoon boat and its drunken crew and the ducks who had turned and headed north. The gap was narrowing and he cranked the speedboat directly in front of the pontoon boat whose crew stopped singing now and clutched the rails as the *Agnes D* pitched violently left to right in the speedboat's wake. The Danes would've hung on except for the barbecue tipping over—hundreds of red-hot coals came skittering across the deck like a manifestation from the Book of Revelation and over the rails the pastors dove. Twenty-four manly forms belly-flopped in the water—only four feet deep, thankfully—as the boat righted itself and plowed ahead toward the shore. Duane steered around the ducks who had split up and, still planing at high speed, he roared past the mourners.

It appeared to Barbara that something about flying had excited her son—yes indeed that was most certainly true. Yes, that was certainly true—the Ladies Circle ladies were studying the stones at their feet as if on a field trip. Pastor Ingqvist was deep in thought. Phrases of old sermons ran through his head—*our earthly journey—incorruptible from the corruptible—dust from whence we have come—the Lord's mercy is measureless.* And then he saw the naked young man fly by, arms spread, harness around his waist, high in the air, a large pink bird. *Oh Absalom, my Absalom—*

"Oh Jesus God, have mercy," said Barbara, and Muffy said, "on us sinners now and at the hour of our death." Mr. Hoppe and

Roger were waving and shouting at Duane to stop. Raoul in his distress at seeing the bowling ball containing Evelyn sink below the waves had pressed the PLAY button and Andy Williams sang "Moon River, wider than a mile, I'm crossing you in style someday" as the naked young man flew in the clear blue sky and the parasail banked and now a hot-air balloon came drifting at low altitude over the tree line.

"Oh dear God," said Barbara. It was startling, as if a barn had come floating into view. "You hired a balloon too?" said Raoul. "Why didn't we have him drop Evelyn off?"

It was blue and green, silver and gold, a magnificent silken bag from which hung a golden wicker basket and the kerosene burner on a frame above it, a man in a white naval outfit and officer's cap, his hand on the rope that pulled the switch that fired the burner, scanning the water below for the wedding couple he was to scoop up and carry away, descending, descending. The naked Kyle spotted the balloon as Duane made the turn and the parasail appeared to be on a collision course with the balloon—Kyle let out a high-pitched yelp, but Duane was busy steering around the men floundering in the water and the giant ducks paddling in circles and the crewless pontoon boat. He had more than enough to contend with!

"God have mercy, Jesus have mercy," cried Barbara. "Jesus have mercy," said Muffy, her hands pressed together, her eyes shut tight.

Fred the theologian had now joined the group of mourners. Mr. Hoppe smelled the dog and picked up a stone and pegged it at him and hit him in the hindquarters. "Beat it!" he yelled. Fred was thrilled by the sight of the Danes floundering in the water, trying to escape from the 18-foot fiberglass ducks, which seemed to be pursuing one after another of them. He was delighted. It spoke to his heart. They had slandered America and gotten drunk on champagne and fled from an old dog and now they were paying the piper.

Suddenly, there came a monstrous roar and a mighty flame burst from the burner of the balloon, the pilot attempting to ascend, but alas he overshot with the throttle and the flame ignited the bag, burnt a hole through the tip of it, and the rigging caught on fire, all in a few seconds, as the naked young man flew on, towed by the crazed Duane, and the ropes parted, the basket and burner and pilot dropped into the water with a great *ker-shroom-mm*—big pieces of burning silk drifted in the air like fiery sails and the naked boy heading straight toward them and a fiery death—"Oh God, no," cried Barbara—and Kyle flying onward threw his weight to the left and the parasail banked and missed the flaming silk by inches—a little burst of dark cloud appeared where he emptied his bowels—and flew on. *Thank you, Jesus. Thank you, God be praised.*

Roger was in the water now up to his knees, yelling at Duane to stop, goddamn it, stop the boat!! The two giant ducks came aground nearby grinding up on the rocks. The Danes were straggling out of the water—one of them, stepping on a chain, fetched up the bowling ball and brought it to shore where Raoul took it in his arms, weeping, Andy Wiliams still singing about the river and the huckleberry friends—and finally Roger got Duane's attention. The blind fool looked up and behind him, where any pilot pulling a parasail should have been focused all along, and saw his friend naked, flying, helpless, and he made a beeline for shore. He promptly caught the edge of the sandbar and ran aground, shearing the pin, and the towrope lifted the stern slightly, then snapped, and the naked man glided overhead on his parasail. *Oh God have mercy. God forgive us.* He glided over the mourners, a great shadow passing on the ground, and cleared the spruce trees behind them, and set down in the field beyond, where Mr. Hansen had his raspberry bushes. He yelped twice and then was silent.

Bennett turned to go to the rescue, and Barbara put a hand on his arm and said, "Let him be. Kyle likes to do things himself." She looked out at the lake strewn with wreckage and dotted with survivors and thought that it was the most exciting day she had spent in years. She was exhilarated. Most memorial services she'd ever attended were quiet sodden affairs and Mother's was nothing but gangbusters. Pastor Ingqvist was hauling these foreign men out of the water slopping and dripping and muttering things in their singsong guttural tongue and Duane waded to shore pulling his speedboat behind him saying that he wished people would watch where they were going for Chrissake and the Swanson twins climbed out of the giant duck decoys and explained that Debbie paid them $25 apiece to do it and what were they supposed to do with these ducks now? And the man in the white sailor suit towed his basket and burner up on the rocks and said that whoever had planned this wedding had done a pretty lousy job of it and he regretted ever having agreeing to be in it. It would be the last favor he would ever do for anybody, that was for sure.

"Debbie went back to California," said Pastor Ingqvist. "The wedding got cancelled."

"Why isn't she here? Why didn't she tell me? Why couldn't there have been a little warning?" He was distraught. "Look at me," he said. "I'm all wet, the balloon is ruined, probably the burner too."

Pastor shrugged. People forget. Especially in summer. Happens all the time.

The chaos was marvelous, Barbara thought. Her arm was around Muffy who didn't get scared when the pontoon tipped or when the balloon caught on fire: her eyes were still closed. "It's okay, baby. Everybody's okay. The dog is gone." Muffy said, "I like some dogs but not that dog." She gripped Barbara's hand. The Danes sloshed around, the giant ducks bumped against the rocky shoreline, Duane stood in the water with his boat and bitched that his eyes hurt and asked Roger to help lift it out of the water for him, the balloonist stamped his foot (*Goddamn!*), the ladies of the Circle huddled like buffalo in a snowstorm, Myrtle jabbering at them about how Catholics don't go in for cremation *for this very reason goddammit,* Raoul was trying to repair the plaster cap that held the ashes in the bowling ball which had jarred loose when it landed in the drink. He knelt with the ball in his arms, tamping down the ashes. "I've got you, my darling," he said. "You're all right now."

And the others—Paul and Bennett, Ruby, Harold, Bud, Mr. and Mrs. Berge—standing in place, calm, looking as if a balloon-parasail-pontoon-decoy disaster was what they had been expecting all along and now it was over and they were waiting to see what might come next.

"Are you all right?" It was Pastor Ingqvist, his hand on her elbow. "Never been better in my life," said Barbara.

24. THE KISS

*K*yle is taking his sweet time coming out of the raspberries, she thought. Probably he was embarrassed about the whole thing and girding his loins to march back and face the music. *Oh sweetie, you don't know how beautiful that was. Why didn't I think to get it on video?*

She asked Raoul. "Did you get it on video?" He said he'd gotten some of it and so then the camera had to be passed around for people to savor the near-collision of the speedboat and the pontoon and the little figure flying under the giant wing. Duane looked at it and Barbara and one of the Danes, who laughed a big Danish laugh, and the balloonist said, "Well, I'm glad *you're* amused. I wish *I* were." And then they heard Kyle singing, or chanting—and turned, and there he was, holding a rhubarb leaf to cover himself. His arms were scratched and he'd gotten muddied up in the landing, but he was walking. Limping, actually.

His face was all red and rubbery. He was crying, poor sweetheart. He came down the slope, saying something that sounded like *I've been so bad, I can't believe how bad I've been.* Bennett said, "Kyle, you okay?"

"Bad," said Kyle. He was trying to catch his breath. And then he saw Pastor Ingqvist.

"I need you to pray for me," he said. And then he started blubbering again.

"Honey, you need to come home and let me put something on your arms," said Barbara.

"I need forgiveness," he said. "I have gone astray." He looked her in the eye. "I did bad stuff, Mom."

"It's okay. I understand—"

"No, you don't. It's wrong!" He turned toward Pastor Ingqvist who had backed up a couple of steps. "I need prayer. Now." And he knelt down on the grass at the pastor's feet and bowed his head. In fact, he prostrated himself. He pressed his forehead to the ground. "Your sins are forgiven," said Pastor Ingqvist, "as Christ has forgiven me, and let us rejoice in the gift of God's salvation."

Barbara looked around for something to cover up Kyle's bare butt. She thought of taking off her own shirt and then thought better of it. "Give me your shirt," she said to Roger. He hesitated, startled. "Just do it," she said.

And then she smelled the dreadful odor of the dog. He came down out of the trees where Mr. Hoppe had driven him. His rheumy eyes were fixed on Kyle and he stepped forward stealthily as if hunting down a possum. The crowd parted for him. "I do not like this dog," said Muffy. Mr. Hoppe looked around for a stick but the dog kept coming. He approached the prostrate figure from behind and greeted him as dogs have so often greeted people and the feeling of that cold wet nose on that exact part of his body shocked Kyle like a live wire—he leaped up with a shriek and dashed into the water and rolled around in the shallows, groaning and whimpering.

Roger took off his good white shirt and Barbara took it and

stepped into the water. "Come out of there right now, I'm taking you home," she said. She got hold of one arm and pulled him to his feet and wrapped the shirt around his middle. "Don't be a crybaby," she said. "We all make our mistakes. Just live with it and try to do better next time." She steered him up the rocky beach.

Mr. Hoppe had put down his Viking sword and gone to fetch the parasail, which was in a rather crumpled condition, some struts broken, the fabric torn. And Bennett waded into the lake and came up with several bottles of champagne. He loosened the cork of one and popped it high into the air and put the foaming bottle to his lips. He gave it to Raoul and opened another for Barbara who handed it to Pastor Ingqvist. "I believe this is yours," she said.

He smiled. "Barbara," he said, "it's okay if you say no, but I have to ask: would you mind if I said a prayer?"

Well, no, she wouldn't *mind* exactly, if you put it that way. She might not feel any strong particular *need* for prayer at this point but she wouldn't *mind* one. She had heard thousands of prayers. What was one more?

He looked around and shushed the Danes and Craig the balloonist who was on his cell phone trying to reach his brother who was supposed to pick him up at two, and they all bowed their heads, including Kyle, who was shivering now, with Barbara's arm around him.

"Our faithful Father in heaven, thank you for this day you have given, and thank you for the life of our sister Evelyn as we commend her spirit to your love and care. And thank you for your safekeeping this afternoon at a moment of danger. And now guide us safely home, Father. We ask it in Jesus' name—"

And before the *Amen* came the voice from heaven singing, "Treat me like a fool, treat me mean and cruel, but love me . . ." The figure under the parachute was golden, flashing in the sunlight, and the voice was sweet and mellow. He appeared to be aiming for the same field Kyle had crash-landed in. Bennett waved his arms in warning and the voice said, "I'm coming, sweetheart. I'm on my way." He came down at a steep angle and then angled the chute expertly to land on his feet on the rocky shore. He was a fleshy man in gold lame and black boots, and he gathered the chute with both hands as it fell around him and he gave them a big lopsided grin. His hair was black and well-oiled and swept back along the sides and his aviator shades rode on top of his head. You could see the tiny microphone taped to his cheek. The loudspeaker was in his fanny pack. He said, "Where's the bride and groom? They in a hurry to start honeymooning?" He winked at Barbara. "I flew in from the coast and boy, are my arms tired." He flapped his arms and shrieked like a seagull.

"This isn't a wedding, it's a memorial service," said Barbara.

Raoul held up the bowling ball. "This is Evelyn," he said. "She's sorry she missed you."

The remains of Evelyn went home with Raoul in his big maroon Pontiac. It just seemed right and proper. Barbara waved good-bye and stopped at the Chatterbox for coffee and pie with her brothers and Muffy had chili and a hot dog and then went back to Sauk Rapids with Flo and Al. Barbara kissed her and went home and pulled the shades and cried for her mother and her daughter. She curled up on her bed with one of Mother's quilts over her and wept a half-cup of tears and sobbed hard until her chest ached and then she blew her nose and got up and took a shower. She had promised Kyle and her brothers and Flo and Al that they'd have a nice dinner at Moonlite Bay, and she thought she'd invite Gladys and Margaret too, and Leon if he wanted to join them, and they could have a cheerful meal together, if she could just hold herself together and keep from bawling. Mother would want her to. So she would do it for Mother. The loose-leaf binder of Mother's letters sat on the kitchen table and as she waited for 6 p.m. when she was supposed to get Kyle, who was at Duane's house, she opened the binder to a letter postmarked Ventura, California.

My darling daughter,

I miss you when I'm away and maybe you don't know that. I miss you listening to me, for one thing, like the story I told you about Hjalmar on the plane to Honolulu and how the champagne went to his head. Who could I tell that story to here in California? Nobody. They'd listen to me for thirty seconds and then they'd be ready with their own story about a drunken old man, a much better one, and they'd get that anxious look like a kid who can't wait to answer the question in class. You get old and you realize there are no answers, just stories. And how we love them. Three different people told me the story about Hjalmar—the complimentary glass of champagne that led to another glass, and then the poor old man strolling up and down the aisle introducing himself to people, and then he made his way up to business class, singing "Honolulu Mama, could she dance, in her pink pajamas when she took off her—Oahu! Oahu! Oahu!" A song so wonderful that it had to be shared with the world. The flight attendants had to restrain him and awaken Virginia, who had been sleeping through the whole thing, doped up on Drama-mine, and she thought they were picking on Hjalmar and she told them that if they had any idea what a good man he is and the good things he has done for others, you wouldn't be treating him like a common criminal. And then she realized he was three sheets to the wind. When they got to Honolulu, she was thin-lipped with anger and he was in a downward spiral of remorse, and also a little unsteady, and they managed to get to the hotel where, alas, their room was not ready, so they had to wait on the veranda, and it was sunny and they both fell asleep, and her purse got stolen. And Hjalmar spotted the perpetrator and gave chase and ran into a stone cherub on the terrace and fell and dislocated his shoulder. And the room was on the 23rd floor which made them sick with fear that they might jump out the window at any minute, so the next day they got on a plane and flew back home. With a fresh pineapple from the airport gift shop. Which gave them diarrhea for a week.

Anyway, you remember the story. Those were just the high points. The real comedy was how Virginia told it. It's really her story. She told it so well, and she made it all sound so perfectly reasonable, which it was. But then other people get hold of it and it becomes a sermon about the perils of drinking or travel or Hawaii—the perils of having a good time—and they kill it. And that's why I love to travel. (And drink. And have a good time.) Because I need to get away from the killers. Righteous people can be so cruel when they go after sinners and infidels, I just don't want to be around to see it. Our people settled out on the prairie because they like straight lines and neat corners. I know these people. I'm related to some of them. And sometimes I'd like to wring their necks. And then it's time to get in the car and go.

I am going to drive up to Santa Barbara today and visit Roger and Gwen. Not sure how long I'll stay, maybe a day. They're very busy with all their projects and things. And then up the coast to Mendocino which I love, love, love. If I could, I'd move there tomorrow, but I'm an old lady and I need to tell my stories to people who already know them and can tell me the parts I've left out. So, I'll head home soon. Can't live with people, can't live without them. That's how it goes. Just one thing after another.

Love, your mother

EPILOGUE

Kyle returned to school in the fall, as a history major, and somebody lit a fire under him, combustion was achieved, and he rocketed onto the Dean's List and aimed himself toward *summa cum laude* and vanished into the library. He was gone from September through June, visited Barbara for a weekend with Sarah in tow, kept his nose in a book, was preoccupied, unapproachable except one night when Barbara told the pontoon story and they laughed a lot, then he left in the morning and spent the summer in summer school, then did his senior year at the London School of Economics, and pretty much disappeared from Barbara's life. Kyle was not a big letter-writer. A few lines by e-mail was all he could manage. *I'm fine. Busy. Frantic. Sort of. Have a paper due in a week. Talk to you soon. When are you going to sell the house?* Sarah sent occasional longer dispatches—*You'd have been proud of your son if you'd seen him read his paper on Woodrow Wilson last night. I don't know if he told you but he won the Abingdon Prize which is given out by the American Union Society here (6,000 pounds—yippee!) and you're supposed to present the prize-winning paper so he did. It was held at the Marlborough Hotel and the*

ambassador was there and the Archbishop of Canterbury and Julian
Barnes and people from the BBC and Kyle was so unbelievably cool in
his three-piece suit (ten pounds, used) and acted like it was nothing, but
me, I was so scared I had to go to the loo and put a paper sack over my
head. But that's done and now we're off to Copenhagen. He got a fel-
lowship to the World Health Organization. I assume he told you.

Raoul died two years later, while on a cruise to the Aegean.
His daughter Carmen called Barbara and told her. He was traveling alone and landed in Ephesus and e-mailed her from the hotel
that he was under the weather and in the morning he called a cab
and went to a hospital and died at noon, alone. The American
consul took care of everything. Raoul was cremated and the ashes
were in the mail. Carmen was busy cleaning out her father's
house on Aldrich Avenue and found a note from him saying to
make sure Barbara got the green bowling ball.

Oliver died. His great heart gave out one day at work and a
customer came in and found his body on the floor of the men's
room. He and Barbara had parted company. The issue was marriage. He wasn't ready. He had to deal with some things. He
couldn't tell her what they were. Things. So she wished him well
and bade him goodbye and only heard about his death six months
later from Dorothy—who saw a story in the *St. Cloud Times*. He
was wedged in between the door and the sink and they had to
remove the door to get him out.

That was the day Barbara finally sold her house. She didn't get
the price she wanted, but it was an okay price, and the buyers
were nice, two dentists, a man and his wife. Dorothy said, "So
what you going to do now?" *I'm thinking I'll go see what Georgia*
looks like. So word got around and one by one, people called her
and wished her well. "Good for you," said Luanne. Wobegonians

are folks who steer a steady course and make fun of people with Big Ideas but by God they admire gumption. They might not say so in so many words, not wanting to encourage their kids to jump the tracks, but they found it darned fascinating that she had *no idea whatsoever where she would be one month from now, no idea, no sir.* And one day soon after that, the angel visited her on her back porch. She was lying on the porch swing, dreaming. She was pretty sure it was a dream. It felt like one. She heard the clacking of his golden curls and he stood radiant and polite by the screen door and said, "Nice town. What's it like here?"

She said, "You're asking me?"

He explained that angels are not omniscient and that in fact their knowledge is extremely limited. The only people he met were dead people and there wasn't much to be learned from them except that they weren't ready to go yet.

"Well, now you've met one more," she said.

He shook his curls *clackclackclack* and said, "No, no, no—this is purely a social call."

"Thank you very much. Then I'm going to Georgia and start a new life," she said.

"No, you're not," he said. "You're going to—" And then he caught himself. "Sorry, I am not supposed to say."

"Where am I going?" she said.

The angel's face went blank, as if his brain had shut down, and then it rebooted and his face resumed its beatific shine. "I know a joke about heaven and hell," he said. "The one with the Baptists." His face darkened. "No, I forgot that one," he said. "Do you re-member it? It had hellfire in it. A good joke." She pointed to the door. "Go," she said. She opened the door. He was making her nervous. "If you're not here on business, then good-bye and good luck," she said. She had no need of a joke from an angel at the moment. But the moment he disappeared, another walked into the room, a woman in a faint blue print dress and big black shoes, her hair tied back in a bun, and in her big rough hands was a glass globe. She spoke in a voice so low Barbara could barely understand her. "I came over from Norway when I was nineteen," she said. "I went to Central High School for eight months and then they sent me out to the prairie to teach in a school. I passed the test. It was an easy test. They made it easy because nobody else was willing to go to western North Dakota and teach. This was in 1887."

"Speak up," said Barbara. "I can't hear you."

"I was betrothed to Olav Olavsson back in Melby, the only man I ever loved, and he couldn't come to America because his mother was dying and if he left it would kill her. So he had to wait for her to die on her own. I understood that very well. I knew about rules. I had to leave because my mother was making me insane. So that was that. I went to North Dakota and lived with a family who I didn't like at all. The wife was sick with tuberculosis and I thought the man would take advantage of me. So I slept in the schoolhouse, with a gun, and I bathed in the river, though it was winter. In the spring I filed for a homestead that someone had abandoned two miles from school. I moved into the shack, which was 10x12, with a woodstove, a chair, a table, a bed, and a copy of the Bible. I hired a man to plow forty acres. It was land that had never felt a plow before, and I walked across the cool earth in my bare feet, and the man came walking after me. He asked me if I was betrothed and I said, yes. And he said, To whom? And I said, Olav Olavsson. And I ran as fast as I could to the shack and closed the door and put the chair against it. He stood out there begging me to talk to him."

"Would you mind speaking up?" said Barbara. "And who are you?"

"He was lonely and I understood that but I didn't want to talk to him. On the night before I left Melby for Bergen to board the ship to America, Olav and I had taken off our clothes and lay together in a bed upstairs under the roof, side by side, naked, so that we would remember each other for as many years as we would be apart. I promised him then that I would wait for his mother to die. She was in the next room and heard me say it and she screamed at me that she had no intention of dying and that I could never have her son.

"The man who plowed the field kept coming back day after day and he followed me to school. He begged me just to hold his hand, or to cook him a squirrel. I said no. I remembered Olav and how his body felt next to mine. The man drowned himself in the river. I lived in that shack for five years, read every book I could find, saved every nickel I earned, planted a garden every year, raised wheat and clover, built a barn, bought a horse and wagon, and I remembered Olav Olavsson. After five years, I got title to the land and sold it and that was our nest egg when his mother died and he sailed to America. I took a train to Chicago and married him a week before Christmas and we spent the night in a hotel by the lake, the waves were crashing on the shore."

"Are you related to me?" asked Barbara.

"Olav got sick from something he ate and he never got better. He was homesick. I told him I would take him back home and we got on a ship in Montreal bound for Oslo. It was a little ship and this was in January and the crossing was terrible. We lay in our bunks and were too weak to move. We thought we would die. One night, he reached over to me and he said, 'I'm not sorry about a thing that's happened to us. I would do it all again, exactly the same.' And that night he died in his sleep. We buried him in the sea and I went back to Oslo and on the way back to Melby, I slept in an inn and someone tried to take my money, a bag with thousands of dollars in it. I had tied it to my ankle and they cut the cord but I woke up and screamed and scared them away. And so I came back home seven years later and I moved in with my mother. She was meaner than ever. She hated me for having left her. She called me by an old nickname I hated—Goat."

"What did you do?"

"What could I do? I kept going. So much misery and trouble, it must lead to something better. And so I cleaned and baked and did laundry and then one day, to my great surprise, I threw myself into the sea and drowned. I thought, 'This is not right.' But there it was. Done."

"Are you an ancestor of mine?"

She didn't get the answer to that. She woke up and the phone was ringing. It rang three times before she could locate it and say hello and it was the mover, he was at the back door, the truck was pulled up in the backyard, he was ready to go.

So was she. Too many ghosts around here, too much history, the mutterings of old worn-out people, even the dogs were tired. Winter was not the problem. She knew that. Dark and cold and you're lonely as a hoot owl but you're used to it. Then spring comes and all that giddy insect music and you think maybe now your life will burgeon and prosper and leaf out and you won't always be this naked little scared person, maybe now you will follow your dreams and be true to yourself no matter what anybody thinks— and then you remember people who were like that and how much you couldn't stand to be around them. Life is a feast but we are only human, we're not tapeworms. The world is a paradise but there are mosquitoes. Winter kills off the weaker strains and leaves us with ferocious ones the size of hummingbirds that bug repellent does not repel, it only irritates. Our cutworms will eat lawn chairs and garden hose. You take a snooze outdoors and they will eat the sneakers off your feet and the mosquitoes will drain you of blood. You doze off in the sweet sunshine and you never wake up. This has happened time and time again. And so we are not a lighthearted Mediterranean people. We're Lutherans, even the Catholics are. And though one doesn't like to generalize about Lutherans, one thing is most certainly true of every last one of them: the low point of their year is summer vacation. They are suspicious of pleasure. An old Norwegian ugly as a toad meets a pale raven-haired beauty who hugs him and kisses him and takes him home to her father, the richest man in the county, and there is a lavish wedding and the couple retire to their French chateau by the lake, a wedding gift from her father, and the pale young beauty takes the old man upstairs and pours him a glass of Chateau Lafite Rothschild 1963 and a minute later appears in her diaphanous nightgown and sits beside him on the bed and says, What do you think, my darling. He says: it could be worse, that is for sure.

Okay, she thought. *Get me out of here, Mother, before I change my mind. I can't bear it.* All of these lonely stoics and their elaborate rituals of reticence and self-effacement that everyone struggles against and finally surrenders to but not her. She would pick up and leave and try again somewhere else. The way to do it was to do it. And that's exactly what she did. She left the mover her cell phone number so he could find out where to ship the stuff and she got in the car and she drove out of town, south, along the river, aiming to make Winona by nightfall and maybe stop there or maybe keep driving, heading for Columbus unless something better presented itself along the way, she was prepared to be lucky. "Isn't this the deal?" said Mother. "In a car and heading somewhere and looking for adventure. Aren't we something. Heaven knows what we'll find but you know everything is fifty-fifty. Either you get there or you don't." And then she was quiet. She fell asleep. And then she was gone. Night fell and Wisconsin passed in the dark, Chicago a distant glow in the sky, and the white stripes raced by, and the radio played one great song after another.